BATMAN

DEAD
WHITE

By John Shirley
(published by Ballantine Books)

DEMONS
CRAWLERS
BATMAN: DEAD WHITE

BATMAN

DEAD
WHITE

JOHN SHIRLEY

Batman created by Bob Kane

BALLANTINE BOOKS • NEW YORK

Batman: Dead White is a work of fiction. Names, places, and incidents either are products of the author's imagination or are used fictitiously.

A Del Rey Mass Market Original

Copyright © 2006 by DC Comics

All rights reserved.

Published in the United States by Del Rey Books, an imprint of The Random House Publishing Group, a division of Random House, Inc., New York.

BATMAN and all related names, characters, and elements are trademarks of DC Comics © 2006. All Rights Reserved.

DEL REY is a registered trademark and the Del Rey colophon is a trademark of Random House, Inc.

ISBN 0-345-47944-0

Printed in the United States of America

www.delreybooks.com
www.dccomics.com
Keyword: DC Comics on AOL

OPM   9   8   7   6   5   4   3   2   1

for my son Byron

You're wearing a mask, you're wearing a mask . . .
—which mask are you?
—IGGY POP, "Mask"

Special thanks to
    Steve Saffel, DC Comics, Julian "Regime," Micky,
Corby . . .
        To El Queso—for his combat notes—
            and of course . . .
                we all owe Bob Kane

1

I'm not scared of him. The Bat? No way. Lots of guys this side of Gotham City, yeah, they're scared of the Bat. Not me. They're a bunch of J-cat bitches. The Bat, he's a maniac in a costume, is all. Or maybe he doesn't really exist. Maybe it's some government psychological-ops program. I read about those, in the Weekly World View. They're screwing with our heads, using some guy in a bat outfit. That's what it is. That's what I told Skeev when I dropped the meth off for White Eyes, last time. Wish I was still dropping boof off instead of the hardware. Crystal meth is easier to hide than guns. Damn guns are so bulky. Makes me nervous we'll get caught. With this armament, the feds could get involved. The feds, puppets of the Antichrist, could be following me right now. I sure as Hell feel like someone's been watching me . . .

This old truck needs a tune-up. That's Skeev's new drop, over there, isn't it? Hard to tell from here, in the dark, with all the streetlights shot out on Simpson. Corner of Courtney and Simpson, he said—one of the sleaziest blocks in town. What'd he say, Rankin's Fish

Depot, by the river? And there it is, RANKIN'S FISH. *Sign's so old you can hardly read it. Fog's murking it up, too.*

Park the truck legal, Skeev said. Don't give nobody an excuse to search it. We don't own every cop in town. That Captain Gordon's got his team, too. Can't trust honest cops.

There's that feeling again. Like somebody's watching me. Watching from . . . up high somewhere. Like you can feel it on the back of your head. But when I look, can't see them. Skeev might've put some dude on the rooftop with a rifle. Can't see anybody up there . . .

Wait. Was that something? Like a shadow moving around.

No. Jumpy. Seeing shit.

Check the watch. 2:53 AM. *Skeev oughta be out here, watching for me, but I don't see him, the bastard. Probably got a speed run on. White Eyes told him not to do the boof anymore himself. He don't listen to White Eyes, going to find himself out in the country, spread-eagled under one of those harrow machines, like Harnie. I didn't mind Harnie's screaming so much—it was the whining before he started screaming, that's what gets on your nerves.*

So where are you, Skeev?

"Trask!"

"Jeez, Skeev you made me jump outta my shoes! Why you sneak up on me like that?"

"What you so nervous about, Trask? You got a tail on you? A tail following you, right? That right?"

Skeev talking a mile a minute, combine that with his southern accent, makes it hard to figure what he's saying sometimes. "I haven't . . . I haven't seen anybody, Skeev. Exactly."

"What you mean, *exactly*? You don't say exactly like you mean exactly. Some people say exactly but they don't mean exactly they mean *exactly*. What the Hell you mean by—"

"Awright, awright—" *Christ, Skeev's buzzing on boof for sure. His little rat eyes darting around. Still over-weight but he's half as fat as he was before. Well, I known him for a long time, I'm not gonna tell the Big White, but Skeev better hope he don't find out he's tak-ing the product himself. Being fat, he's liable to have a heart attack on the shit. Stick to the steroids like the Big White does.* "Chill, Skeev, I just—just had a feeling, that's all. Nerves. Hey—you got a guy on that roof over there?"

"What, where, which roof, where, that roof, that one there?"

"Yeah, I thought I saw somebody just now . . ."

"No, fuck no, maybe it's the Bat, man!"

"The 'Batman'?"

"No, the Bat, man! It could be him! He hammered down on Joe Bliney last night. Joe's whole crew, boom, slammed to mush."

"The Bat killed 'em?"

"They're alive, just busted up. I don't know how the cops can take 'em in when they find 'em tied up to the stuff with those black ropes, that bat-shaped deal on 'em, I mean, what's that, proof? But it's good enough for that bitch DA, and they went down, man, they're all in the city can, gonna go to the joint for sure, and for why? Because of the Bat. You better get this damn ugly-ass truck of yours outta here . . ."

"No can do, Skeev, White Eyes says I deliver no mat-ter what. The Bat comes, I'll be ready. Those other guys,

Bliney's crew . . . I dunno, I think it's a put-up job, I think it's all just a bullshit story about the Bat, the cops are gassing people, maybe, to knock 'em out, like something illegal, that's what I heard—and they're saying the Bat done it. Come on, one guy taking out five, more than five? No one man could do that, not without guns, and he don't use guns . . . if he exists."

"I seen him, man, you going to call me a liar, are you? That it, I'm a damn liar, right? I'm just running my mouth here?"

"What? No, Skeev, jeez, put away the piece, man, don't wave that gun, if a cop drives by what ain't one of ours, sees you waving that niner around—"

"I tell you I saw the Bat myself! About a year and a half ago, a little less, just when he started showing up, before I was working for the Brotherhood—we had a chop shop set up, ten new cars in there waiting to be stripped, and the window explodes and down he comes like black lightning, man, *wham!*, that fast, three guys go down before the Bat even lands on the floor, two more in the next second, he moved so fast—just like that!—and his face, man . . . *he ain't got a human face!* He's some kinda genetic crossbreeding thing, like a mutant—he's half animal! He's got bat genes, I figure, and he's got this look in his eyes, make your blood run cold, dude, and I don't ever wanna see that again . . . I ran for my life, and I was like half a block away, and *whack!* he shoots something or throws something and it hits me in the back of the head . . . Woke up cuffed to the wheel of one of those Jags. My lawyer got me off 'cause there was a witness says I went down on the street instead of in there with the cars, but I tell you what, I don't ever want to see the Bat again. I know at least one guy died of a heart attack just looking in the Bat's face!"

Pretty obvious Skeev was loaded that night and seeing things. Hallucinating on boof. Take enough, you get paranoia vision. On and on, rattling and tweakin' at me, boofin' out. Halitosis, too. Don't wanna talk to him no more. We gotta get these guns moved in.

"White Eyes says we deliver, Skeev. You gotta get your boys out here, unload the stuff."

"No, man, you move it around to the loading dock. I'll tell 'em to get it in. But I ain't sticking around. The Bat's been hitting the Alley for a while now. This whole parta town's his turf. Those chink whores that come in on the ship? The ones that didn't die in the hold? They were supposed to work a good three years whorin' for Venko, but the Bat kicks ass on the bodyguards, lets the trim go. Bitches run off into the streets. Guess he don't care about enforcing the immigrant laws—but you chain up a whore, it makes him mad. He busted some arms on Venko's boys when he found out they'd—"

"Skeev? I'm gonna move the truck. Get your boys around back."

"Sure, sure. The Bat. The Bat. The Bat's out there. I can't stay for this. I can't stay here, with the . . ."

Driving around the back. Pull up at the loading dock next to that fence. No choice: Gotta tell White Eyes about Skeev. He's out of his gourd on the shit. Whoa, stinks back here. Pile of dead fish parts. So they really do ship fish through here, too. Good cover. What cop wants to look close at a place smells this bad? Rankin, for sure it's rank, man, there's maggots on that one, enough to make you—What was that? Was that some-

thing on the roof of the warehouse? Like a black shape with horns, in the fog?

No. Seeing things again. Nothing there. So who are these weasels with Skeev? I don't know these guys.

"These guys down with White Eyes, Skeev?"

"Yeah, yeah, Trask, this is Sancho, this is Tar, this is Ronson, they're gonna move the shit out, I gotta go, my nerves can't take it, just put the gear in there . . ."

"You don't even want to see the goods? I'm supposed to show you, you're supposed to say *yeah that's the goods.* Look here, the crate's not even nailed shut. Check it out."

"Looks like a damn machine gun—or a cannon—or both."

"Shotgun-machinegun. Auto-shotgun, some call it. We got some other stuff you wouldn't believe—it's going to be the cutting edge of the revolution against the Legions of the Antichrist, man. Centrifugal gun—wait'll you see that one. This one's loaded. I'm gonna have it right here in my hands, standing guard. These things got hella range and power. I got this one loaded with flechette shells. The Bat shows, I'll cut him in half."

"Don't mention him! You mentioned his name! Don't say it! He'll know, if you say his name, he'll hear it and he'll know and he'll come!"

Look at that, the big tattooed guy, Tar, and Ronson, pale lean son of a bitch in his faggy earrings—both of them laughing at Skeev without making a sound. That Sancho looks like he's got that one cold expression and nothing else. That let's-get-this-over-so-I-can-get-my-money look. Tired of guys like him. Need something to believe in besides the next score, the next hit, the next drink, the next ho. That's what White Eyes gives you . . .

And the world's gonna be ours. Then you got it all. The women, the highs—and the power. That's something to believe in. These guys are all so shortsighted . . . Skeev still babbling at 'em . . .

"Hurry up! Hurry, Tar! Get that stuff inside! He could be . . . he could be watching us right now, he could be right there, right up there in the . . . the . . . in the . . ."

Funny, Skeev running down like that. He never runs out of words that quick. What's he looking at, his mouth hangin' open . . . ?

Oh, my God.

It's him. Up there. Letting us see him against the fog, the moon. Spreading his wings for the jump. Like a bat-shape cut out of the gray sky. His eyes like red holes in the night. Those horns—or bat ears? Like spikes. The gleam of his teeth—

The Bat.

I've got the Thunder—right here in my hands. Let him have it! But he's moving too fast, too fast—too fast!

He could have hit them before they ever saw him coming. But Batman had deliberately let the gun smugglers see him—the criminal nervous system tended to lock up at the sight of him, giving him the extra split second he needed to really take them *down*. It was good for the legend, too, spread the message of fear he was sending to the underworld.

Black cape streaming behind him, Batman leapt down at his targets, knowing he was going to connect solidly. He could feel it. Skeev's thugs were reacting slowly, and Batman's movements had been perfectly coordinated with his perception of the exact placement and types of the men he was taking down. Only one of them had a weapon in his hands—an unusual weapon.

Batman had hit "the pocket," as he thought of it. Maybe some would call it the Zone—but it was deeper than that. It'd taken more than a year to get that feeling, consistently, when he was out on a Mission. First year he was still floundering, trying this and that, making mistakes. Now he was getting his groove.

No room for mistakes. The places he'd trained in the Far East hadn't countenanced mistakes. When you've got Perfect Presence, the right flow of *chi*, complete fusion of attention with action, there is no excuse for mistakes— so his teachers had said. But he'd made them anyway until he started to feel "in the pocket"; that internalized knowledge, intelligence in motion, like a cellist hitting the bass note at just the right moment in the symphony, the dark symphony that was the Gotham night. This would go right—unless . . .

There was always an *unless*. He knew that, too. There was always an X factor. His combat choreography was at best just probability.

Still, as he struck the muscular, heavily tattooed thug, and the wiry one with the earring, Batman felt a simple, profound satisfaction in the way the double blows of his fists conveyed the momentum of his plunging weight: hammer-downs, right and left almost simultaneously, catching one on the right temple, the other on the bridge of his nose, the cartilage bursting. Batman could feel the kinetic energy passing through his gauntleted fists, into his adversaries, knocking them into unconsciousness as definitely as a light switch flicks a room into darkness. The chunky balding overseer of the operation was running for it—Batman knew him: Lon "the Skeev" Skeven, two-time loser for grand theft, total of nine years in State Pen behind him, rumored to have been a member of the Ku Klux Klan in Alabama before coming to Gotham City.

Batman struck the pavement with his booted feet, expertly absorbing the shock in the bend of his knees, aware of the swiveling muzzle of that big, almost cannonlike gun in the gangly red-haired man's hands—and already sidestepping as the man pulled the trigger.

Multiple shotgun blasts, missing—Batman was too close to catch the shotgun-spread effect, but flechette rounds tore through one side of his cape, two flechettes razoring across his lightly armored upper right arm, a double streak of cold instead of pain, for now—the pain would come later, but he was used to that: pain was as much a part of Batman's Mission as sleet was of Gotham's winter.

Some part of Batman's mind noted that the auto-shotgun had blown the wooden fence beside the truck to splinters. The weapon had tremendous kick, wasn't something anyone but a strong, well-planted man could aim effectively, and the terrified red-haired thug was staggering.

Batman spun on his left foot, kicked out with his right, as the gunman, pausing in his strafing, tried to bring the weapon to bear. Kevlar-reinforced boot striking the gun muzzle upward, Batman knocked the top of the breech into the gunman's face, so that he shouted in pain and the gun spun from his fingers. The Dark Knight was already spinning to chop down with his left hand at Sancho, who was bringing a .45 to bear. The karate blow struck the skinny gangster's hand just behind his thumb, breaking a small bone and knocking the gun to the ground; less than a split second later Batman's right fist connected with Red's chin in an uppercut. But Red was flailing backward from getting the gun knocked into his face, and the blow didn't connect solidly. Sancho howled with pain and, clutching his hand, turned to run. Batman's left hand, as if moving on its own initiative, had already plucked a Batarang from his belt, was spinning it after Sancho, who was running off, but still only a few steps away . . .

Sometimes, during a fight, it seemed to Batman that other people were moving in slow motion: perception of time was subjective to your personal rate of movement; to your capacity for absorbing detail. And to your adrenaline.

A bullet struck his chest armor, making him take a step back to keep his balance, and at the same moment he caught the muzzle flash, someone shooting from the corner of that wharf building. Three other incoming rounds hissed past his cowl. Panicky shooting—that would be Skeev. *Lucky I didn't catch one in the teeth,* Batman thought. *Bruce Wayne'd have to spend a lot of time in dental surgery.*

It was thirty yards to the shooter, just at the end of effective Batarang range, but Batman took three bat-shaped shuriken from his gauntlet; he flicked the "throwing stars" toward the muzzle flash while ducking back behind the rear of the truck. Doing two, three, sometimes four things at once was an absolutely necessary skill for nearly every Mission.

He heard a shout of pain. Running feet. Stumbling into a trash can.

Batman could see that Sancho was down, out cold, but the redheaded guy who'd driven the truck had taken advantage of Batman's distraction to run around the corner of the building. Sirens were approaching. The gunfire had drawn the cops as the smell of blood draws sharks.

Batman didn't like to work with the police around. Technically, he was a vigilante. And some of Gotham's Finest were taking bribes. They knew the underworld had a price on Batman's head. Besides—cops brought an additional element of chaos to the Mission. Batman liked to stay in control.

His instinct said that Skeev wasn't badly hurt. So he was left with a choice—pursue Red or go after Skeev. Probably didn't have time to pursue both men and get what he needed from the crime scene.

The truck had an out-of-state license plate. Pennsylvania. Interesting: Skeev was a local boss.

Batman jumped into the back of the truck, shining a light from his utility belt. Found nothing but the crates— and an object fallen into a crevice under the passenger cab. He pulled it out, expanded a sample bag from his utility belt, and stuck the object in. He jumped from the back of the truck, picked up the weapon Red had dropped, and set out after Skeev seconds before the cops arrived.

Batman slipped around the corner of a boathouse beside the river just as the first cruisers screeched up at the back of Rankin's Fish Depot. He ran along the wharf, pressing a stud in his gauntlet that would summon the Batmobile. Skeev wasn't hard to follow—there was a spotty trail of blood. Chances were the shuriken hadn't hurt him badly, but they'd scared him into giving up the fusillade.

The trail led to a crumbling old dock, a gull-speckled wooden ladder, and a big abandoned chunk of concrete embedded with rusty iron that someone had used for an anchor. Skeev was in a motorboat at the bottom of the ladder, frantically trying to start the engine, a nine-millimeter pistol in his free hand. Unmoored now, the boat drifted just under the ladder.

"Good to catch up with you again, Skeev," Batman said, leaning the auto-shotgun on a post. Batman's voice was as designed as his cowl and costume. It was the voice Bruce Wayne had carefully chosen for Batman: deep, a little raspy, and with a whispery quality around the edges—like something you hear at the tail end of a roll of thunder.

"The Bat!" Skeev squealed, turning to fire the pistol up at him.

Batman didn't bother to dodge aside. Long before Skeev was ready to pull the trigger, Batman could see that the pistol was aimed too high and to his left. The bullets cracked by a good two feet off target. Skeev was too out of it to know how badly he was shooting, and Batman pretended to catch one of the bullets in his hand. Aware that Skeev was in a state of superstitious terror, he pretended to look at the bullet in the palm of his black glove—though there was nothing there. "A niner, I see. Too heavy for you, Skeev. You'd shoot straighter with a .22 caliber."

Skeev's eyes widened. "You . . . you're a . . . you ain't . . ."

"Human? You'll find out if you don't tell me what I need to know." The Batmobile was approaching the foot of the dock. The cops were looking toward it. They'd heard the gunshots. "Where'd the fancy shotguns come from?"

"I don't . . . I don't . . ."

For just a moment, looking into Skeev's terrified eyes, Batman felt a kind of disorientation—a disconnection from the Mission. For a moment he felt that he was Skeev, looking up at Batman. A terrifying figure in black and gray; a personification of violence in a sinister cowl.

Batman clenched his fists, bringing himself back to the Mission. Strange, though—that lapse in confidence, that doubt about his approach, had never happened to him before . . .

He forced himself back on task. "Skeev—am I going to have to come down there, to that boat? Just the two of us, down there?"

"No, no, no!"

"Then tell me who shipped the guns here!"

"It's the Big White! It's White Eyes himself! I don't know where he is, he just sends them for the Brotherhood—I don't know nothing else!" He dropped the gun, turned back to the motor, tried to start it again, babbling to himself. Hands shaking. Drugs, maybe, Batman decided.

Skeev was low-level. Probably telling the truth. The cops were coming over here . . .

"That's a Briggs and Stratton four-stroke, Skeev," Batman said matter-of-factly as he ran the magnetized thumb of his right hand over the remote steering-control screen on his gauntlet, turning the Batmobile toward the river. "You need to twist that throttle, you want the boat to go." He straightened up, adding, "Or you could ride the boat straight down to the bottom of the river."

And Batman pushed the old concrete anchor with his boot so it fell directly into the wooden boat, smashing through the bottom. Skeev yelped as the boat began to sink. He flailed for the ladder, missed, and fell into the water. Batman tapped another stud on his gauntlet: the coded combination of taps told the Batmobile to track him, and meet him with close timing.

"Hold it, you!" a cop shouted, running up the dock. "You in the cape, dammit, don't you move! Freeze!"

Batman spread his hands, clasping his cape in a small, ironic gesture of regret, then turned, sweeping up the auto-shotgun as he went, sprinted to the edge of the dock about thirty feet away—and jumped off.

"Shit!" the cop yelled. "Where's my flashlight! He's gonna drown in there with all that gear on!"

"There's a guy trying to climb up the ladder here!" yelled another cop. "Hey, it's Skeev Skeven! We been looking for you, Skeev!"

Batman jumped directly onto the back of the Batmobile—which had gone into amphibious mode on striking the water. It sped off down the river, sending up a fantail of ichorous water behind it. A group of cops watched with amazement and grudging admiration as Batman ran forward to the Batmobile's now open cab, dropped in, and took the wheel. Its sensors recognized the touch of his gauntlet, and the wheel responded. He put the amphibious vehicle into high gear and rocketed across the river to a boat-launch ramp on the opposite shore. Up the concrete ramp, onto the streets, and away toward the country roads that led to Wayne Manor.

A shame the red-haired one had gotten away. He'd have to fire up the computer, look at some computer mug shots, see if he could ID him . . .

I did it, I got away from the Bat! He'll have to live with losing Red Trask! I thought I was a goner when he kicked the gun from my hand. I owe one to that speed freak Skeev. But hey, the Bat wasn't so tough. I saw him stagger when that bullet hit him. Kevlar. Just a man in a costume. I don't have to be scared of him.

Oh, God. Please don't let him find me.

2

"And how did you know, Master Bruce, that there was contraband in the back of that lorry?" Alfred asked, putting a silver tea service down at Bruce Wayne's elbow. Alfred had bandaged the wound on Bruce's upper arm, but the double cut had been deep enough that it throbbed as Bruce worked. Now he sat shirtless in the chilly spaces of the Batcave command center. He was a sturdily handsome black-haired man with brawny shoulders, chest and arms bulked by muscle—not exaggerated Mr. Universe muscle, but impressive. He still wore the lower part of his costume, and his gloves.

The command center was directly under the sprawling old Wayne Manor. Close at hand were racks of spare costumes, grappling devices, throwing weapons, and the entrance to a gallery of chambers containing the Batmobile and other aptly designed vehicles—highly customized motorcycles, and even planes, like the new VTOL stealth jet.

"Oh, I *didn't* know what he was up to," Bruce said absently, studying the image in his mug-shot program. He'd typed his subject's characteristics into its search engine, and it had given him a probable ID on the one who'd gotten away—the truck's driver was likely Douglas "Red" Trask, three-time loser for carjacking, armed robbery, amphetamine dealing. "I was watching from the roof of an apartment building on Winslow," Bruce went on, "and I noticed a truck, at almost three AM, driving in a way that suggested someone was trying to lose a tail."

"Did you say he was trying to *lose a tail,* sir? Is this an allusion to his evolutionary status?"

Eyebrows lifted, Bruce glanced at Alfred, whose deadpan affect and Oxford accent gave away little. Smoothing his small gray mustache with a forefinger, Alfred admitted, "I was speaking facetiously, sir. In actual fact I recall the expression *lose a tail* from a novel by Mr. Raymond Chandler. Your quarry was trying to elude pursuit."

Bruce smiled, glad that the aging English butler was here. The Mission could be achingly lonely at times. Alfred Pennyworth was his only confidant.

"More likely he was worried he *might* be followed," Bruce said, "so he was taking precautions—lots of pointless turns. I took a shortcut across the rooftops, followed him to Crime Alley. Simpson Street. And when a guy with a record of grand theft cracks open crates full of automatic weapons at almost half past three in the morning, it's a good bet those guns are illegal."

"Illegal they certainly are," said Alfred, who had inspected the auto-shotgun himself. "The weapon is completely unregistered—and in violation of nearly every gun-control law in the books."

Bruce nodded, glancing thoughtfully at his cowl; it stood like a knight's helmet beside the flechette-torn cape on an examination table nearby. The cowl stared sight-lessly back at him, above Batman's armored cuirass, which leaned against the leg of the table. The empty cowl, the cape drooping off the edge of the table, the chest armor with its bat insignia, glossy black against flat black—all of it together was like a Batman ghost, watching him. Waiting for its moment. When Bruce Wayne put on Batman's cowl, he *became* Batman—he underwent a psychological transformation. He deliberately cultivated that changeability in himself. Just now he was simply Bruce Wayne—not the Bruce Wayne the world knew: the head of Wayne Enterprises, the feckless playboy. He was Bruce Wayne, the planner, the researcher—the detective. Curious to think that Batman, a man in a mask, was somehow more real than the Bruce Wayne known to the world. In a way, Bruce Wayne, billionaire playboy, was his real mask.

Sipping tea—the exquisite china cup looking absurdly small and delicate in his gauntleted hands—Bruce moved his computer's mouse, activating the soil-analysis program to see the results on the dirt scraped from the object he'd found in the truck. "Silver, copper, iron . . . traces of sulfides and tellurides . . . the sort of clay that may also bear gold flakes."

"Indeed, Master Bruce? And the object itself?"

Bruce picked up the object from a specimen table beside his computer. It was a small circle of aluminum, from which extended three equally spaced rods of some other gray metal, converging in a smaller circle: the outline of a truncated cone.

"It's quite enigmatic!" Alfred observed. "It might be anything."

Bruce chuckled. "Actually it's very distinctive—it's a dredge nozzle, Alfred. Used in amateur gold prospecting. Combined with the ore sample, it suggests that the truck was used, not long ago, by someone prospecting for gold."

"Do people still engage in individual prospecting, sir? I had supposed it was all done by multinational mineral rights concerns."

"Gold prospecting's never disappeared in this country. There's a whole cottage industry supplying prospectors. They use metal detectors, handheld dredges, magnets to separate iron flakes from gold, all kinds of things. People do it in the mountains—but which mountains? This soil sample could come from the Rockies, the Ozarks—maybe the Cascades."

"Still, would it be a clue suitable for a detective?" Alfred prompted.

"It is, Alfred. I'm going to follow up on it. Skeev mentioned someone he called the Big White—aka White Eyes. I've heard rumors he's the head of something called the Brotherhood. If that's the Bavarian Brotherhood, I can tie them into at least two execution-style murders in the last year."

"And I take it this Brotherhood is not a monkish organization, sir?"

"Hardly. They're white supremacists—part of the so-called Christian Identity tradition—they have nothing to do with legitimate Christians, of course. They're caught up in a fantasy about a Zionist conspiracy and the United Nations, under the control of the Antichrist, taking over the United States. Various domestic terrorists and racist militias have more or less the same notion."

"I have read of them. Some think they're making alliances with Muslim extremists."

"It's possible—both groups are anti-Semitic. Disastrous if domestic terrorists work with international terrorists . . ."

"So you'll head for the mountains to investigate this gold-mining connection, sir?"

"Don't know yet which mountains." Bruce took another sip of tea, carefully putting the cup down—Alfred would have given him his iciest look had he damaged the heirloom. He got up from his seat and strolled over to the big swathe of window screen edging the natural dais of rock that separated his command center from the great, stalactite-dripping cavern of the Batcave. Bats swooped and twittered beyond the cave, coming in during the predawn, stirring the air with the musty aroma of bat guano—Bruce and Alfred were quite used to the smell by now. "So I'll be looking in Gotham City first. The Brotherhood appears to be active here. I need to know exactly what those guns were for . . . and then where they're from. Was there a hallmark on that gun?"

"No, Master Bruce. No maker's mark of any kind. Your weapons design scanner came up empty as well: no known gunsmith or professional manufacturer."

"That was my impression. Not a single part seems factory-made. They've been machine-shopped somewhere privately. Very privately."

Bruce shook his head ruefully. This was ominous. Who was designing and secretly constructing such elaborate weapons—and to what purpose?

There was a fluttering at the mesh—then the flutterer clung to it.

"Alfred—our friend is here." A medium-large brown bat was gripping the mesh with tiny claws, his furry reddish brown belly pressed to it, his wings spread out, his muzzle poking through the little feeding gap Alfred had made in the mesh. Bruce knew this bat by the slight hole in his left wing, near the bony peak that ended in a claw. "Same bat we fed all week. Seems to know us. Has that same hole in his wing. I came home with holes in my wings, too, little guy . . ."

Strange to think as a kid I was afraid of bats. He reached through the feeding gap and scratched the bat under his furry jaw . . . *How could I be afraid of this fellow?*

"Ah, yes!" Alfred said, coming over with the jar he kept for bat feeding. "Our *Eptesicus fuscus*—or simply, the big brown bat. You know, this species isn't common here in the cave—they've joined our northern long-eared bats—which, as you know, are *Myotis septentrionalis*—"

"I was *just* going to mention that," Bruce said dryly.

"I believe the presence of *Eptesicus fuscus* in the cave indicates cold weather coming. They only take to deep caves at such times." He handed the jar to Bruce, like an adult letting a child feed an animal at the petting zoo. "Bats, you know, are not flying rodents, as people suppose; they're in a family more closely related to primates. They're closer to us than they are to rodents."

"The 'rats' are on the street," Bruce murmured.

He pinched a mosquito from the jar to feed to his provisional pet as Alfred continued, "What a shame it is that so many bats are killed by pesticides intended for insects—when bats are far more effective at controlling pests than pesticides. Do you know how many tons of mosquitoes they eat per day, Master Bruce? Why—"

"I think I may catch a few hours' sleep," Bruce interrupted gently. "I wonder if you could turn down the bed." Though he had a deep affection for his butler—really, his most important employee, factotum, and best friend—he knew that once he started, Alfred could pontificate for an hour on any subject dear to his heart. Alfred sometimes gave in to a nostalgia for the years when Bruce was a little boy, the survivor of his parents' murders outside the opera house, and Alfred had been a surrogate father, in charge of Bruce's education as well as care and feeding.

"Naturally, Master Bruce, the bed has been turned down for hours," Alfred said coolly. "Just in case *anyone* in the house should feel the need for a normal, sensible, restorative night's sleep."

Bruce nodded distantly, feeding another mosquito into the bat's small, needle-toothed muzzle. Its little gemlike eyes glittered as it tilted its head to look at him. "Keep an eye on the cave," he told the bat. "I'm going to roost awhile."

Gotham City PD Detective Cormac Sullivan, sipping rancid coffee at the workstation of his cluttered Precinct One cubicle, was finding it difficult to focus on the big case that had landed in his lap. He had a truckful of auto-shotguns, an illegal weapons design that no one had known about till the night before; he had rumors of other radically designed weapons hitting the street. He had the Bavarian Brotherhood dealing speed and hot guns and getting into street wars with black gangs. Add to the mix the interesting complication that was the Batman. All of this, normally, would consume his attention so thoroughly he'd forget to eat. But all he could think of, right now, was his teenage son, Gary.

Should never have left the kid in LA with that witch Rosemonde, he thought, compressing the Styrofoam cup in his fingers so that it was in danger of bursting. His ex-wife had seemed to be cleaning up her act, and after twelve years as a freelance detective, bodyguard, and skip tracer, Cormac had decided he needed the financial stability of the job offer with the GCPD. Alimony was a bitch, and to pay it and the child support he'd needed a more consistent paycheck than he got working freelance.

Looking at the photo of him and Gary together on the wall, Cormac took out his cell phone and speed-dialed his ex. When she answered, her voice was slurred. "Huh-loo-oo . . ."

"Rose. Cormac. The boy there?"

"Gary? He's not back. Haven't heard from him. Gone."

Cormac's heart sank. He managed to ask, "You okay?"

"I'm as good as I'm gonna be. Like you care if I'm okay. You the one left. Not me."

"You were loaded all the time."

"You didn't care. You just blew me off when I was having problems."

"Rose, I tried for years—more than ten—"

"Now Gary's left me, too. Now it's just me and the little orange ovals. Me and the ovals. Gary's gone and—"

"You know where he went to?" Cormac interrupted.

"Almost four years you're over there in Gotham City, you see the kid only every couple months, all of a sudden it's where's Gary, where's Gary."

"I wanted custody of him so he *could* see me all the time. You wouldn't give me custody."

"Kid needs his mama."

"Mama needs child support, you mean." He shouldn't get into it with her this way, he knew. But she knew how to get under his skin.

"Hey, kiss my ass, you're the one who left."

"He gets busted for tagging, drinking—you don't tell me for months, I have to find out from—"

"He hasn't got a father, what else is he going to do? He'll spray his name on buildings, he'll drink some hooch. Stole some of my pills, too, if you wanna know. You're the one who—"

"You already said that. Three times. Where's the kid? You must have some clue. You looked for him?"

"I don't know, Cormac. He's probably in Venice, or Santa Monica. He's got friends in Venice Beach. But I don't know where exactly. I'm not going to go snooping in those places. Scary places the kid goes. No way."

"You call Murcheson? I gave you his number, said I'd pay . . ."

"I don't want to send your sleazy bounty hunter friends after my son. The kid'll come back when he gets hungry, like a damn house cat."

"If he's . . ." He didn't want to say it. *If he's not dead.*

"Where's my check?"

"I sent it already. Try getting up off the sofa and looking in the mailbox." He hung up.

Cormac shook his head. The boy's resentment over the breakup—and maybe over his mother's erratic behavior—had erupted into some serious acting out. Three misdemeanor busts already. One for pot, one for underage drinking, one for vandalism. Worse, Cormac himself had found a bindle of meth in the kid's bedroom, when he'd come to pick him up in LA. Left there by another kid, Gary claimed. Cormac wanted to believe that story . . .

He didn't want to think his son was becoming a full-blown drug addict.

He knew the stats. Some drug use was down, in some

places, but crystal meth use was up across the board. GCPD routinely had to arrest paranoid kids, psychotic after a week without sleep. Sometimes, instead of having to arrest them, they had to scoop what was left of them from cars wrapped around streetlight poles.

Captain Gordon had personally supervised the bust of one speed lab; Batman had left broken bones and smashed equipment at another. Groaning speed dealers eager to confess. *Just keep that Bat thing away from me!*

But even Batman couldn't stem the tide of the toxic white powder. It was all over Gotham and it was all over LA. And Gary had disappeared.

"Detective Sullivan?"

Startled, Cormac looked up to see Gordon standing at the entrance to his cubicle. "Captain? Cormac's only two syllables, you know."

"Cormac then. How you doing? You're going to spill that coffee . . ." Gordon was a medium-sized man in an off-the-rack dark blue suit with a perpetually serious expression, dark eyes, sandy hair, and a mustache showing some gray. Looked more like an accountant than a cop—but Cormac had heard that Gordon had knocked more than one gangster out cold with his fists alone.

"Uh—I'm okay, Captain. I just . . . I was thinking about that pile of hardware we lucked onto."

"Wasn't exactly luck. *He* busted that one open for us."

Cormac knew who Gordon meant by *he*. Gordon rarely used the *B*-word around the precinct. He knew that the chief and the mayor frowned on "the Bat." Cormac himself had mixed feelings about Batman. On the one hand, Cormac had been something close to a vigilante himself, working as a skip tracer, chasing down guys who'd skipped on their bail out in LA. You could do some good, working around the edges of the law. And Batman had done a lot of good in the year and a half or so he'd been flapping his cape over the rooftops. On the other hand, Batman was technically a criminal. Guilty of breaking and entering (never had a warrant when he broke in on a criminal), assault (you couldn't say that every time he'd knocked around a punk he was stopping a crime; lots of times it was just interrogation), driving an illegal vehicle—and there was probably more. Hell, there were laws against vigilantism itself.

"Yeah, about him, Captain. You ever wonder—how sane is a guy who dresses the way he does, and does the things he does? Night after night?"

"Sure I wondered that. But this is an insane world. People adapt. And the guy's got a mission . . . Hell, he *is* his mission."

Cormac could hear the admiration in Gordon's voice. He wasn't objective where Batman was concerned. But then, if you stayed too coolheaded—did you get anything done?

"So—Cormac. Any luck tracing those guns?"

"Nah, Captain. The lackeys we picked up with the guns didn't know where they came from. Truck's driver got away."

"Who's the truck registered to?"

"License plate was stolen from another vehicle, about a week ago."

"We've still got Skeev."

"Skeev is out of his mind, incoherent. I can't make head or tail of his transcript."

"Somebody try to get a maker on those guns?"

"We brought in two ordnance experts. Best they can

tell us is that the weapons were made in a private machine shop somewhere; there's not a single mass-produced part. I figure they did it that way to cover their tracks."

Gordon nodded. He looked around the cubicle, shook his head. "Whoever invented office cubicles should get about ten to twenty years in one, with no possibility of parole. They used to give us an office. Not a big one but . . ." He shrugged and looked at the picture, several years outdated, of Cormac and Gary, pinned to the wall, Cormac holding up a couple of trout on a fishing line, Gary offering up a frozen, ironic smile. Typical teenage disdain. But it was still the best photo of Gary that Cormac had. The kid hadn't smiled for the camera since then.

"That your boy?"

Cormac felt a lump in his throat. *My boy.* "Yeah, that's Gary. He's out in LA. Once this case is over, I'm gonna need some time to go see him."

Gordon nodded. "Sure." But his mind was somewhere else, you could tell. "What if we go see Skeev again? He's had all night to come down . . . might have something to say to us now."

Skeev woke up crashing.

He was flopping around in the jail cell bunk in a clammy sweat, had finally slept, with the meth wearing off, and only the maddening clamor of a cellblock could've awakened him. "Goddamn them, why couldn't they keep their mouths shut," he muttered. He felt like somebody had opened up his belly and torn out his guts and sewed him back up again and for some stupid reason he was still alive. He felt that hollow and he felt that dead and he wished it was real death . . .

But then again, when he thought about death, he

curled up like a fetus and gnawed on his knuckle. *No. Have to hang on. Don't let 'em kill you, man.*

He wanted to die and he was terrified of death, at once. That was a speed crash, all right. It made clinical depression seem like something you could hope for someday.

He put a shaking hand on his head and sat up, his head ringing from the shouting that echoed through the cellblock.

"Hey ya Jew hymie bastud! Kiss my ass!"

"Whuzuhhellinyewazzholesyellinaboutshuddahellup!"

"Hey who's gonna be my girlfriend when we get to shower huh? Somebody here gonna be my girlfriend!"

"Your right hand's the only girlfriend you'll ever get, nigga!"

"I'll show you what my right hand can do to your face you—"

On and on like that. Demons, Skeev figured, they were all demons, working for the Antichrist, trying to torture him. He should've listened to White Eyes, he should've been careful, he should never have . . .

The Bat. *The Bat!*

He saw the Bat in his mind's eye, a dark-horned silhouette against the sky, spreading death-colored wings to soar down at him—coming to get him.

He covered his eyes. "Cut it out, cut it out, damn you, man . . . The Bat's not here now . . . get it straight, he's not coming in here, you're safe from him . . ."

"That's right," said the stockier of the two men standing on the other side of the bars. Both of them plainclothes cops, gold badges clipped to their belts. They'd stepped up while his eyes were covered. "You're safe from the Bat here. And from the Big White. We can pro-

tect you, Skeev. But you've gotta help us, too. Who knows
what kind of deal we could cut if you help us out . . ."

The cellblock had gotten eerily quiet with these two
big cops in here. The quiet made Skeev almost as nervous as the noise.

"That's right, you could cut yourself a sweet deal,"
said the other cop. "Or—it could get ugly." Big man, a
scar on one cheek, hair cut in a flattop. Looked like he
might be half black. Shirtsleeves rolled up, navy SEALs
tattoo on his arm. Don't screw with that one.

Skeev licked his lips and flailed out desperately with,
"I'm crashing bad, man. Can you . . . can you get me
something, you know, to make me feel better?"

"We can't get you any speed," the older cop said.

Skeev remembered who the cop was from the TV
news. Big-shot cop name of Gordon.

"But we can get you rehab," Gordon went on.
"Maybe they'll give you some Valium, for a while, help
you through it."

"Yeah, Valium . . ." Valium sounded like heaven right
then. His nerves were trying to crawl out through his
pores. "Maybe . . . I dunno . . ."

"We need to know where the goods you brought in
were made," Gordon said. "We're pretty sure it's White
Eyes' people but . . . we need details. And testimony."

"I dunno. I can't. But . . . maybe."

"Maybe is a start," Gordon said. "You think about it.
I'm Captain Gordon, this is Detective Sullivan. I'm gonna
leave word here that if you want to talk to us, they're to
get in touch with one of us right away . . ."

But Skeev was staring past Gordon—at a cop he
had seen at Brotherhood meetings. Breen, the cop who
worked with the guards for Precinct One. Red-faced

guy, receding white hair, swag belly bursting his uniform shirt. Stubby fingers, the nails chewed to hell, toying with his little walkie-talkie as he stared warningly at Skeev.

Forgot the bastard was here. And he's on the Big White's payroll, too. Did he hear me saying I might cooperate with them? If he did . . .

"Everything okay here, Captain?" Breen said, with a slight Irish accent.

"Yes. We're going to leave Mr. Skeven here to think awhile." Gordon nodded to Sullivan, and they started out.

"Wait!" Skeev said, looking desperately at Breen. "Captain—I didn't mean it! I mean—I never—I can't—"

"Just think about it, Skeev," Sullivan said.

Then the two men went through the door at the end of the cellblock, leaving Skeev alone with Breen.

"I swear, Breen, I didn't—"

"Shut up. Just keep your mouth shut. Right now," Breen hissed. And he walked out after the other two.

Like magic, the cellblock shouting recommenced.

"Hey whuttayabastadswaitinforIwantmydamn breakfast—!"

Bruce Wayne, in Wayne Manor's gym, was doing his eighth set of bench-press reps. He had increased the bench weight to three hundred pounds and it was feeling like he couldn't do a seventh set without tearing something. As it was, he felt like his chest was going to explode with the thudding of his heart and the aching labor of his lungs. Sweat dripped from his forehead, burned his eyes.

His muscles hurt like a son of a bitch. And that was good. Serious workout pain, short of snapping a tendon, was Batman's friend. It meant he was pushing the envelope, reaching the absolute outer limit of his endurance—and going beyond. He had to attempt the impossible. Because the job was impossible. It was him versus every criminal predator in the world . . . starting with the vast underworld in Gotham City.

Alfred, wearing purple workout togs—though his only workout was a brisk walk twice a day—was spotting for Bruce, his fingers hovering nervously over the free-weight bar, ready to direct it back on the stand if Bruce's muscles should suddenly fail.

But Bruce Wayne . . . Batman . . . would tear a muscle before he'd fail to finish a rep. As it was, he just got the weights back on the stand and lay there panting, a fog clearing from his eyes. The clock on the wall said 5 PM. He'd do some leg lifts, some gymnastics, try to get that backflip perfected—have to put the costume for the gymnastics on so the body weight would be right—and then rest forty minutes or so in the Jacuzzi while he took care of some Wayne Foundation business on the phone.

"You had a call about the Wayne Foundation's charity ball, Master Bruce . . ."

"Which charity?" Bruce asked, sitting up, toweling his face.

"Something about free counseling to help prostitutes, sir."

"Oh, yes. One of our new ones. Get them away from pimps, into job training. Good charity, but I don't think I'll make it . . . I'll want to start patrol early tonight. The mayor will be at the charity ball, and the governor. Maybe an actor or two. It'll do very well without me."

"As you like, sir. I took the liberty of mentioning the event to a lady who called for you—she said she knew you from . . . overseas. She thought she might attend the ball."

"What lady? I'm not interested in any dates, Alfred, I'm much too busy right now. When I need to put up the playboy veneer again, I'll call, oh . . . I don't know, someone. Della or Angelina."

"Very good, sir. If Teia calls again, I'll tell her you're not at home."

Bruce turned and stared at Alfred. "Did you say Teia?"

"Shall I make an appointment for you with a hearing specialist, sir?"

"Teia! It can't be . . . Alfred, I'm going to finish my workout. Lay out my best tuxedo. I'm going to the ball."

"We got to get that nigger out of here," Breen said.

He and Van Wyman—the only Gotham City jail guards in the Brotherhood—were standing just outside the door to the cellblock, looking through the mesh window at Cecil Wilson, the brawny black guard who had just finished giving out the evening meals. Cecil was stopping to talk religion to one of the boys. Waving a Bible, trying to get his Pentecostal Christianity across to these slime. Waste of time. Foolish deviltry, anyway, since all black men would eventually go to Hell, as White Eyes had explained, being as niggers were the Descendants of Cain, and their black skin was the mark of Cain, the accursed of God. Fit only to be slaves. But Breen knew better than to voice any of that aloud around here, except quietly to Van Wyman: pale and tall and big-nosed and with big, sleepy brown eyes, Van Wyman had the right attitude.

"I seen the Big White ignore niggers when he's out on the street," Van Wyman said. "He figures he'll catch up to 'em later when the time is right. He won't care if Wilson's around."

"Wilson'll report the damn incident," Breen pointed out. "Starting with an unauthorized visit."

"Yeah, okay, good point, I'll get him outta there, keep him busy." Van Wyman opened the door. "Hey, Wilson—you got a family call, some kinda emergency!"

Wilson looked over in alarm. "What kind?"

"I dunno. They said come right on home, don't even bother to call! I'll cover for you here, man!"

"I'm coming!" Wilson almost ran up the hallway, pushed through the door, ran past them toward the locker room, the Bible like a football under his arm. Just in time, too, because Breen's beeper went off.

The man himself was here . . .

Skeev was pacing back and forth, three steps this way, three steps back, the diagonal length of his cell. Now and then he kicked angrily at the seatless toilet. When he walked toward the back of the cell, he was pretty sure he wanted to tell the cops to go to Hell. When he walked to the front, he wanted to make a deal with Gordon.

Because then he thought about all the time he'd do, with his record. He thought about how badly he needed to get away from the boof. He thought about the street . . . and the Brotherhood, and what they might do to him anyway.

He turned away from the bars and paced the other way.

Back of the cell—cops go to Hell.

Back the other way—maybe he'd play. *Back of the*

cell, cops go to Hell; turn the other way, maybe he'd play. Back of the cell . . .

"Hello, Skeev."

Skeev froze, feeling like he was trying to swallow a golf ball as he stared at the enormous man standing on the other side of the bars. He had seen him in person only one other time, at the Brotherhood Hall, up on Hatchet Mountain. Up this close, he looked even bigger: the Big White. It was all muscle, too, Skeev knew. White Eyes was so big he didn't quite fit into that charcoal-colored suit. The cloth strained at the seams. He was tanned, contrasting sharply with his eyes and eyebrows; the brows and his flattop hair were flaxen, his eyes so gray they were almost lost in the whites. You had to watch a long time to see them blink. His lips were almost nonexistent—his mouth just a wide line in his face above that lantern jaw. His left ear was mostly missing. There were stories about that. Some said cancer. Some said a grizzly, some said "a nigger with a machete—but you shoulda seen the nigger when White Eyes got done."

On the middle finger of both of his side-of-ham fists was a big silver ring. They were identical rings, each with an iron cross cut into it.

White Eyes cracked his knuckles. "Open it, Van Wyman."

Sure, Van Wyman was there, too, but Skeev hadn't even noticed him. You wouldn't take much notice of those little asteroids when you were staring up close at Jupiter.

Breen unlocked the jail cell door, and White Eyes slipped in, moving all that bulk with no wasted motion.

Skeev took a step back. "Yes sir. How are you, sir."

White Eyes shook his head at Skeev. "Don't you back off from me. That is not what a White Man does. A White Man does not back away."

"No sir." But Skeev stayed where he was. And he was noticing the strange hush that had descended over the cellblock. The others were listening. Waiting . . .

"You back off from a challenge, Skeev? First, the temptation to use the Product. I have told my people about that. Only the Supreme may use enhancements. You used amphetamines. Not good. Second, you ran from a homosexual lunatic. He wears tights and a cape— the man is a homosexual for certain, Skeev. And there are indications of great wealth around him. That car of his suggests as much. Therefore he is, in all probability, a Jew, stealing money from the hardworking White Man. Yet you ran from him."

It took Skeev a moment to realize that White Eyes meant the Bat. "Oh—sir. He's not . . . he's no human being. He's . . . he works for the Antichrist. He's a demon, is what he is. I seen it. You didn't see him up close, sir."

"We could have punished you for snorting up our Product and running from that faggot Jew in the tights, and then forgiven you. But you committed a third crime: you buckled for the slaves of the Antichrist. You were going to tell them everything. Weren't you, Skeev."

"No sir! No, I—"

It was a blur of motion: White Eyes went from dead-still, out of reach, to standing over Skeev with his hand around his throat, all in that flicker of an instant. And a moment later Skeev felt himself lifted off his feet, as if by a jib crane, but it was White Eyes' right hand, lifting

Skeev—who was a big man himself—right off his feet, squeezing, not seeming to feel it when Skeev thrashed and clawed and kicked. That implacable grip never wavered, with 241 pounds of man struggling in it. Struggling more and more feebly. Just looking into those dead gray eyes that never blinked and trying to scream and unable to. Fingers trying to pry just one of White Eyes' fingers loose. Just one. If he could just pry a thumb away . . .

A buzzing black darkness, like a swarm of jet bees, seemed to emerge from those flat unblinking gray eyes, and the buzzing filled his ears, filled all the world . . .

But for an instant, just before he died, Skeev felt a strange gratitude to White Eyes—who was, after all, setting him free.

Captain Gordon was thinking of calling his wife, telling her he'd be late again, wondering how he'd justify it to her this time . . .

He forgot all about it when the cell phone rang. Not his personal cell phone. The special one. It had been simply left on his desk, one day, in an envelope that also contained a piece of paper showing the bat insignia. The rooftop Bat-Signal wasn't always practical. He'd satisfied himself the cell phone was untraceable.

The ring came again—a high-pitched *eeee* sound. Like a bat makes?

As Gordon drew the small black cell phone from his inside coat pocket, he glanced at the open door of his office. The precinct station was noisy: computer printers going, phones ringing, loud conversations, prisoners bitching as they were booked in. With all that noise, and no one around, he didn't think it necessary to close the door. But just in case, he rolled his chair over to it, pushed with his foot, then turned his back to it . . .

. . . so that he failed to see, as he spoke on the special cell phone to Batman, that the office door didn't quite fully close.

"You there?" Gordon said.

"I'm here," came the familiar voice. It wasn't a voice you'd want to hear in a dark alley. Only, you'd be wrong about that, unless you were a criminal. "You make a deal with Skeev?"

"Tried. Going to be hard to make a deal with him now. I just got word he hung himself in his jail cell. We've got safeguards—not sure how he's supposed to have pulled that off."

There was a pause before Batman asked, "Any other prisoners see him die?"

"Nope. His cell faces a blank wall."

"Coroner's report?"

"Not yet. Awkward coroner's reports have a way of getting lost around here."

"You think the Brotherhood has infiltrated the department?"

"I don't know. I know we have some dirty cops I haven't been able to get Internal Affairs interested in. I did get a tip that there may be another gun delivery in the Alley tonight—this time in the old Drago building. Sometime after one in the morning. I'll have some trusted guys on it—but I don't want them too close, too soon. If we *are* infiltrated, word would get out . . ."

"I understand. I'll be there in advance."

"Thanks. Listen, I was wondering, maybe we could talk about . . . hello?"

Dial tone.

Bruce had lifted the cowl from his head, to put it away after his costumed gymnastics exercise, when a flicker of motion, a dark ripple in his peripheral vision, made him turn to stare into the cave's primal darkness, beyond the window screen.

Bats, he supposed. But then again, it was now after dark; he'd already heard the voluminous whirring of their thousands of wings as they'd flocked to the entrances and out into the countryside to hunt.

The motion had seemed . . . very human.

He put the cowl back on, in case someone should be there—some wayward spelunker, perhaps—and stalked over to the screens, looking out into the caves. Thought he saw a shape move there, once more. Then it was gone. He kept watching, but saw nothing more.

He moved to the surveillance panels. All lights were green, and when he flicked the monitors through the various views, the infrared cameras showed no one. There were only the stalactites and a few sleepy bats. None of them was flying.

He checked another panel: the motion sensors on the lawns around Wayne Manor were on, and they had detected nothing. The cameras on the grounds showed nothing special. A jay, hopping from one shrub to another. A raccoon prowling. The motion sensors were sophisticated enough to filter out birds and raccoons— anything larger would set them off. He hit the intercom. "Alfred—any indication of intruders, people on the grounds?"

"No sir. Shall I check the surveillance panels?"

"I already have . . . I'm going to have a quick look. Probably a trick of the light . . ."

Batman went to the door that led out into the Batcave, down the spiral stairs. He stepped to the stone floor, stood motionless in the chilly, damp space—he could feel the vastness of the cavern opening up around him; he smelled guano and minerals, heard the drip of water from somewhere. Another sound came sometimes, like someone winding an old-fashioned windup watch—but he knew that was a noise bats made, the part of the sound you could hear when they were echolocating. The remaining bats were heading for the night sky.

He watched, and waited. Saw no one. He slipped deeper into the darkness and found the small UV goggles he kept in his utility belt. He slipped them on and looked around the cave, the ultraviolet making its naturally vaulted ceilings, its cathedralesque spaces an almost abstract composition of red and blue. Saw no one . . .

Wait. There. Up atop that melting ziggurat of stone that led to a stalagmite column—was there someone, almost blending with the stalagmite's craggy base?

It was a man, wasn't it, in a cape? A man with half a face—and horns?

Or was it . . . his costume? An empty Batman costume, standing there, looking eyelessly at him. Reminding him of that moment at the dock when he'd seemed to see himself as Skeev had—more symbol than human being. A threat in the shape of a man. But this wasn't his current Batman costume he was seeing—it was the very first costume he'd made. He and Alfred had sat up, sewing it like a couple of women stitching Halloween costumes for the children. It hadn't lasted that first night out intact. It'd taken two bullet holes and four knife slashes. Wasn't that it, standing there without a man in it?

He stalked toward the apparition—and almost instantly lost sight of it. Had it vanished—or had the figure slipped behind the column of rock? He ran to the column and circled it . . . and found no one, nor any tracks in the thick mat of guano under it.

He was quite alone, in the gravelike silence of the cavern.

"They fell for it, sir," Breen said as he came into the penthouse suite in Gotham City's best hotel. Looking out at the dusky city, hands clasped behind him, White Eyes was silhouetted against the sunset-washed plate-glass window.

He didn't bother to turn around as he replied, "It remains to be seen if they fell for it, Breen."

"I heard Gordon talking to Batman in his office—he thinks I don't know, but some of us do: he's got a special cell phone the Bat calls him on. The lunatic in the cape will be there tonight, sir. The Bat don't like to leave things unfinished."

"We'll see. We'll be waiting for him. Did you arrange for the coroner to see the wrong body? Or should I say, the right body . . ."

"I did, sir."

"Then we'll divert the centrifuge shipment—but we'll have a sample of our new hardware on hand, just so we can test it out on this Bat thing, and any uniformed slave of the Antichrist who shows his face there . . ."

"Where's the main shipment going, sir?" Breen asked.

"Need to know, Breen."

"Need to know so's I can try to protect 'em, sir. We may have to pay off Sergeant Felucca. Burris and Median are ours, of course—they'll cover for us, if we know what to cover."

White Eyes considered, then grunted assent. "The other side of town," he said. "An Italian restaurant,

Uncle Gnocchi's. We've paid some of the Italians to cover us but best to keep the police out of the way entirely. Interesting—I see a billboard, down below, advertising a movie about a nigger air force general. Can you imagine? The Jews continue the indoctrination—continue to make their gorillas appear to be legitimate human beings, and no one calls them on it. Though nigger leadership is a contradiction in terms."

"It is that, sir! Why this afternoon I was telling Van Wyman that the media is taken over by—"

"Breen?"

"Yes sir?"

"Shut up and see that there are only friendly patrols in the vicinity of that restaurant."

"Yes sir. Anything else?"

"Have you any more intelligence on the bat Jew?"

"No sir. Just that Gordon's tight with him."

"We'll eliminate this Batman first, then Gordon—when the time's right."

"Yes sir." Breen waited, but White Eyes said nothing more. Breen shrugged to himself and turned to walk out, reflecting that the great man hadn't even bothered to look at him, not once, in the entire conversation. That didn't sit well with Breen. That feeling that he was so far down below White Eyes that he wouldn't even look at him. But, after all, White Eyes would one day be absolute dictator over all the United States.

So it was something Breen would just have to get used to.

In a place like this, Bruce thought, *you can pretend, for a while, that the world's not so bad. That it's about people smiling, dancing around and around. Anyway, you can try to believe it.*

"Bruce, you look like you're having a good time!" Della said, in her slight Georgia accent as she walked up to him at the open bar. The lights of the Wayne Center Ballroom's chandelier played over his tuxedo and scintillated in Della's glittery blue dress; dancers gyrated across the shining ballroom. "I am just mired in ennui at this thing . . ."

"I'm having a great time—now that you're lighting the place up," Bruce said, slurring the words just enough and beaming his big, gleaming, carefully constructed playboy smile at her. He tossed off the "champagne"— it was actually sparkling apple juice, but he wanted Della to believe it was champagne—and set it down on the table with a pretend awkwardness, so that it fell over on its side with a *clunk*. "Whoopsy."

"I think you'd better dance with me," said the young socialite, "just so I can whirl you away from the champagne bottles, big guy." She was a blue-eyed, dimpled professional model, her glossy blond-red hair piled artfully on her head, her swanlike neck set off by a jeweled choker. She bobbed her head to the music—a tango, with some classical flourishes from the orchestra Bruce had hired, the musicians dressed in white tuxedos on their golden bandstand.

The dancers whirled across the floor in designer gowns, glittering jewels, platinum cuff links, carefully displayed Rolexes. Orchids spilled from wicker baskets on the walls; enormous silver-framed mirrors returned the light of the chandeliers and duplicated the gaiety of the murmuring crowd. The mayor was dancing with an up-and-coming young movie actress, and the governor's wife was dancing with an aging movie star. Several other men, good-looking young guys in tuxes, were looking dourly on as Bruce and Della passed through the crowd to the dance floor.

"Looks like you disappointed some of those guys," Bruce said. "They'll wait their chance and cut in. Maybe I'll be lucky and they'll fight for who gets to cut in first, knock each other down."

"If they try to cut in, *I* may knock them down! I've been waiting to get you on a dance floor—at least—for a long time, Bruce Wayne . . . Whoa, you've been working out!" She was genuinely startled, laying her delicate fingers on his upper arm for the dance. "That's like a fence post. You flexing your muscles to impress me?"

"No—would it work?" They went into their dance positions.

"Doubt it. But I might enjoy it anyway."

Bruce knew he should pretend drunkenness, just to be consistent, but he could never resist a tango. He danced with energy, exactly on the beat, never falling behind, though the song fairly raced along. He caught her up in his arms and whirled her into the *abrazo,* exactly in the pocket of the music, with an overpowering yet gentle control that made her gasp, surged color to her cheeks. Tall though she was, she held herself gracefully, and she felt light in his arms. He swept her around to the end of his reach, so they drew apart, each with an arm stretched to the other—and their gazes locked. Her eyes glittered and her sweet lips parted invitingly . . .

In the space of a second, a flash of insight that took place between dance moves, Bruce Wayne imagined the fullness of another life entirely. He saw himself married to Della—not a vapid woman, like many models, but bright and well spoken, a great beauty who would age very well—and he saw them with children; he saw himself sharing his secret with her, and she sadly accepting it, though it meant many nights alone while he was Batman. Why not? Why *couldn't* he have that life, if she was willing? It was a sacrifice for him, as well as for her. Then he imagined her loneliness, night after night, her increasing shrewishness as she nagged him to take time off, finally begging him to let Batman go entirely. He envisioned his refusal, his attempt to explain, yet again, his Mission, the oath he had taken at his parents' graves, the boundless fury that burned in his breast like the flame at the Tomb of the Unknown Soldier. He saw her walking out on him. He saw the book an angry woman might write. *My Life with Batman.* The destruction not only of his secret identity, but of his sacred cause.

Saw it all in a second . . .

And then the music called for quite another position. They moved into it with rhythmic accuracy, but something had shuttered in Bruce Wayne's face, and a subtle disappointment flickered across Della's expressive lips, though she could not have consciously said how he had disappointed her.

Then the dance was done. He offered her his arm. She took it but looked quizzically at him, shaking her head. "You're not even breathing hard."

"I . . . jog. Have to, with my lifestyle."

"Oh, what lifestyle?"

"Show you sometime."

"Mighty generous of you," she said, with arch sarcasm. "I'm more in the mood for a waltz, right now—could you get them to play us one? It's your orchestra!"

"Slavery's illegal, I believe, nowadays—I only rent them. But . . ."

Then—he saw her. There, near the orchestra risers. *Teia!*

". . . but I'll ask. Um—in the meantime . . ." He snagged a flute of champagne from a white-jacketed waiter's passing salver; with his free hand he took Della's and kissed it, then placed the glass in it. Did it swiftly but without spilling a drop. He inclined his head, smiling apologetically—and hurried off to the orchestra. He caught the conductor's eye and mouthed, *Waltz.* The conductor, who knew very well who was writing the checks, nodded and signaled for a segue into a waltz.

Teia was watching him approach across the ballroom floor, smiling faintly. She stood there, very self-possessed and still, so still he thought of a dark flower in a place no wind could stir. She was much shorter than Della, her hair glossy black, spilling over her bare, golden shoulders and her silken burgundy gown; her eyes were so brown they were almost black, and the pupils seemed impossibly deep. Her lips were full, her compact body taut and delicate at once. He could detect no makeup on her.

The delicacy, he knew, was an illusion. He had seen her break through a brick wall with a single kick.

"Bruce. You look well. Strong."

"And you look beautiful," he said. She'd always looked beautiful, even in the simple black pajamalike outfit they'd worn during the training retreat. Only a few such remote training centers admitted women—and she was one of the few women who had qualified.

"But there is something . . ." She pursed her lips, just slightly—it didn't ruin them at all—and looked at him with her head cocked. ". . . a shadow of something, perhaps, yes? Something bothering you?"

He laughed gently, as they drifted over to a refreshment table. "Two years since I've seen you and you act as if we were just parted for an evening, ready to start up the conversation again."

"Oh? What conversation was that?"

"You were always trying to draw me out . . ." She'd tried to talk to him about his parents. A touchy subject. A painful subject. "Champagne?"

"Just some juice. Thank you."

"Teia—it's good to see you." He meant it. He didn't usually drop the Bruce Wayne mask—he was either Bruce Wayne, playboy, or Bruce Wayne the philanthropist—but he realized, in that moment, how much he'd missed her, and he let something show through he didn't usually permit anyone to see. He cleared his throat. "What . . . what brings you to Gotham?"

"I don't like to lie," she said. "But I had made one lie up for you: I came to collect donations for the Tibetan Freedom Fund."

"I already—"

"I know you do. But your friends here don't."

"I'll see what I can drum up for you. So—how is your collecting for the fund a lie? You do a lot of work for it."

"Yes—but how did you know that? I only started after we went our separate ways."

He didn't want to admit he'd had her discreetly checked out—just to see if she was all right. "I don't know, I heard it somewhere."

"I do work for the charity, but . . . It is not approaching from a position of strength to admit this—but I

really came to see *you*. I thought . . . I just *felt* you
needed to talk to someone. And I needed . . . to see you."

She dropped her gaze at that. She was usually so confident, it was a rare thing to see her embarrassed.

"I missed you, Teia." A moment of awkwardness—he
felt something else was called for. "Would you . . . care
to dance?"

"I don't know these dances. And you do it so well.
Perhaps a walk . . . ? There is a garden outside?"

"Something that passes for one. But you'll brighten it
up. Come on . . ." He offered her his arm, and they
crossed the ballroom—where he spotted Della, flamboy-
antly dancing with a star quarterback. He saw her wince
as the big guy stepped on her foot. She was careful not
to look directly toward him, but he knew she was
watching as he and Teia went out an exit, into the
Wayne Center's sculpture gardens. Abstract sculptures
rose from beds of roses, and a fountain burbled, surrounded by birds-of-paradise.

" 'Just felt I needed to talk'?" he prompted. She didn't
answer immediately and he added, "That's a pretty
good long-distance line you've got to me. Working on
telepathy?"

She sighed. "Oh! I hear that mocking tone! You were
always so skeptical! But *There are more things on
heaven and Earth than are dreamt of in your philoso-
phy,* as your Shakespeare says."

"We can't really lay claim to Shakespeare, here in
America," Bruce said. "We've got Poe, however. What
you said about a shadow makes me think of Poe's
'Shadow: A Parable' . . . *And lo! from among those sable
draperies where the sounds of the song departed, there
came forth a dark and undefined shadow—*"

He broke off, feeling incongruous, reciting prose—the night after knocking people out cold and ducking the cops—but the rest of the line came to his mind, unspoken: *a shadow such as the moon, when low in heaven, might fashion from the figure of a man: but it was the shadow neither of man nor of God, nor of any familiar thing.*

"There is a gloominess in you," she murmured, looking at him, as they stopped beside the fountain, "a dark place, that you try to hide . . ."

"Do I? You'd be surprised. Sometimes it comes right out."

"And you have been troubled by something," she said, reaching a hand to catch the spray from the fountain. "I *did* feel it."

He hesitated. He did want some advice—her philosophical background might help him. Though Bruce had adopted no specific spiritual tradition, Teia was a practitioner of a variety of Vipassana Buddhism that he could relate to. Like the most ancient Buddhism—Gotama's own—it was less a religion than an inner movement toward deeper consciousness, toward less identification with desire; it was about intelligent self-control, and inner freedom. He respected her grounding in that tradition, and he suspected that what he'd experienced might be more metaphysical than physical. But he couldn't tell her much about it without revealing that he was Batman. No way he could tell her about the uncharacteristic moment of doubt he'd had, gazing down at Skeev. The thing in the Batcave, though . . .

"I saw something last night, Teia. There's . . . a place underneath the manor. It's dark in there."

"A wine cellar?"

"Close enough. I thought I saw something there, a . . . a shape. A visitor where there shouldn't be one. It was as if it was mocking me. I have enemies—it could be they found a way in . . ."

"What enemies are those?" He could feel her close scrutiny. Perhaps suspecting paranoia.

"Everyone with enough money has . . . enemies. Potentially."

"You mean—kidnappers? Terrorists?"

"Could be. These are grim times—maybe that works on my imagination. I suppose I'm imagining things."

"A dark visitor. There is more than one type of 'visitor,' Bruce." She looked up at him, her face catching the light—passing headlights mixed with streetlights, the urban version of the lover's moon—and for a moment he felt the space between them as clearly as he felt his own body; a space filled with a subtle electricity, with longing. "Perhaps, Bruce, loneliness makes you see things worse than they are. Where I come from, we have the legend of the Mountain Ghost. He is an evil magic beast who is said to carry children away. Once at night when my parents had left me at home, and the wind was crying in the darkness—I thought I saw the Mountain Ghost, skulking along in the shadows, coming toward the house. I wanted to know. I had nowhere to run, and did not wish to be a little cowering victim, so I picked up a burning stick from the fire and ran toward the creature. And I saw that it was just the stump of an old tree—but in the starlight, and the shadows, my mind had made it look just like the Mountain Ghost. And you—your parents have been gone, too, since you were a child. You have no one but Alfred . . . Perhaps, in a way, what you see is—the Mountain Ghost. And your Mountain Ghost, too, is a projection of your own mind, Bruce . . ."

"Maybe your ghost took a shortcut here—under the mountains." He smiled and shrugged. Shouldn't have brought it up.

She was gazing at him in a way that made him feel like she was looking right into him. It was a feeling that made him ill at ease—yet he didn't want it to stop.

"Bruce . . . do you remember . . ." Her voice became husky. "That night beside the stream?"

She put a hand up, and he enfolded it in his own. "I remember, Teia. It was spring. There were blue crocuses, soft grass—and it was quiet. There was only the stream, and the wind—and a bird was singing, just one bird in that willow by the stream, and you said he was calling to someone . . . He just kept calling and calling . . . And you let me kiss you . . ."

He had almost lost himself in her, that night. Almost surrendered his heart to her.

She raised her face to his, and he kissed her now— enfolded her in his arms . . . Kissed her once more . . .

And almost, almost . . . almost surrendered to her once again.

Bruce felt he was fairly flying over the rooftops, under a moon sliding behind racing clouds. He was actually only leaping from one rooftop to the next, sometimes using his newest projection-grapple to swing over whole streets, but it almost felt like flying. *Teia!* He stopped for a moment on a roof across from an apartment building where, through a window, he could see a father reading to his small daughter as she lay in bed, Mom smilingly watching from the doorway. Perhaps they lived modest lives, in that creaking apartment building, but right then it felt to him that their lives were somehow much bigger than Bruce Wayne's. Something in him ached to carve out a home for a wife, a child—to create a whole different quality of life. He couldn't surrender his Mission—but maybe there *was* a chance he didn't have to be alone. Of all people, Teia would understand . . .

Then the dad got up, and turned off the light, and went out of that little room with his wife, shutting the door.

Shutting the door on Bruce Wayne.

Wait. I'm Bruce? Bruce dressed as Batman? That's a mistake. And mistakes aren't allowed. I can't be Bruce and do what Batman has to do . . .

He moved hurriedly on, his movements now not as sure. He crossed another rooftop, shot the grapple across to an old stone building; it latched onto a gargoyle and held firmly. He swung across the street, hit the COIL switch, and it pulled him up to the gargoyle—an almost batlike figure with its scalloped stone wings and animal face eyeing him, the lower part of that face eroded by the acid rains—missing, just like the lower half of the face he'd seen in the Batcave; like that mocking shadow.

He winced, climbed atop the gargoyle, pulled himself from there to the rooftop, ran across the roof, an image of Teia sharp in his mind . . .

And came to a dead stop, on the corner of the taller building overlooking Drago Storage and Supply across the street. Peering over the edge, he saw some men eight stories below, moving furtively into the building through a side door . . . and one of them was carrying a crate.

Time to get serious.

He had left Teia at her hotel—she didn't invite him in, though he could tell she was tempted, and it was good she didn't because he would have had to say no. Reluctantly—but he'd have said no. Yet when he'd summoned the Batmobile to a warehouse parking lot near the hotel, took the costume from its trunk, and changed, he'd been *whistling* while he was doing it. Whistling a tune from De Hartmann he'd heard Teia play on the piano, once. *You don't prepare to be Batman by whistling a damn tune!* he reminded himself. Disgusting adolescent state of mind . . .

He chuckled at himself, just once, and then decided Bruce had to go away now, and Batman had to be here, and only Batman. He closed his eyes, balled his fists, and remembered that night, out behind the Gotham City opera . . .

The boy walks with his parents out of the opera house, into the shadowy side street. The dark figure steps from the shadows, brandishing a pistol, and demands Dad's wallet; grabs the wallet, then snatches at Mom's jewelry. His father sees the man reach for his mother and instinctively steps in front of her, knocking the man's hand down. Reacting mindlessly, the man pulls the trigger, again and again. Dad falls. Mom screams, and the man shoots her—shoots his mother!—shoots her to stop the screaming, and Bruce throws himself over his parents' bodies, crying out in disbelief and shock, feeling shot himself though no bullet has touched him. And the man hears the sirens and runs. The cops tear Bruce away from his parents' bodies. Then comes the realization that the man got away and probably won't be caught . . .

The funeral, the burial. The vow at their graves.
And Batman is born.

Now, on that Gotham rooftop, Bruce Wayne had left
the costume. Batman was back.

His eyes narrowed, his pulse quickened, the Batman
feeling swept over him, all-consuming: a fury tempered
by calculation; a heat in his spine, a focused intensity
chilling his nerves: a one-pointed attention, a two-
pointed cowl.

Batman assessed the street, saw the quickest way
across and down to the Drago building. He fixed his secondary grapple onto a solid cornice, ran to the rear of
the building he was on, long-jumped off—it'd been a
year and three months since he'd gotten used to simply
leaping off buildings many stories high, diving into space
without a net—and his momentum carried him out to
the end of the grapple line. He turned at the end of the
swing, pulling his kinetic force back through the motion
so that it redoubled, carrying him *whooshing* past the
front corner of the building, up and over the power and
phone lines, over the intervening street, and down to
the roof of the Drago building below. He hit it at just the
right angle, some of his falling energy soaked up by the
cable as he manipulated the gripper, so that he broke
neither his ankles nor the roof. He gave the gripper
the exact twist and tug that would send a signal to the
grapple, which unhooked itself and coiled back to
the grapple launcher in his hand.

Most of this was watched, on the sidewalk below,
by a droopy, marginally intoxicated bag lady pushing
an overflowing shopping cart. She wasn't sure if that

flying black-winged man was real, or one of her hallucinations. Probably seeing things again. Hell, though—it
was a good'n.

Batman saw that it was an old-fashioned building,
with a trapdoor roof hatch for maintenance—the newer
ones, more burglar-proof, didn't have them. It struck
Batman as a bit too convenient, their having a rendezvous
in a building with that trapdoor, which might've been built
just for him. He turned his back on it, went to the corner of the building, looked over the edge. There was a
guard, with an ordinary 12-gauge shotgun in his hand,
down there, a white man in civilian clothes and a black
watch cap. The man glanced toward the rooftop, sensing something, and Batman drew back a little—but
the sentry didn't see him. The gunman went back to
strolling back and forth in the alley and Batman, using
UV binoculars, immediately recognized his face: it was
bisected with a scar he'd given the guy himself, about a
year before, when he'd thrown him through a plate-
glass window. It was Tommy Dench—speed dealer and
rapist, reputed to have been an admiring correspondent
with the late, unlamented Timothy McVeigh. Seemed
Dench had gotten out of jail again.

Batman drew a Batarang from his belt, attached it to
a grapple cable, worked out the angle, and whipped the
Batarang down so it encircled Dench's neck, caught in a
loop, and pulled tight; he jerked Dench off his feet,
winding the other end of the Batarang around an iron
ventilation pipe. Dench's fingers tightened on the shotgun, as Batman hoped they would, and the 12-gauge
fired. The shot echoed through the empty streets. Dench
dropped the gun and clawed at the loop around his

neck. It wasn't tight enough to choke Dench to death anytime soon, Batman knew, not with Dench's hands free, but he also knew it'd make an interesting sight for the other Brotherhood thugs spilling from the side door at the sound of the gunshot. It was all a decoy so he could get behind them.

"What the Hell, Dench!" one of them yelled. "Someone cut Dench down!"

"Look at that thing on the rope there—shaped like a—"

"It's a bat! The goddamn Bat's here!"

Batman was already at the back of the building, dropping down another cable, crashing through a window into the main room of the building, accompanied by a shower of broken glass as he dropped past an old earthmover to the floor. The first three stories of the building were taken up by one big room, storage for outdated construction equipment and old trucks, even a mid-twentieth-century fire truck. In the cleared space on the dusty concrete floor near the front was an open crate—with nothing in it.

"So you thought *you'd* decoyed *us,* you cross-dressin' lowlife?" came a low gravelly voice from behind.

Batman heard the click of a weapon . . .

He was already throwing himself aside, landing on his right shoulder, rolling as bullets strafed just a millisecond behind. He threw himself behind an old backhoe, amazed to see the rounds from the weapon tear the engine cover off the old machine, rip the engine apart, turn it into shrapnel. A powerful gun.

One of the rounds ricocheted around the room until, spent, it rolled to a stop against his boot—the bullet, made of some shiny alloy, was as round as a ball bearing, like a ball from an old muzzle loader, but smaller.

Batman clambered quickly to the rear of the backhoe, poised there, crouched, looking down to see White Eyes grinning from the center of the floor. Damn, the s.o.b. was *big*.

"Come on down, cape-boy!" White Eyes called. "You look like a fairy in that outfit! I got some *real* manhood for ya right here! Come and get it!"

The weapon in White Eyes' hands had a disk lying flat atop it, a drum that gave off a hum as it spun within itself, the whole thing like a machine gun from World War One, in outward appearance—inwardly it would be something far more sophisticated.

Centrifugal gun, Batman thought. *A Dread.*

He'd seen prototypes blueprinted in Wayne Industries' intelligence report on new ballistic technologies: the "Dread" gun was one of them. It fired thousands of small spherical bullets with a rapidity and force, delivered by centrifugal energy, far in excess of an ordinary machine gun. This was the Brotherhood's homegrown version of a Dread. With weapons like that in the hands of an army of enough racist criminals, the balance of power in the United States could shift . . .

"Fancy moves you got, Bat-thing!" White Eyes jeered. "Like one of those pretty-boy figure skaters! Your costume'd look good out on the ice, skatin' to 'The Blue Danube'!"

Batman was moving along the top of the backhoe, almost crawling, keeping its bulk between him and White Eyes.

"He's up there!" one of the Brotherhood shouted. An auto-shotgun roared, again a millisecond behind Batman as he leapt to the right, onto the old fire truck. He vaulted over its mildewed canvas hoses, came down onto another Brotherhood sentry on the other side, this one armed with an Uzi. Batman's right foot smashed into the man's gun hand, breaking every bone in it, his left boot heel slamming into his forehead, cutting his scream short.

The guy was out cold before he hit the ground—with Batman landing on his chest. He leapt off, ducked behind a road grader, circled it to try to flank White Eyes . . .

He stepped over the prostrate form of another man, this one in uniform: an unconscious security guard, a small Filipino, with an egg-shaped lump on his forehead where someone had coldcocked him. Batman heard the man groaning, stirring. "Stay down, play dead," Batman whispered as he passed. "I've got it covered."

As he spoke he threw a Batarang over the grader, so that it rebounded from the wall on the other side of the building. White Eyes reacted, firing a burst from his whirring centrifugal gun at the decoying Batarang. Batman had his grapple ready now, stepped out and fired it toward the gun in White Eyes' hands, tilting it down so the claws of the grapple caught the gun; he gave the exact twist and tug needed, making the grapple recoil to him, pulling the gun with it.

"You sneaky son of a whore!" White Eyes roared, clutching at empty air as the gun vanished from him, clattering onto the floor at Batman's feet.

"You afraid to fight me without a gun?" Batman asked, deliberately goading him.

"Let's go!" White Eyes shouted.

"Without your little troop of Neanderthals backing

you up?" Batman said, stepping out into the open. "That's too bad—but I'll get to them later." His right hand had drawn his cape up in front of him, so that he seemed a dark, indistinct shape with horns and gleaming eyes— till he spread the cape open, his gloved hands spread wide as if ironically offering an embrace. "Well? *Let's go*, Big White."

Looking at the Bat face-to-face wasn't exactly what White Eyes had anticipated. He didn't see the clownish figure he'd described to Skeev. He saw a shape carved from the darkest heart of a thundercloud; he saw a figure pulsing with a hunger for vengeance. Like Skeev had said: a demon.

Seeing Batman, in that moment, White Eyes had a momentary nightmare premonition . . .

But he suppressed the feeling, angrily deciding Batman had somehow induced in him the superstitious dread he cultivated on the street.

Not me, he thought. *That's no demon. He's a man in a costume, just a guy in a mask, and he's going down.*

"Stay back, Brotherhood!" White Eyes bellowed, "the Bat-thing is mine!"

And then he rushed the guy in the mask.

Batman waited, not even tensing, as the big man charged him, then let the *Taijutsu* move that he'd already selected unfold itself: the way of evasion and redirection, the striking at the enemy's soft places while he rushed past you off balance.

Batman slipped aside at the last possible instant, driving a knee into White Eyes' soft parts, under his rib cage, feeling it jab past the hard muscles to slam his innards.

The Dark Knight drew back, spun to set himself for his adversary's recovery. White Eyes, faster than he looked, had managed not to fall and was already coming back at him, big hands held like thick swollen talons in front of him, face rigid and white as the onrushing grille of a semitruck—and showing glints of pain that let Batman know he'd hurt him.

Batman let White Eyes' second rush seem to knock him back but instead he rolled onto his back, took the big man on his boots, and propelled him over and past, so that White Eyes flipped over on his back with a thump that shook the whole building. Batman jumped to a standing position in a blur, whirling, sweeping his cape out of reach with his right hand.

The man who would someday be known as the Caped Crusader was aware that his cape was sometimes a liability—it provided extraneous material an enemy could get a grip on and use against him. But it had advantages at other times, involving psychology and camouflage in dark places, that made it worth the risk.

White Eyes was up almost as fast as Batman, but gasping, the breath knocked from him by the fall onto his back. Big White took a deep snarling gulp of air and his muscles swelled with his fury, so that his clothes ripped at the seams; veins stood out on his neck, his eyes bugged, his teeth bared, his hands clutched, and Batman knew that if this man got a good hold on him for even half a second he'd break his spine in two.

"Cops outside!" someone yelled. "We gotta get outta here, Big White!"

But roaring so loudly the windows rattled, White Eyes rushed again and Batman feinted left, then dodged right when White Eyes went for the feint. He grabbed the big man's left arm and twisted, using momentum against him, throwing him in a classic Judo move—again White Eyes was flipped painfully onto his back.

Batman was dimly aware that, in the background, the security guard, a spindly little man, was up, staggering toward his own fallen pistol. "I help, I help, Batman!" the little man shouted hoarsely.

Don't help! Batman thought as he set himself to kick White Eyes in the jaw as the big man started to get up—but this time White Eyes rolled away and swept up the centrifugal gun, kicked to him by one of his minions. White Eyes cackled in triumph as he turned it toward . . .

The security guard, who was running between the two men.

"No!" Batman shouted. He dove to put himself between the little man and the big gun, knocking the security guard aside even as White Eyes opened fire.

Batman was turned sideways in the air as he leapt, facing White Eyes, and a burst from the gun caught him square across the chest, so hard and fast he felt his armor cracking, one round striking his cowl in the right temple—so that opacity splashed across his senses like black paint over a window, blotting out the light.

So this is death, he thought—until that thought was blotted out, too.

4

Gotham Police Detective Cormac Sullivan was just stepping into the doorway of the Drago building when he
saw Batman leaping to block the gunfire from White
Eyes—taking a strafe that otherwise would have cut
down the security guard.

The little Filipino guard had sprawled to one side as
Batman was jerked by the impact of the bullets to change
his trajectory in midair, like a football player intercepted
by a lineman, slammed in a completely different direction to lay limply up against a tall stack of forklift
pallets. The stack overturned, collapsing onto Batman,
burying him. Cormac had his gun out, was aiming it
toward White Eyes.

"Drop it, damn you, drop it!"

White Eyes pointed the centrifugal gun at Cormac,
squeezed the trigger—nothing happened. It was out of
ammo—but Cormac's shot, fired while White Eyes was
bringing his weapon to bear, cut the air by the stump of
the big man's missing ear. White Eyes ducked behind the
road grader as Cormac shouted for backup and ran
through the empty, dimly lit spaces of the room in pursuit. Moments later he found an open door behind the

grader—and beyond it a black SUV, without a license plate, roaring away into the darkness. White Eyes was making his escape.

"Somebody get after that vehicle, now! Black Explorer, no plates!" Cormac shouted. "Go!" A patrolman ran to his cruiser to take up the chase but Cormac didn't think it was going to work—the SUV had too much lead and chances were White Eyes had his escape route planned out. Probably would be transferring to another vehicle soon.

Cormac turned to see the security guard dazedly pulling wooden pallets from Batman's still form. "He saved me . . . saved my life . . . ," the guard said wonderingly. "He knew . . . he took it for me . . ."

"Yeah," Cormac said, crossing to help, "that's how it looked to me."

They'd gotten the pieces of wood off Batman—and Cormac could see he was breathing, anyway, but apparently out cold, when he looked up to see Sergeant Breen and a jailhouse cop with a name tag that said VAN WYMAN standing there, guns in hand. The guns were pointed at Batman.

"Best move away from him, Detective," Breen said. "He's dangerous."

Cormac glared at them. "What're you two doing in here? Call an ambulance and get after the men who were in here—the men who assaulted this security guard."

"They're long gone, before we got here, most of 'em," Van Wyman said. "I mean—that's what it seems like to me. I only saw that one big guy and he's . . . he's, like, gone, dude."

"What the Hell are you doing here, anyway, Van Wyman?"

"I was passing with the sergeant here and, ah, we heard a shot and thought we'd lend a hand, like. So that's the bat guy, huh? Look, he's bleeding. Human as you and me, dude. Let's get his mask off—"

"No," said Cormac flatly, stepping closer to Batman and tapping his pistol warningly in the palm of his hand. "You won't."

The security guard looked back and forth between them. "I am going to the maintenance office . . . call for more help." He loped off toward the stairs.

Van Wyman was staring at the gun in Cormac's hand. "Breen—what the Hell is he doing?"

Breen chuckled, holstering his gun to defuse the tension. "Oh, he's worried, Van—right, Sullivan? You're afraid, are you now, that we'll hurt the man if we take off his cowl, with the wound and all? Why, Detective, he's shot in the head and chest—he's a dead man anyway. And there's a reward for this man. He's a vigilante, is what he is—a criminal! I say we unmask him—and you leave him to us, after that. We'll take care of him while you go after the perps in this case. What do you say now?"

Cormac glanced down, saw Batman's eyes fluttering. Looked like he was struggling to regain consciousness. Maybe hearing what was going on. Despite wounds in the chest and head, there was a chance that this man would live to fight crime again. Gordon believed in Batman—and Cormac believed in Gordon. More than that, he'd seen Batman make himself a human shield to save the life of someone he probably didn't know, someone a lot of people would've thought of as inconsequential beside the big players in town. But Batman didn't think a mere security guard was inconsequential. Batman was willing to die for him.

Plus, Batman had done a lot of good in the last year or so—he wouldn't be as effective if people knew who he was.

And finally, Cormac didn't like Breen or Van Wyman. He was pretty sure they were dirty cops. He reflected that Van Wyman was the one who'd found Skeev hanging in his cell, a supposed suicide.

No way was Cormac going to let these scumbags take Batman's mask off. Maybe it had to be done—the guy was technically a lawbreaker, after all: a vigilante. But Gordon would be here soon. Let him do it if it had to be done. "If Captain Gordon wants to unmask him—he will. I expect the doctors will have to do it at the hospital. But you two? No."

"Have to insist, Detective—best for the community to know . . ."

Breen knelt, reached for the cowl.

"I'm warning you, Breen, back off from him!"

"And I'm telling you, Detective—the mask comes off!"

So Cormac drop-kicked Breen in the face.

It felt good, too. He'd been frustrated as all Hell with the Gotham City PD. Every time he'd tried to get something done some dirty cop like Breen blocked him.

Right now Breen was sitting on his ass, clutching his bleeding nose. "Why you nigger shit-heel, you! I'll have you up on charges, I'll turn you in to Internal Affairs."

"You do what you want, you mick prick," Cormac said.

Van Wyman was scowling, fingering his gun, and Cormac knew he was seriously thinking about using it.

Cormac stepped over and shoved his own pistol in Van Wyman's face. "You'll drop that gun, toss it away—now! That goes for you, too, Breen, or you'll clean his brains off your uniform!"

The two cops hesitated—then tossed their weapons clattering aside.

"Oh you're going down, my friend!" said Breen. "Behind you are two patrolmen—they've just seen you threatening a brother officer with a gun . . ."

"Say, uh, what's going down here?" said one of the patrolmen, a young white rookie, walking up. "Detective?"

"Hey, that's the Bat!" said the other, a tall black officer. "Let's take off his mask!"

"No!" Cormac bellowed, spinning to point his gun at the startled uniforms. He was in too far to back off now. It'd all be meaningless otherwise. He could feel his career in Gotham slipping away . . .

"Look, Detective, you're in deep shit, you keep pointing that gun at us!" said the black cop. "That bat bastard is wanted for breaking and entering and questioning on all kinds of stuff—last year, I remember, he—"

"What the devil is this all about?" demanded Captain Gordon, stalking in. "Sullivan! Lower that weapon!"

Cormac swallowed, and holstered his gun. "Yes sir. Misunderstanding. Heat of the moment."

"Bullshit!" Breen yelled, getting to his feet. "He kicked me in the face!"

"Did he?" Gordon said, covering his mouth with one hand to hide a smile. "Shame I wasn't here. I mean—to stop him." His voice trailed off as he noticed Batman in the debris, stirring slightly. Saw the breaks in his chest armor leaking blood, and blood dripping from under his mask—the blood a different manner of mask for the lower half of his face. They heard the siren, saw the whirling light of an ambulance pulling up outside. "Good timing. We've got to get this man to the hospital."

"We could pull the mask off first, Captain!" Van Wyman said.

"No," Gordon said, calmly enough. "That'd be like taking off a motorcycle helmet when a man might have a neck injury—let the surgeons do it at the ER."

The ambulance attendants, a couple of gaping white-trash-looking yahoos to Cormac's eye, were rolling the gurney up beside Batman. It took Cormac's help to lift the masked man onto the gurney. Gordon wouldn't let them touch the mask, either.

One minute later Cormac and Gordon were riding in the back of the ambulance with Batman lying on a gurney between them . . .

Leaving Breen and Van Wyman to glare after the ambulance as it drove away.

"Guy over here out cold," the black cop said. "Has an Uzi with him."

"That's our collar," Breen said, intending to let the man go at the first opportunity. "We'll take care of him. You two go out and . . . secure the street."

"Sure thing, Sarge."

When the patrolmen had gone to their cruiser, Breen slapped the fallen man till he woke then sent him on his way, out the door to the alley. Then he turned to Van Wyman and growled, "Let's get to that hospital. We'll get our chance. We'll make it look like a suicide."

"Make what look like a suicide, Breen? I mean what exactly?"

Breen smiled. "I'll personally cut the Bat's throat in his little white hospital bed."

The ambulance drivers, Ed and Berdoo, two brothers from Texas who'd moved to Gotham City together, were passing a small flask bottle back and forth as they raced, sirens blaring, up the narrow streets. Berdoo was driving—as usual with his mouth hanging open. There was an unlit cigarette stuck in the corner of his gaping mouth. Ed kept expecting to see it fall out, but it was stuck there good.

"Head for Courtney Boulevard," Ed said, picking his nose with one hand and reaching for the flask with the other, "it's a wide road. I don't like these here narrer streets, Berdoo, they're devilish tight. The way you drive you'll sideswipe another goddamn bus. You're lucky you haven't lost your license."

"You just want that ol' Courtney Boulevard because them whores is out there," Berdoo said. "I don't have time for you to dog no whores. There's a couple of goddamn cops in back, and that lunatic's with 'em, and he's a big newspaper story. We can get interviewed on that, sell it to the *Enquirer*."

"Nobody going to care about our opinions! You are so full of shit the fertilizer companies is makin' bids on you."

"*You're* so full of shit you don't need a toupee 'cuz you got so many flies on yer head."

"*You* are so full of shit—what the hell is that?"

A funny-looking low-to-the-ground black car was pulling up in front of them, blocking their route, just before the turn onto Courtney—and it was slowing down.

Berdoo hit the brakes, blooped and beeped at the flat-black car, but it ignored them. He couldn't see into it. Tinted windows. Then, all of a sudden, moving in a way no car should naturally be able to move—all four wheels turning 180 degrees at once—it whipped sideways to block the road completely. The car made Ed think of the *Nautilus,* like he'd seen at Disneyland, only it was a car, not a submarine.

Ed and Berdoo gaped at each other, then back at the car. The wing doors of the strange, low, oddly finned vehicle raised up, like a bird lifting its wings in a mating dance. They could see right into the car.

There was no driver.

"Ed—it looks like . . . like there ain't no . . ."

"It couldn't be."

"I got to go look inside 'er."

"You can't, we got to back up, get out of here, we got a patient!"

But Berdoo was already climbing out, walking over to the vehicle . . . it was empty all right. He turned to spread his hands in a theatrical shrug at his brother—then stared past the cab of the ambulance at the two cops carrying the bat guy between them. They'd taken him from the back and were now helping him walk past Berdoo and to the empty car.

"You can't drive, friend," said the cop with the scar to the bat feller. Dark-looking guy, Berdoo thought. Maybe half colored.

"Won't . . . have to . . . ," the masked feller said. He climbed painfully into the car and sank into the seat. The wing doors shut with a shooshing sound, the car lit up and hummed—and then drove itself away.

That's how it seemed to Berdoo, though he couldn't see into it.

It just . . . drove itself away.

"Now look here, you hounds," Berdoo began, "how'm I going to—"

"It was a hoax call," Gordon said, counting eighty dollars out of his wallet, tucking it into Berdoo's shirt pocket.

Berdoo stared. Then he put his hand out, palm upward. "What about fer my brother?"

The dark cop sighed and pulled out his wallet.

Alfred was waiting anxiously at the entrance ramp in the cave when the Batmobile drove through the hidden doors, into the cave itself, and right up to him. It drove at him, but he didn't flinch, and it stopped on a dime, as he'd known it would, inches from his knees. The wing doors raised up, and Master Bruce tried to climb out— and fell back, gasping with pain. Alfred helped him.

"How bad is it, sir?" Alfred asked, helping him up toward the infirmary.

"I don't know . . . till we get this gear off . . ."

"Times like this, Master Bruce, I wish we had some help . . ."

"Someday."

Ten minutes later Bruce was lying on his back on an examining table as Alfred gingerly peeled off the damaged breastplate. He stared at the wounds on Bruce Wayne's chest. In the lesions were what looked like old-fashioned musket bullets, only shinier, perfectly round, four of them embedded in the muscle of his chest, each one sunken in most of the way, but still quite visible. The armor had soaked up most of the impact, but so powerful was the centrifugal gun that its bullets had broken through anyway, when others couldn't. Luckily the projectiles had spent most of their force by that time, wounding Bruce only superficially. The wound on his head was a minor scalp contusion requiring half a dozen stitches at the back of the hairline. Alfred, who had acquired almost as much medical training as an ER intern, looked into Bruce's pupils with a small penlight and said, "I believe you have a mild concussion, sir. On the whole, however, pending the X-ray, you've been quite fortunate . . . I wonder, Master Bruce, just how long you'll continue to press your luck."

"Have to press it, till it breaks sometime," Bruce said, faintly. "Stitch me up."

"Morphine, sir?"

"No. Need a clear head. Just get it done, please."

Alfred sighed. "Very good, sir. But you've lost a good deal of blood. You're going to need rest . . ."

It was all over for Cormac in a little more than a week. Oh, he could have fought the termination, gotten the inquiry stretched out for months. But he was disgusted that the chief was taking Breen's side over his. Refusing to consider the corruption allegations. Then there was the whole issue of what had happened to Batman. *He jumped out of the ambulance? Jumped into a car on his own, did he, all shot to pieces? Likely story, Sullivan . . .*

Cormac had insisted that Gordon be left out of the inquiry. He claimed Gordon had left the ambulance before Batman had, called off somewhere. Gordon had a job to do—he let Cormac take the fall. Because it was a fall he was going to take no matter what.

So Cormac had been fired. Which removed his last reason for staying in Gotham City.

"I'm still grateful to you, Cormac," Gordon said, walking Cormac from his apartment building out to the street so he could catch a ride to the airport. "We're both grateful."

"I was going to take a leave of absence anyway, see if I can find my son. So now it's a permanent absence—so what?"

"Maybe not so permanent. We'll work together again someday, if you're willing. You'll see."

They stood on the sidewalk, Cormac putting his luggage down and looking around. Gordon had said he'd arranged a ride for him to the Gotham International Airport. He'd expected to see a patrol car, one of the friendlier local cops driving—but there was no one out here. "You did say there was a ride?"

"Yeah—least I could do. Not one of ours. A limo. More or less."

"A limo? Why the Hell not. Any luck on that case?"

"White Eyes? No. He's dropped out of sight. Story is he's left town, gone to some secret compound somewhere. I got word that a big gun deal went down in Italian Town. There's rumors of a domestic terrorism move coming—I'm trying to get the Department of Homeland Security on it, but those guys—"

Cormac shook his head. "I know. Believe me."

"What are you going to do now?"

"I've got some friends looking for my son out in LA—I'm going to need money. Sent most of what I had to my ex. Alimony settlement. So I got a one-off job in San Francisco—should be over real quick. Then it's down to LA to follow up on Gary."

"What type of job?"

"Skip trace. My old specialty." Cormac looked at Gordon to see what his attitude would be—some cops looked down on bounty hunters.

"Something to be said for bounty hunting," Gordon said wistfully. "Take a job, get it done, take some time off . . . Not so much responsibility . . ."

"Has its ups and downs. Maybe I should call a cab. I don't see—"

"No need—here comes your ride."

A low, Bible-black car drove around the corner, pulled up in front of them, almost silently. The wing door on the passenger side lifted open.

Cormac stared at the Batmobile—and the silhouette of the masked man driving it. "Somebody call for a car to the airport?" came the low, unsettling voice from within.

"I cannot believe I'm doing this," Cormac muttered. The Batmobile was taking turns at speeds that would have flipped an ordinary car. Batman, glancing at him, noticed that Cormac was digging his fingers into the meager upholstery—he slowed a tad, though there was really no danger of a crash. He drove with small, expert movements of his fingers, fully focused. They were still a couple of miles from the airport.

"I mean," Cormac went on, clearing his throat, "suppose we get stopped by the highway patrol or something? How do you avoid that, anyway, when they see this thing? You can't outrun them all when they call for backup."

Batman didn't answer for a moment, trying to decide if he should reveal some of his methods. He owed this man—he could tell him just a little. "First, I have a device that tracks almost every cop in the area. If I can, I drive where they're not."

"How do you track them all?" Cormac asked.

Batman shook his head. He wasn't going to tell Cormac about the Wayne Enterprises satellites, with more than one function—their spy functions known only to him and Alfred. Nor would he tell him about the small bat-shaped RPVs, the remote-piloted vehicles that sometimes surveilled the city for him. He also didn't want to mention the Batmobile's camouflage, the digitally impregnated skin that could copy its backdrop when activated by an electric current, so that if he pulled over with the digital camouflage on, a cop in pursuit would drive past without seeing him. But the license plate? Why not. "They don't always get interested when they see the car: license plate's digital, doesn't really show any definite set of numbers, changing all the time. Looks like a different plate to everyone who sees it."

"Got to be more to it than that." Cormac commented.

Batman nodded but didn't elaborate. They were pulling into the airport complex.

Cormac looked at the dashboard, puzzling over all the indicators and dials. There were small computer monitors, mini television screens, the surveillance screen tracking a detailed topographical image of the city. "What—no iPod hookup?"

Batman smiled thinly and shook his head.

Cormac looked closer at him—couldn't see much in the shadowy cockpit of the Batmobile. "How you feeling, uh . . . Batman? I mean—you were, you know—shot up pretty good."

"Wasn't as bad as it looked." Actually, Batman was still in a lot of pain. The cowl hurt his head; driving hurt his chest. He was going back to Wayne Manor after this. He needed another few days before he could go on a Mission without popping his wounds open. "We're almost there . . ."

As they pulled up at the airport passenger-drop-off area, Batman said, "I wanted to tell you personally, Cormac— I owe you. If you need my help—need it badly—call Gordon. Tell him you 'feel like you're howling at the moon.' Give him a phone number. I'll call back—and if I can help, I will." For a moment, as Batman pulled up, he met Cormac's eyes.

Those eyes! Cormac shivered, looking into them.

"Your war," Batman said, "is my war, Cormac. Remember that."

Cormac stared at him, then nodded. The door hushed open and he climbed out. The door shut, silently and almost seamlessly, and the car drove off. Somehow his luggage was waiting behind the car.

A fat, red-faced airport cop came jogging up, pointing at the Batmobile as it drove away. "It looked like . . . when the door was open . . . was that . . . ?"

"Nah, man. Costume party. Wish I coulda gone with him. But I gotta make a plane."

Cormac picked up his luggage and walked into the airport. He just wanted to get to California, put this damn spooky town behind him.

He just wanted to find his son.

5

"What precisely am I to look for, sir?" Alfred asked.

"I don't want to say exactly. I want you to see it on your own," Bruce said.

They were standing on the natural floor of the Batcave itself. It was mid-evening, after the bats had left for the night. The two men stood on the great stone floor beside a rock wall leading up to the stalactite-fanged ceiling of the main chamber. They both wore helmets with lights on them, and in their beams the wall showed outcroppings of moonmilk, clusters of aragonite, dripping stone pendulites glistening with microbial slime, and a thin stream of water that flowed away into a spill sink at their feet. Arthropods scuttled in and out of the grooves of calcite-flowstone.

"There," Batman said, pointing at the wedding-cake-like base of a gigantic column about twenty-five yards away.

"I see only an interesting speleogenic formation, Master Bruce," said Alfred, approaching the column. "Fascinating to consider that the column is formed in the macrocavern by the fusing of the stalagmites and stalactites. Over millennia, the dripping carries mineral deposits, which, by slow degrees—"

"Yes, thank you, Alfred," said Bruce, "I know. But—stop where you are and look over there. Beyond the column—there, in the shadows under that farther column—in the calcite flow, see it?"

"Ah—I am sorry to disappoint, sir. But I see only stone and . . . the shapes *are* rather suggestive to the imagination."

"Yes. It could be that. But if you don't mind, Alfred, we're going to search this cavern."

"We've never found the end of it, sir. It would take a team of speleologists weeks, months to—"

"I mean the main chamber, at least. Come on."

"You cannot describe what we're looking for?"

"If I do—you'll imagine you see it. Suggestion works on you, too. But it's more or less shaped like a man . . ."

They searched the main chamber and some of the adjacent passages, but they saw nothing that shouldn't be in the cavern; heard nothing but their boots crunching in cave scat, the drip of mineral water, the occasional clicking of subterranean fauna.

Yet Bruce felt sure something was there, watching him. He sometimes glimpsed it out of the corners of his eyes . . . just in the place he'd been looking before.

When he looked back—it was gone. But he felt sure, somehow, it was merely hiding.

A bat flew over a biker bar.

The bat circled, then landed on top of a tin lamp shade over the lightbulb illuminating the sign and the front door. The bat made a slight metallic *clink-clink* when it landed—because it had metal claws. Between the lamp and the door was a sign:

HAWG HELL
Bar and Grill

The bat's artificial head swiveled on its simulated-fur shoulders, and tilted to look down at the front door. The microcameras in its eyes focused. It opened its mouth, the tiny directional mike coming into play.

In the Batcave command center, Bruce had removed his costume's gloves so he could use the keyboard and joystick more accurately as he controlled the bat—actually a small remote-piloted vehicle. The "bat" was made from cutting-edge Wayne Technologies components, the newest combination of hardened plastics, light alloys, compacted batteries, and surveillance gear that the CIA was just now getting around to testing. Bruce had spent hours practicing, over the past week, controlling RPVs like this one, and all the training was paying off. Its surveillance gear was working, too; he was getting a pretty decent down-angled digital-video transmission in the computer monitor, and good-quality sound as the bar's door opened and two shaggy bikers came out, wearing only leather pants, boots, and vests in the unseasonably warm weather. He couldn't see their faces very well from this angle, but one of them had a bald spot on the top of his head, and both had ARYAN NATION tattoos on their shoulders. Probably had done time together.

One of Batman's snitches had heard on the street that some of the Brotherhood frequented this bar. The bikers came outside to smoke, and for two nights Batman had been listening to their talk as they puffed Camels and passed joints.

"It's like goddamn Indian summer out here," the taller of the two bikers said, lighting his cigarette.

"Yeah. It's that global warming shit. Man, I gotta pee."

"Don't piss on the front of the building again, Dinky'll break a pool cue over your head. Weather's supposed to change in a day or two, though . . . Maybe go for a run first on my bike . . ."

"You get them new glass packs in that custom Dyna of yours?"

"Yeah, man, that sucker's *loud* now."

"That bike was already loud enough to wake the dead."

"Now it wakes 'em up and makes 'em put earplugs in, bro. I'm telling you, I hit the street at one in the morning, every freaking light goes on in the block. It's beautiful."

"Yo, you got any tree to put into that cigarette?"

"Naw, you wanna blunt, talk to Squeaky—or Rick. Unless he's gone to his meeting."

"There a meeting tonight?"

"Not the Nations. The Brotherhood. Come to think of it, Rick oughta be here tonight 'cause his Operations meeting's not till tomorrow night . . ."

"Tomorrow? Maybe I oughta go. I was thinking of volunteering."

"They're having a hard time finding guys for this one. I don't know what the Operation is—I guess it's a one-way trip, though . . . You wanna go, they're interviewing guys over in that beat-up old Y, on the West Side. One of those after-midnight things."

"That Y where we banged that Puerto Rican chick? Oh yeah. What a shit-hole that is. You not going to the meeting?"

"I ain't volunteering for that shit. I'm telling you, you ain't coming back from this'n, dude . . ."

"When they gonna get us those weapons they promised?"

"Don't even talk about that out loud, man. There was a snag. But we'll get 'em when the Major Move comes, Brethren all over the country gonna get their orders and tear the Jewboys a new one." He sucked on the cigarette and coughed. "Gotta give these things up. Bad for the health, man. Come on, I'm gonna do me a line and some Jell-O shots."

The two men pushed through the door into the bar and Bruce leaned thoughtfully back in his chair.

Tomorrow, after midnight . . . Batman should make that meeting, too.

"Master Bruce?" Alfred's voice on the intercom.

"Yes, Alfred?"

"Dinner will be ready in forty-five minutes—and the lady will probably be here in half an hour."

"I'll come up and change."

He stood and hit the key combination that would return the RPV to the Batcave and went to find an appropriate suit.

Bruce had done a fair amount of strolling with pretty girls in the moonlight, as he was doing now on the grounds of Wayne Manor. But with Teia, it felt different . . .

She tugged her wrap more tightly around her, though it was a fairly warm night, the oaks and poplars decked out in fog. He thought perhaps she was hinting he might put his arm over her shoulders, but he wasn't sure, and held back. Then he shook his head, amazed at his own uncertainty. He simply wasn't used to feeling nervous around women.

"The skiing accident does seem to have left you moving stiffly, Bruce," Teia said, reminding him of yet another lie. She reached up and touched the bandage on his head, with no more pressure than a lighting butterfly. "Does the wound on your head hurt you?"

"Mostly it itches. It's just a slight wound. I had a concussion, but that's passed."

"Your chest is bandaged, under the shirt?"

"Yes. Ran into a couple of tree limbs. Shouldn't drink before skiing."

She looked at him sharply—but it wasn't to reproach him for drinking and skiing. He could tell she simply didn't believe him. She knew he didn't drink much.

"Here we are," he said, as they came to the center of the rose garden maze and found a linen-covered table decked out with china and silver service.

"What! You sneak, you said we were going to look at the grounds before dinner—I thought we were going out!"

"You'd prefer to go out? I can call the car, Alfred'll drive us anywhere you want to go."

"No! This is wonderful! But you know I'm a vegetarian . . ."

"I haven't forgotten. Alfred brought in the best vegetarian chef in Gotham for this. I said, 'Oh, a vegetarian pizza from Domino's will do for her,' but he insisted—"

She laughed. "You liar! This was your idea! Mmm, it smells wonderful!"

She was only joking, calling him a liar, but it hurt anyway—because he was. Being Batman meant Bruce Wayne had to do a lot of lying. It was all for a good cause, he told himself. He didn't lie to women about his intentions; he didn't lead them on. But he often had to make excuses . . . *Most nights I like to go out on my own, check out the nightclubs—sometimes head over to the casinos at Atlantic City . . . I'll be working late tonight at Wayne Enterprises . . . Oh that? A skiing accident—I had an impulse to fly to Aspen . . .*

Lies. But what else could he do? He was far from ready to tell her about Batman—probably never would.

She was lifting the covers off the serving dishes. "Oooh! Braised tofu and shiitake! Ginger-fried rice! You remembered!"

He drew her chair back for her, and she sat, with a swish of her white silk dress. He poured sparkling water for her and sat vis-à-vis, smiling. "You look great in the moonlight . . ."

"I can't believe the weather is cooperating so much! My pantheist friends in the hills back home would say the sky gods had decided they approve of us."

"We also had a very exact weather report."

He served the food up himself, and she gave it her full attention; not gluttonously, but with conscious appreciation. Afterward, they sat holding hands—it felt natural to just sit there with her small hand in his.

Maybe, he thought, sipping mineral water. *Maybe I could tell her . . .*

"Bruce," she said, "is there anything you want to tell me?"

He almost choked on the Pellegrino at the synchronicity of her question. Was it just coincidence—or had she read his mind? Like many people deeply trained in consciousness meditation, she could be spontaneously intuitive. He tried to block off any thought of Batman, just in case. But he had to ask: "Anything I want to tell you? What, exactly . . . ?"

"Just—you seem to have something you're brooding about. Something . . . I saw a man in a cape . . ."

He stared at her.

". . . in a musical. What was it called? Oh yes—*The Phantom of the Opera*. Sometimes you seem to brood like he does, like some part of you is watching from the shadows . . ."

He shivered. Maybe it was just the gathering chill out here. "I—I have been thinking about that 'visitor' . . ."

"Have you seen it again?"

"Yes. Briefly. Yesterday evening. I tried to get Alfred to see it . . . No go."

"That doesn't mean it wasn't there." The lighthearted young woman had vanished; the sage appeared, speaking with the conviction of understanding. She had studied certain things longer than he had. "You must acknowledge this thing—*meet it,* to know what it is, Bruce. You will have to give this darkness its proper place within you, to subdue it. Perhaps it is another 'I' within you, which you must consume and digest, before the ghost can be released."

"So—you think it's just psychological? Like a 'shadow self' from Carl Jung . . ."

"Perhaps it's more than 'just psychological.' What is a poltergeist? Is that only psychological? No. But is it really a living being? Not really that, either. The substance of the world's own mind reacts to our minds—and will create things, temporary beings, made from our obsessions. They may be quite fearful. Or they may be just . . . what do you call it in English . . . Harbingers? Omens?"

"Yes. But what do you mean—consume and digest it? How?"

"You do that by seeing its part in you . . . by observation. By being watchful."

"If that's what it is—is it dangerous? I mean—I'm not—"

She smiled and raised a hand to interrupt him. "I know you are not a coward, Bruce! I remember when we went to Katmandu, on an errand for the Rinpoche—we got lost looking for the incense shop, and those men tried to rob us. You knocked two of them down, like a lightning strike, crash!"

"I remember *you* knocking them down."

"That was their friend. Only one. I used the no-shadow kick."

"I remember! They never saw it coming."

She put her wrap over the back of a chair and stood, kicked off her pumps. "Now—I have learned a thing in the Philippines called Arnis—I'll show you, if you want, and I'll try not to hurt you!"

He had to grin—she weighed about 120 pounds, if that. But he knew better than to underestimate her. "What, here, next to all this crystal? Come on, over here, then, away from the table, Alfred would never forgive us if we broke anything . . ."

"Now, this particular move is called *gunn-ting*—the scissors. You know it?"

"Not really." He knew of it—but that wasn't mastering it.

"Strike at me here—"

Bruce struck, careful to pull his punch up short, but using good form, and she ducked the blow and tapped at the inside of his wrist with two fingers as it passed.

"Ow!" he blurted. "Hey—my hand's numb!"

"Oh, I didn't mean to do it for real—not quite so much! My poor little Bruce, and you're already injured! I've hurt you!"

"But what a great move, you struck the nerve cluster—temporarily disabled my hand."

She took his tingling hand in hers. Her touch was so sensitive—and so full of life.

"I'll massage it . . ." She rubbed his hand. "Any sensation returning?"

"Um—no," he lied. "No, it's dead as a doornail."

"Really?" She pressed his wrist to her lips. Her voice was softer, and husky as she asked. "Anything then?"

"I think . . . *almost* . . ."

She turned her face up to his, to be kissed. He complied. Then she whispered, "What about now?"

The sun was shining off the bottles in the trash can, making Cormac squint. He was digging bottles and soda pop cans out of the plastic recycling box on the sidewalk and putting them in a black trash bag, all the time watching Lunder's house without seeming to. It was a tall, narrow blue house with a balcony that seemed never used, wedged between a white house and a gray one, all built in the 1940s. He was pretty good at watching the house without seeming like he was watching it.

It was a breezy day, but not too cold, nicer here than Gotham City anyway. So clammy and cold in Gotham this time of year. Good-looking houses, too, this part of

San Francisco, he reflected, even if they were crammed together. How long had Lunder had this one? Guy was such a lowlife, he'd probably let it go to seed.

"You know, that's kinda lame, taking stuff from a recycling can, considering you're just going to sell 'em to the recycler anyway," remarked a bucktoothed young guy in a mesh jersey, walking by with his sniggering boyfriend.

"Shut *up*, Roland," said the young guy's small Asian boyfriend, staring at Cormac—at this big, scruffy-haired guy in a gray hooded sweatshirt, too warm for the day. The sleeves were pushed back to show a fading navy SEALs tattoo on one forearm.

"This here's the way I get my beer money," Cormac said, all the time watching the little garage door. All these houses had tiny garages, tiny driveways, just barely big enough for a compact car. "You don't want me to go without my beer money." But they were already moving on, and the garage door was opening.

Lunder backed the gold metal-flake four-door BMW out, and Cormac adopted the slack, blinking look that usually made people look past him when he needed them to. Lunder was thick-bodied, muscular, blond, maybe thirty-two, in a Hawaiian shirt. Cormac started to amble away, mumbling, weaving toward his battered van—but then stopped, seeing that maybe he wasn't going to have to follow the guy after all.

The BMW had stopped in the driveway, and Lunder opened the car door, put a foot on the ground, got partly out to scowl at the fender. He had scratched the left front fender, just faintly, backing out of the narrow garage space. "Goddammit," he muttered. Not a big car, but too big for the Munchkin garage. Shaking his head, he started to get back in it.

But Lunder froze partway in as Cormac pressed the cold round rim of a beer bottle against the back of his neck and said, "Don't move or I pull the trigger. It's a forty-five, man. It'd mess up the car and I don't want to do that."

He had decided not to carry a gun right on him unless he really had to. Legally risky to use a gun on a skip trace bust. The taser on his hip, his hands, and a little deception—those were enough. But of course there was the 12-gauge in the van, just in case.

"What the hell do you want?" Lunder growled, trying not to sound scared.

"Your ass and your car, both intact," Cormac said. "Step forward, squeeze in, standing up, between the Beamer and the car door. Good—now reach down and grab the outside door handle. It'll be uncomfortable. But do it, and I won't kill you."

"Goddammit," Lunder said. But he did as he was told.

"Okay. Just don't even twitch, Lunder," Cormac said.

"You know my name?"

"What did you think this was?" Cormac had transferred the bottle to his left hand, reached back through the car door, twisting to unlock the car's back door as he spoke.

But Lunder was staring into the mirror on the car door. *"Goddamn beer bottle!"*

He threw himself back, wrenching sideways, slamming at Cormac's face with an elbow.

Cormac caught the elbow glancingly on the right side of his head, at almost the same moment smashing the bottle down on Lunder's forehead. Both of them staggered, blood gushing over Lunder's eyebrows.

Okay, Cormac thought, Lunder hadn't been as scared as he seemed.

Lunder squared himself, jabbing Cormac just under the left side of his rib cage. Cormac grunted, feeling it, but he got his feet under him, shifted his center of gravity forward, hooking a sharp right into Lunder's head so he'd fall away from the car. Never damage the asset. Cormac managed to get his right hand on the taser as Lunder tugged a .38 from the back of his waistband and turned it, cocking, toward Cormac's belly.

Cormac's left hand reflexively chopped Lunder's wrist so the gun fired wide. Cormac winced, hearing glass break across the street behind him, the *crack* of the gunshot echoing down the street—

Oh, Hell. What have I done this time? Come without backup to score the whole fee and this is what happens . . .

—shoving the taser hard into Lunder's gut, giving him two full blasts. The crackle of electricity, smell of burning cloth, and then Lunder was staring, gagging. He went rigid, then limp, sliding to his knees. Cormac caught the gun as it dropped from his stiff fingers.

"Asshole," Cormac muttered, shoving the gun in his waistband, putting the taser away in its little holster. He found the cuffs he kept in his back pocket, bent and twisted Lunder's arms behind him, cuffed him, and muscled him into the BMW's backseat, facedown. He had to go to the other side of the car and pull Lunder under the shoulders to get him fully inside the Beamer.

Cormac was sweating as he turned, chewing his lip

with worry, to squint at the other side of the street. A window? Or . . .

Lunder was coming out of it, squirming, cursing, as Cormac crossed the street. He could see a bullet hole in a trash can. The breaking glass must've been a bottle. He bent to look at the back of the trash can.

Oh, shit. The bullet had gone through.

He found it, wedged visibly into the wooden frame of a garage door, and he felt better. The bullet had stopped here, so no one was hurt.

Sirens, as he crossed the street, but still some way off. They might not even be coming here. San Francisco PD was world-famous for its inefficiency. What was that statistic? They personally investigated fewer than one-third of assaults, only a fourth of robberies.

Still, if they did come, they weren't necessarily going to give him the benefit of the doubt. He was ex–Gotham City PD, not ex–SFPD.

So he got into the BMW quick, and drove away as fast as he could without risking the Beamer.

Lunder was gagging in the back, like he might heave. Not good. "Don't throw up, Lunder, we'll have more depreciation on this car. You'll be stuck with that much more to pay. You're the garnishee, dumb ass, don't make it worse."

"Who . . . the Hell . . ."

"Don't tell me you didn't know your car was gonna be repo'd."

"That . . . all this is . . ." He paused to gag. "A god-damn . . . repo?"

Cormac grinned. "This is a twofer. This is gonna pay my rent for three, four months. I got the fee on the repo *and* the skip trace. You think moving up here from

Cache Creek is going to hide you? They ran a credit check when you leased this place, Lunder. You don't think that leaves a trail?"

"A scumbag bounty hunter . . ."

"Bounty hunter, repo man, clean up after horses in the parade—whatever. This is my first twofer in a lotta years—but then, I've been on the job in Gotham. Anyhow, Lunder, if you'd used some of your winnings from that Indian casino, cleaned up your delinquency, paid your fine for all those DUIs, man, you'd be out chasing tail and not lying there gagging. "

"This is illegal bullshit . . ."

"Lunder, I got all the papers, folded up under my sweatshirt. I was gonna serve you. I'll show you when we get where we're going. Better just drive the car to the lot, get it out of here before the local PD shows up. I mean, I'm legal but I don't like having to prove it, you know . . . Damn, now I'm gonna have to take a cab from there back to my van . . . Maybe I can get the agency to give me a ride? I mean, I'm freelance, but they might do it. What you think, Lunder?"

"Screw you."

Cormac chuckled. Then he saw a teenage boy striding up the street, and he thought about Gary. It was a big ugly tough cold harsh world full of guys like Lunder— even lunatics like White Eyes—and Gary was out there in it, too, somewhere. Alone . . .

Batman was still feeling his wounds, but so far the ligatures were holding. He didn't seem to be bleeding as he climbed up the fire escape and vaulted onto the roof, into the flickering light of a failing street lamp.

He imagined Alfred saying—he often imagined Alfred's voice, chastening him—*Master Bruce, was it nec-essary to vault onto the roof? You might've climbed the ladder and not risked your injury. It's not long since I pried bullets from your chest.*

But being Batman meant moving like Batman.

He crossed the rooftop, looked into the alley. "The old West Side Y," they'd said. This derelict building on the West Side was an old-time YMCA. So far he hadn't seen anyone here—saw and heard nothing but trash blown by the rising wind, the hiss of a thin rain. Weather was turning colder.

He removed a small spindly metal device from his belt and screwed it into the tar rooftop so that it penetrated a support beam. He activated it with a touch of his glove; a soft chime in the headset built into his cowl told him it was scanning the building for human voices. The chiming stopped and it transmitted the sounds it picked up from the interior.

"If you're really serious—"

"Am I really serious! I have been chosen for this, how serious is that? The hand of God on my shoulder, how serious is that? Is that serious enough for you, huh?"

Two male voices. One of them guarded, manipula-tive; the other shrill, manic.

"Listen, Coreno, we got to be more committed than those rag-head terrorists—and they're committed enough to blow their asses up just to get you."

"I ain't got no fear of dying, I know they're gonna take me out. I don't want to die like Tim McVeigh did, strapped to a table. I told him he should never surrender and he didn't listen. I want to die fighting the Anti-christ."

"Uh-huh. Dutch? Bring that piece over here. You see

this, Coreno? This is what we call Steel Thunder. Some call it the Dread. It's our own update on the Dread— carries twice as many rounds. Now, you take this in your hands, and you kill them all, and you do it on the schedule we give you—not before, not after. We're takin' a leaf outta them towel-heads' book—simultaneous attacks in many places. But since you look like that page, you gonna do the most spectacular job—once they're back in session. We kidnap the page, you take his ID and clothes and his pass. Our man in their kitchen's going to leave the gun where you can find it— it's comin' in the supply truck. But you got to be cool- headed to pull this off—

"*That's what worries me about this guy, Rick—*"

Another voice, a skeptical growl. Must be "Dutch." Lot of guys went by Dutch, but Batman suspected this could be "Dutch" Hoosker, a biker not long out of the pen after doing six years for dealing skag, known to have close connections with the Aryan Nation and other white supremacist prison gangs. The biker connection— Batman's source of the rumored meeting—and the racist tie-in, together with the moniker, argued for Hoosker. Coreno, however, was new to him, an unknown.

"*—you telling me this guy's gonna be chill before the hit when he's all talking about being God's chosen little angel, Rick? I don't see it.*"

"*If I am chosen, I am chosen! But that don't mean I can't be chill! You want to see me be chill? I can sit here without moving, like a spider a-waitin' in his web, just watching and waiting and hungry waiting, hungry wait- ing, hungry waiting—*"

"*Lord, Rick, the guy is—*"

"*Maybe so . . . we're gonna have to talk it over, in the*

*next room here, Coreno. Just wait here—and give me
that weapon—"*

"*If I give you this weapon, what you gonna do if you
decide I'm no good for this? I don't know, don't know if
I should give you this weapon, man, you better stand
back, mother—"*

"Uh-oh," Batman muttered. He checked the listener's
directional indicator—it was pointing toward the southeast corner of the building. He retrieved the device and
jumped to the low wall along the edge of the building—
if he ran across the rooftop, the men below might
hear the drumming of his feet. He padded along the
tin-sheathed rim wall to the southeast corner. A crow
squawked up, flapping angrily out of a nest under the
roof's cornice, and he nearly lost his balance. He squared
himself again, waved the crow away, and knelt, testing
the drainpipe with one hand. Seemed solid enough.

Batman quickly lowered himself to the drainpipe, descending hand-over-hand, braking with his feet, in three
seconds coming parallel with the only window showing
any light, at a height equivalent to the second floor. He
climbed sideways over to the window ledge and hunkered, holding on to the window frame, looking in at
three men standing below him at the edge of the cracked
tile of the old dusty, dry swimming pool that was the
centerpiece of the two-story room. It was a grimy, cobwebby room, with heaps of empty wine bottles and rot-
ting blankets left by squatters, and only one working
light dangling in a farther corner. The three men were
about thirty feet below him, in the nearer corner—and
the short, stocky one in a sleeveless Levi's jacket with an
odd haircut, cut into the shape of an iron cross seen

from the top, was waving a centrifugal gun at the other two, keeping them at bay.

Batman considered the window—not an easy one to get through. It would tilt up and partway open, but he'd never fit through the opening—and it was edged in metal that would make it difficult to break through and still control his fall. He removed a small laser cutter from his belt—it stored only enough power for one or two decent cuts—and burned through the bolts holding the window in place, catching the window section before it fell. He set it quietly on the ledge, all the time listening to the conversation below him.

"You know what I got in this backpack, don't you, Coreno?" the blond man asked. He was heavily tattooed, swag belly, leather jacket with Gotham Goths colors on it—and over one shoulder he'd slung a backpack. "Got my hand in the backpack, Coreno. Know what I mean?"

"You're trying to psyche me out, is all!" Coreno chattered, shifting from foot to foot. "I can look right into your hearts and see, I can see, I can see you're getting taken over by the Antichrist to stop me, because I'm the One and you had better fight it off because—"

Tweaker? Batman wondered. But he suspected this wasn't a case of drug psychosis. This guy felt like a natural-born paranoid-schizophrenic. Cannon fodder for the Brotherhood.

"Look at the backpack," Dutch said. "We can't risk anybody running loose who's not going to keep his mouth shut—and you seem incapable of it. If you get caught with that gun, you'll start babbling and then the whole thing goes down the tubes. So I took an oath—"

Batman was now moving along an interior ledge running under the windows—poising—

That's when Dutch caught the motion, looked up right into Batman's eyes. Batman held his eyes as he leapt, coming down right at them as Rick—the tall lanky greasy-haired one—turned and yelled, "Oh, shit. The Bat!"

Batman slammed into Dutch with a boot heel to his face, launching the biker backward into the dry pool. The other boot struck Rick hard on the side of the neck, slinging him over to the left; recovering in midair from these impacts, Batman flipped to land on his feet to Coreno's right.

"Stay away from me! No human being moves like that!" Coreno yelped, fumbling with the gun, failing to take the safety off—he had a round head, ears that seemed too low on his skull, a snub nose, a spiderweb crudely tattooed on each of his cheeks. Batman whipped a shuriken at him, followed by a Batarang. The shuriken stuck deep in the back of Coreno's gun hand, cutting into tendons, making the hand spasm, loosening his grip—and a split second later the Batarang knocked the weapon away. The gun went clattering, spinning, ending up near the edge of the pool as the Batarang spun back to Batman. Coreno howled in pain and backed away, drooling in fear, his eyes pinpoint. "Stay away stay away stay away from me!"

Dutch was inert in the pool; Rick was groaning, getting to his hands and knees, and Batman used his boot to almost casually roll him into the dry pool with Dutch.

"You're a demon thing, is what you are," Coreno sputtered, clutching his hand to himself. "Just like Skeev was sayin'!"

"Skeev was right," Batman said, making his voice hit its lowest register as he approached Coreno, cape swept up in one fist like a bat enfolding itself in its wings. "But you and I already know that—when I visited you in your dreams, in another form, we both knew, right, Coreno?" Batman assumed that a sick puppy like Coreno had more than his share of nightmares.

"You know my name? You *are* him! The one from my dream! *You are Satan!*"

Batman smiled coldly. "So you do know my name! What form did I take in your dream, Coreno? Do you remember?" Batman was backing him against the wall—well out of reach of the fallen gun. "This is a test, Coreno—what form did I take?"

"You were a big black dog! You were that crazy vicious dog Sam that talked to the Son of Sam! And you were telling me what to do! But I wouldn't listen!"

"No, you wouldn't listen, would you, Coreno? I couldn't fool you. You knew who I really was. So you know who I am now . . . You know you can't hide things from me! I know all about what you are going to do. You are going out on one of the Brotherhood's Operations— a mission to kill my devils! But I wonder if you have the guts to fight my devils, Coreno. Do you?"

"I will! I will! I will kill them and I will kill dozens of them, and the others will strike at the same time!" Coreno was beginning to foam at the mouth. "I will kill them! I will destroy your minions, Satan!"

Batman hulked over Coreno now, fixing his eyes on the lunatic's. "You're too confused to do it, Coreno. You don't even know what day the Operation is—!"

"The great day is coming! The great day is January—"

"Coreno, *SHUT UP!*" Dutch bellowed, climbing up the ladder onto the edge.

Batman turned, saw Dutch with his face splashed

with blood; his teeth red with it. He had the backpack in one hand.

Coreno was running past Batman, going willy-nilly for the edge of the pool. Dutch grabbed Coreno and jerked him over the edge into the empty pool below, falling to lie stunned beside Rick.

Batman reached for a Batarang as Dutch—a look of cold determination coming into his face—put his hand into the backpack . . .

There had to be a bomb in there—and Batman had only one chance to live through the blast. He threw the Batarang with all his strength and speed, so it struck Dutch in the forehead, knocking him back into the pool.

Batman turned and threw himself flat in the corner.

The explosion shook the whole building, brought down a large part of the nearer interior wall of the pool and a section of ceiling, blew out the windows and filled the air with raining debris. Batman felt the blast's heat and shock wave only glancingly—most of it had been absorbed by the walls of the dry swimming pool.

He sighed, standing up, coughing with the dust, annoyed with himself for not separating Dutch from that backpack.

He looked over the shattered edge and confirmed it: It'd been a big charge—and they were blown to small pieces. No time to sift a mess like that for clues—the cops would be here soon. Even the centrifugal gun was destroyed—a tangle of torn metal, half buried in rubble.

This wasn't the outcome he'd hoped for. Three of the Bavarian Brotherhood had gone down, but they'd taken valuable information with them . . .

He looked up at the window, then noticed an exit door blown open at the back of the room. No reason to go the long way. He circled the crumbling pool and went out the exit, tapped his gauntlet to summon the Batmobile from around the corner, and was away well before the police arrived.

Racing through the countryside, on his way back to the camouflaged cave entrance, Batman assessed the fruits of the evening's Mission. He had blown it, in a way—but he'd learned some things, too:

The Brotherhood were now using suicide bombers to keep their secrets. They might continue their imitation of international terrorists and use the same weapons in their assault on the so-called Zionist Conspiracy. But their main plan seemed to be to arm domestic extremists with unusually powerful light arms.

There was more: they seemed to be planning to copy al Qaeda's pattern of multiple simultaneous assaults. And their first big assault would be sometime in January— weeks away.

They'd referred to a *page* and a group of people coming back *in session*. That suggested that one target was the US Capitol—and the United States Congress.

It was time to get the word, and the sample autoshotgun, to the DHS, the ATF, and the FBI—through Captain James Gordon, Gotham City PD.

Gordon would be discreet about his source. The feds, after all, weren't used to getting tips from Batman.

6

"Sullivan? *Cormac* Sullivan? To see the boss? I don't think so, no," said Old Randy, shaking his white head, making it snow on his shoulders. "I don't think Benny wants to see him. No. Not him. Uh-uh. No freakin' way. Jeez, I thought we were done with him when he took that cop job out east in Gotham. That place eats cops alive . . ." He said everything with the same inflection, short and rat-a-tat sharp, like he was drumming instead of talking.

Old Randy was talking to Mrs. Cortland, the secretary, who was almost as old as he was, and making no effort at all to conceal his disregard from Cormac, who was standing three yards away in the waiting area of Kennedy Bail Bonds. It wasn't a waiting room, because it was all one room, partitioned by a greasy oak rail with lathed posts, a feature that was, on purpose, like something you'd see in the courtroom. It was supposed to give the bondsman's office an official look, as if it were an extension of the court. Behind the rail were half a dozen putty-colored steel desks, each with a dwarfish computer monitor, an untidy heap of forms, and a much-scribbled-on desk calendar. There was a water-

cooler that had been dry as long as Cormac could remember, and a coffeepot that produced sour coffee no
matter how freshly it was made. On the wall were shelves
of forms and a cobwebby seascape. Two closed doors
led into the only back offices, Lenny's and the one that
had been Lenny's dad's before the old man had died.

Lots of bail bonds outfits had gone to a friendlier, less
institutional look, investing in warm and fuzzy TV com-
mercials about how they *understand* and they *only want
to help*—but not Kennedy Bonds.

"I thought we ought to ask Lenny, anyway, if he
wants to see the man," Mrs. Cortland was saying.

Good for you, Mrs. Cortland, Cormac thought. No
longer in street camouflage, he unconsciously straightened his sports jacket. He hadn't seen Lenny in a long
time.

"So you're working this side of the street again?"
Mrs. Cortland asked, tamping some papers into a pile.

"I am, for the time being. I had a job up in San
Francisco—came down here to see my boy, got a message
on my cell there might be some work for me here . . ."

He heard someone sobbing, glanced at the interview
desk. Darrel Cohen was sitting at his desk with a distraught thirtyish black lady with long wavy hair. With
that hair she might be from Tonga.

Cormac thought he'd never been in a bail bonds office
without seeing a hand-wringing, weeping lady or two.
Your basic distraught woman was the bail bondsman's
bread and butter. The lady had her back to Cormac but
he could see by the movements of her arms she was
twisting a kerchief, or wringing her hands. "I didn't
think he could . . . he said, so many times . . ." drifted to
Cormac. ". . . I thought . . . I should have . . ."

"Yes ma'am," Darrel said, typing into his computer. "I know how that is. It's a Hell of a thing, what people do. What was the appraised value of your house, when you got the second mortgage?"

Lenny popped his head out the door of his office. A round, balding head, thick glasses, dimpled cheeks, fixed smile turned toward Randy.

"Randy," Lenny said, "can you look and see if that tracer from Louisiana is still . . ." Then he saw Cormac. "Oh—you showed up!"

"What, him?" Old Randy said, turning his craggy, skin-tagged face toward Cormac, but talking to Lenny. "You *invited* him here?"

"It's good to be home," Cormac said, smiling. It hurt to smile, a little; there was still a touch of swelling on the side of his head from Lunder's elbow.

"This ain't your home, bruiser," Old Randy said, looking at Cormac directly for that one. "You run off to be a cop in Gotham City. Mr. Bigshot Detective. Must've blown that bad and come whinin' back here."

"Why, Randy, LA's my home," Cormac said mildly. "And this office is my home away from home."

"Hell it is," said Old Randy.

Mrs. Cortland went back to her desk, sighing, rolling her eyes at Cormac, a bit theatrically. She'd been a minor character actress in the 1950s and '60s.

"You back from Gotham City for good, Cormac?" Lenny asked, pushing his glasses back on the bridge of his nose with his index finger. "Going to be in La-La Land awhile?"

"Maybe." It depended on Gary. Cormac had already gone to his ex-wife's place. Found her sleeping on the sofa, with the TV on. She'd scowled at him, said she hadn't seen Gary yet, didn't know where he was. Cormac had some guys out looking. When they got a lead, he'd search for his son personally.

Lenny was gesturing for Cormac to come back to his office, so Cormac went through the gate in the rail, past Old Randy.

Settling into his desk chair, Old Randy muttered, "Jackass."

Cormac went into Lenny's office: not much more than a cubicle, papers everywhere and framed pictures of racehorses—Lenny had made *almost* as much money as he'd lost, breeding racehorses.

"Close the door, Sullivan, will you? Thanks. Have a seat."

Cormac sat. Lenny grunted and so did his swivel chair as he settled into it, pudgy fingers tapping his computer keyboard before he'd quite finished sitting.

"Sorry about Randy," Lenny said, squinting at the computer screen.

"He still blames me after, what's it been, eight years?"

"Just the way it played out. The skip you bring in sues us, the old man dies a week later."

"Your dad was a friend of mine. Had a bad heart for fifteen years."

"Sure. But you know, Old Randy's got to have some beef to get his own pulse going."

Still, there was something in Lenny's voice . . .

Like he wasn't sure if Cormac *wasn't* the cause, after all. Sent out by Kennedy after a minor drug dealer who'd skipped on his bail, Cormac had body-slammed the guy so he fell onto a fire hydrant, hit him just right—or just wrong—and the guy went paraplegic. Crushed spine.

Cormac could have shot him, since the guy was carrying a gun. He'd body-slammed him so he wouldn't *have* to shoot him: lawsuit was dropped for that reason. But back at the time, the skip's lawyers were yelling for ten-million-dollar settlements.

"You wanna talk about what happened in Gotham?" Lenny asked. "The cape guy? I'm too curious to mind my own damn business."

Cormac looked at him in surprise. "It didn't make the papers, far as I know. What'd you hear?"

"We got a guy picks people up for us in Gotham. Said you were hooked up with that vigilante wears the cape?"

"Not hooked up. Just . . . tangled up."

"You get tangled in his cape? Make you trip?"

"Funny."

"I mean, jeez, how can you take a guy like that seriously, wears tights, leaps about on the roofs, wears a mask, thinks he's the Phantom or something."

Cormac had asked himself that one, too. "Um—that's what I thought for a while. But when you're around him—you do take him seriously. The guy's larger than life. Maybe he's crazy, I don't know. But he fills that costume. You just take him seriously when he's standing there looking at you. Like if you were looking at a . . . I don't know . . . a mountain lion, up close. You don't say, *Oh, that's just a kitty-cat.*"

"So he's impressive in person. Okay. You tell him to come work for us. We'll pay him same as anyone else, cape or not."

"He works free, Lenny."

Lenny stared. "He *is* crazy."

Cormac shrugged and looked around. "This office is smaller than your dad's. Not my place to say, but wouldn't he have wanted you to . . . you know . . . move into his?"

"Probably. And Darrel wants me to sell the building, refinance, start new with a softer look. And maybe . . ." He glanced at the door, which was still half open, and didn't have to say, aloud, *Retire Old Randy.* "But . . . I can't get myself to change it yet. I grew up in this place. I feel like . . . I'd look funny in another place. Like . . ." He shrugged. "Sometimes I just want to sell the business. You see that lady out there? You know how there's a law against guys who know they got HIV but give it to people anyway? She's got HIV, that lady, because hubby gave it to her. Guess who she's trying to bail out of jail— and he's in there on a charge of giving it to her."

"Christ."

"I mean—it's business, we got to do it. But sometimes I just think . . ." He couldn't finish saying it. Just grimaced and looked at the window.

"Sure, I know." That was the best Cormac could do. He didn't want to act like he was Dr. Phil or something.

There was a long silence. Finally Cormac said, "You got work for me, for real, Lenny? Or you going to serve me a summons?"

"I wouldn't do that . . . in person." Lenny flashed a set of perfect white teeth. "I do have something. I heard you had some guys looking for your kid—Murcheson told me. Well . . . when this came up I thought my old man, he liked you—I figure he'd want me to give this to you."

He pushed a folder over and Cormac scanned its contents. A skip named Gimby, Samuel Gimby, aka Moth. Possession of amphetamines with intent to sell. Gimby's sister had put up bail, risking her property, and Gimby had jumped. The Santa Monica Detective Agency had word he was somewhere in the vicinity of Santa Monica Pier. No luck actually finding the guy. Santa Monica police claimed not to be able to find him. Meaning they hadn't really tried.

Names associated with Gimby: a teenage boy known only as Dirk, a teenage girl who called herself Kruella, one Lawrence Murch, one "Donkey" Dipsey . . .

And a teenage boy thought to be one Gary Sullivan.

Cormac froze in his chair. His sight seemed to dim. Then he made himself turn the page and scan for further references to Gary. Nothing more.

"You think that's your boy?" Lenny asked. "Wasn't he into that Goth stuff? It's the right age. You brought him one time, he had that streak in his hair, clothes all in black, that stuff."

Cormac licked his lips. "Could be him." Thinking: *Possession of amphetamines with intent to sell.* "That could be my son."

"Almost a bull pup of some kind," Egerson said. "But then again it's not."

"Ain't no bull pup," Grenoble said, glancing up at Egerson, whose lined, lean face was tanned from two weeks of deep-sea fishing in Hawaii.

Bill Grenoble was a black man, dark as an eggplant, in ATF inspection overalls. Though in fact, like Egerson, he was a special agent, not an inspector. "Was me out there fishing," Grenoble said, extending the butt stock on the auto-shotgun, "I'd find me a spot in the shade, under a palm tree. Case of beer. Makes me sweat just looking at how you burned up out there. Not that I'd burn, God knows . . ."

"Can't drink beer," Egerson said, leaning over Grenoble's worktable, one hand on the back of the big man's steel chair.

Except for an outdated Rigid Tools calendar on the wall, the metal table, with a few small toolboxes on it, was the only feature of the firearms examination room in the Bureau of Alcohol, Tobacco and Firearms' Gotham City Field Office. On the table was a big black automatic shotgun. Grenoble had never seen this model before.

"Why can't you drink beer, once in a while, for Chrissakes, you're no alky," Grenoble said, adjusting the gooseneck magnifying glass.

They were both frowning over the gun as Grenoble used an Allen key from a gun-cleaning kit to remove the fixing screws holding the magazine cover.

"Well, I can't drink beer because it makes me fat, Bill."

"It makes you fat. Bullshit! You were never fat."

Grenoble said it feelingly: he was sixty-eight pounds overweight. He carried it pretty well, being big-boned and somewhere over six feet, but at fifty-six, he was feeling it more every day.

"Sure, I was fat. I was seventeen pounds overweight."

Grenoble looked up from the gun to give Egerson a look of disgust. "Seventeen pounds. Piss off."

Egerson chuckled, a creaky sound like rawhide being twisted.

"So where'd this come from now?" Grenoble looked at the paperwork. "Captain James Gordon, Gotham City Police Department. Says there's rumors of weapons like this, and some version of a Dread—"

"Nobody's got a *working* Dread, anywhere."

"Maybe they do. Says there's rumors they're going to

be used by domestic terrorists. Possible Bavarian Brotherhood, possibly in January, possibly against Congress."

"Somebody tell the Department of Homeland Security?"

"Do they listen? They're not interested in militia types. Some of those guys voted for the president."

"There you go, bashing the president again. You going to take that gun apart or not, Bill?"

Grenoble was already working on it. He made sure the spring motor was unwound, then turned the winding key counterclockwise. He pulled out the center pivot shaft from the magazine and lifted the magazine from the cover assembly. The smell of gun oil was strong in the room. "Huh," he said. "With that ammo drum, almost looks like one of those old Machine Gun Kelly things . . . But for shotgun rounds . . ."

"Almost like that. That's an automatic, Grenoble. Look at that receiver assembly."

"That sure as hell is. What, fourteen rounds, shotgun shells, gone in three or four seconds . . ."

Egerson snorted. "They work up a really good belt, they could cut down a tree with that thing. A shotgun-machinegun."

"Shit," Grenoble said, looking closer at the drum. "That thing was machined, man."

"What'd you think?"

"No, I mean—it was *machined*, like, expertly."

"Here you are" came Downing's gravelly voice from the door. "Double espresso mocha. Christ. You can't drink java, Egerson?"

Grenoble could smell the mocha, the espresso, in the plastic coffee cup Downing was handing to Egerson. "Oh, man, you got to drink that in here?"

"What," Egerson said, sipping, "you going to get secondhand caffeine fumes?"

"I miss that shit. We got a great coffee place next door. Drink coffee all my life. Goddamn doctor . . ."

He held the gun assembly under the gooseneck magnifying glass, peered at the cartridge primer. "You know what this is . . . somewhere I've got a manual for something called a Street Sweeper . . ."

"Sure, this is a variation on a Street Sweeper, but the drum is bigger, the whole piece is bigger, more powerful, better cut on the bore." Egerson leaned close to the ammo drum, putting on his glasses. "How many rounds you say?"

"I haven't counted the slots yet, but it looked like—"

"It's not fourteen rounds—look closer, man. It's twenty-one."

"Twenty-one! Jesus!" Grenoble stared at the gun. "And they can make a few changes so you could switch out a drum pretty quick. Twenty-one twelve-gauge rounds in four, five seconds . . . "

Egerson shook his head. "You know something? Wrong people making the right weapons—that shit could get ugly."

Gordon was waiting for Batman in church.

It wasn't really a church anymore, not a working church. Like so much on this side of Gotham City, the church had failed, its members moved to other towns in search of jobs, and now it was a dusty hulk, the nave shot through with dust-dulled colors projected by a bright streetlight on the other side of the stained glass. Gordon had come in the side entrance, which was missing its doors entirely. There was a moldy sleeping bag, left by some homeless camper, under the crucifix on the other side of the chancel. The stained-glass image on the street side, showing Jesus flanked by angels at his resurrection, had sections broken out by vandals where phlegm-yellow light beamed through. One of these shafts of light fell on the newspaper, today's *Gotham Register,* that Gordon had tossed onto the only remaining pew, up front. Sitting beside it now, waiting for Batman, Gordon read again the sidebar article beside the main piece on the explosion at the old YMCA.

"THE BAT" A BOMBER?

The costumed vigilante known by the underworld as "the Bat" and calling himself "Batman" was allegedly mixed up in the possible terrorist bombing at the ruins of the old West Side YMCA in the early-morning hours yesterday. Police sources quoted unnamed witnesses, passing the derelict building at the time, who saw and felt the explosion that shook the entire neighborhood. "I was at a stoplight," said one witness, "and I saw out of the corner of my eye this big flash, and I looked and *boom,* the windows blew out and I'm just sitting there staring with the traffic light turning green, and a few seconds later I see Batman coming out of a door, getting into that [expletive] weird-ass car of his and driving away."

FBI Agent Roland Corning said this morning that tests indicated the use of an explosive of a kind associated with the hate-crime attacks on two synagogues in upstate New York in September and November of last year. But a source in the police department, who insisted on anonymity, suggested, "There are reasons to believe Batman himself may have set the explosive as part of his campaign of terror against perceived criminals." If so, this is the first known incident of this caped vigilante resorting to outright homicide.

" 'Unnamed sources' are popular," said a low, yet carrying, voice, just behind Gordon.

The hairs stood up on the back of Gordon's neck, but he managed to keep himself from spinning around. He knew who it was, after all, and he liked to keep his dignity. "They are. I figure the unnamed source in this case is Breen or maybe Burkhart."

"Who's Burkhart?" Batman asked, coming around to stand between Gordon and the stained-glass window. He made a Witches' Sabbath silhouette against it that some Christians might've found unsettling.

"Lieutenant Burkhart, new in homicide, came here from Boston PD. I suspect him of having neo-Nazi connections. He's at least a Holocaust Denialist—part of the New Right."

"And the article quotes an 'unnamed witness,' too. Word for word."

"Burkhart was taking statements from witnesses. That much I know. They going to be using bombs, too, now, you think?"

"To cover their tracks, at the moment. Later, maybe in January, they'll be part of their big move. You tell the feds?"

"ATF and FBI. I tried to talk to Homeland Security, they recorded the conversation, but they don't seem worried about militia types. Their orientation is to look at foreign nationals, radical Muslims—you know. The other bureaus said it was 'all rumor.' They already know about the guns, of course, after the bust at Rankin's. But they figure that's organized-crime stuff."

"And they're going to do what about investigating the plot to attack Congress?"

"Near as I can figure, they're more concerned about coming up with a new color-coded alert system."

"They're not going to move?"

"Against who? White Eyes? They know about him but they don't know where he is. He had a compound out in Idaho, but it's deserted. Word is, he got nervous, moved back east here somewhere. Or he could be right here in Gotham. One guy I talked to said he thought he heard the Brotherhood moved camp to somewhere out in the Appalachians—upper Pennsylvania, north of the Susquehanna. But that's a big area. They don't know Big White's real name. No one does. They don't even have a reliable photo of him. They'll send a warning to Congressional Security, sure. But how do I tell them I got the information? Batman heard a couple of guys talking right before they conveniently got blown up? They wouldn't trust the source. There's advantages to you working outside the law—and disadvantages."

"They're planning a major attack . . . there should be a national alert . . ."

"We need more proof. It's that simple."

"This attempt to hang the bombing on me going to stick?"

"In the department? I don't know. Seems like stretching logic to me. But they'd like to question you. Then again, they're already looking to question you for a dozen things. And I don't think I can use the Bat-Signal anytime soon—let them know where you're going to be. We'd better stick with the cell phone for now."

Batman nodded, just once. His eyes were in shadow, but Gordon could sense the Dark Knight's searching gaze on his face. "So every time you're seen to be working with me—you risk your career. Maybe your freedom."

Gordon shrugged. "I'm trying to keep it quiet. But I owe you a lot. And you've saved lives. I can't turn my back on that."

"If meeting me starts to be a danger to you . . ."

"I understand," Gordon said. "You let me deal with that risk. There's something else I wanted to run by you. House out on the edge of town, big old place, used to be a bed-and-breakfast, gone to seed. At the end of Red Oak Road. Leased to some thugs I think might be in the meth trade. Reports of chemical smells coming out of there. Smoke at all hours."

"Speed lab?"

"I've got a snitch who says it's that and more—says that the Brotherhood is about to make a major push into the ghetto with a form of amphetamines mixed with PCP."

Gordon heard a sound from Batman that might've been a curse word, hissed under his breath—and might not. If so, it would've been the first time in Gordon's experience. Batman was usually unflappable—despite the cape.

"Deadly combination," Batman said, after a moment.

"Lots of death in the ghetto when that happens. They're calling it 'angel ice.' It'd be just like White Eyes to make a lot of money selling the dope and all the time essentially be selling poison to people he regards as the enemies of his race."

"And you think they're making it in that house."

Gordon stood up, stretched. "Damn church pews always did give me a backache. Yeah, story is, most of the dope's stored in the attic. Hundreds of pounds of the stuff—big financial investment for the Brotherhood."

"And you don't raid it—why?"

"I tried to get a warrant. But I've only got rumors." Gordon stuck his hands in his pant pockets and paced over to the chancel to look up at the crucifix hanging crookedly over what had been the altar. He was struggling with his emotions. The runaround he was getting from the DA and Vice was maddening. "Vice is all caught up on the other side of town—and there are speed labs all over the place. I can't get 'em to make this one a priority. No proof this is the big one. But if someone were to get in there and . . . call attention to the place. Either attract the cops by kicking some ass—or maybe destroying that supply—I could get some choppers in the area on some pretext. Say—tonight?"

"Someone could do some good . . ."

"That's what I was thinking," Gordon said, turning. "But maybe it'd be too—"

He was speaking to the shadows. Batman was gone.

"Hello?" No response. Gordon sighed. Then he looked around in puzzlement. How had Batman gotten out of there so quickly? He'd had his back turned only a few seconds. The nearest open door was at the other end of the big room. No tracks in the dusty floor. There was nothing to hide behind—all the pews but one were gone—and he couldn't imagine Batman hiding behind something to fool him, anyway.

He thought back. A moment after Batman had said, *Someone could do some good,* Gordon had heard a faint hissing sound. He'd heard it before—the sound of a cable that Batman used to draw himself up the sides of buildings. Or . . .

Gordon looked upward. There were rafters, far overhead, running close to a hole in the ceiling that led onto the roof. He caught the flutter of a cape up there, going out the gap. So that was it. Batman had gone straight *up,* to disappear like that.

He shook his head. Were theatrics like that necessary? Couldn't the guy just walk out the door and drive away?

No. Batman was a state of mind, Gordon figured. You could sense it—the guy had to *be Batman.* There was no other way to make it work. That meant consistency—*being Batman* around an ally like Gordon, too. Batman coming, and Batman going . . .

Like a bat, vanishing into the night.

Three people—two losers and one in the making—in a hot, chemical-reeking kitchen crowded with improvised lab equipment.

Duck had worn the grimy Donald Duck T-shirt, way too small for him, for such a long time that it was almost indistinguishable from his skin; so long it had become his nickname. He was a bearded, twitchy little guy, his wire-rimmed glasses taped together, one lens cracked. His thin arms crawled with jailhouse tattoos. He was horning up a couple of lines of the crystal meth he'd made two hours before on a broken piece of mirror. He straightened up, noticing that the mirror fragment was shaped like the head of a bat, with those two hornlike ears. That was some weird shit, that was; he hoped it wasn't an omen.

At his elbow, turning down the heat on the burners

under the nearest meth cooking pots, was Bev—anorexic, in the dictionary under *white trash*, a stiff bottle-blond hairdo, missing a couple of front teeth, thirty-five and looking closer to sixty, a single clumsy jailhouse tattoo of the Virgin Mary on the back of her right hand. Four stoves were lined up in the kitchen, three of them brought from a junkyard, all of them with pots and glass vessels, distilling equipment cooking on their burners. On a stained table to one side were boxes of over-the-counter ephedrine and the caustics they used to separate them out. Most of the caustics bottles had skulls and crossbones on them somewhere. Bev used a burner to light a large blunt . . .

Beth stood in the hall doorway, looking into the kitchen: a teenage girl in a tank top and jeans, pierced navel, with an iPod plugged into her ears—the iPod was a gift from Del Derbinsky, but what Beth didn't know is that one of Del's Operative Teams had taken the iPod off some black dude two minutes after he'd bought it at Best Buy. They'd crippled the black guy.

Her shoulder-length hair was mousy, her cheeks were sprayed with brown freckles, but Beth had large caramel-colored eyes fringed in minklike lashes, and sweet lips, and though she was slender she wasn't cadaverous like the others. She didn't do boof.

She wanted to ask them if she could go outside, the air, poisoned by the speed lab, was making her sick again, and there was nothing on TV right now. She had been here all day, but she'd eaten only once, some Pizza Pockets for breakfast. Maybe she could ride that old bicycle out back to the convenience store, a mile up the road at the highway, get some Fritos or something . . .

Duck looked over at her, trembling as the tweak unreeled in him, his eyes pinning, and she changed her mind, backed out the door, not wanting to launch him into a speed rap that would be all paranoia and no comprehension of what she was asking for.

"You see that, she's on them earphones alla time, how you know she isn't getting signals from the cops on that gear, the spooky little bitch," Duck said.

"Don't be talking that shit," Bev said. "Del likes her, he hears you talk that way about her, he kick your ass."

"She been here three weeks already, she don't do nothing but watch TV, read paperbacks."

"Ain't much to do, she can't go into Gotham, we supposed to keep her here, he wants us to, and that's all, Duck. Does seem like a waste. I could find something for her to do—I was workin', her age, best time for it."

"That's right, she could be turnin' tricks and earnin' her keep."

Beth, just on the other side of the door, heard all that talk about turning her onto the street. You think you're at the bottom of the barrel, and you lift it up and there's another bottom under that one.

And her iPod was dying on her. Needed to be recharged, which she'd have to ask Del to do . . . But she dreaded seeing Del.

Beth wasn't going to let them put her on the street. She was a survivor. She'd been surviving people like this, and worse, all her life.

She thought: *I can't stay much longer . . . I have to go out on my own, someway . . . Wait for the right moment . . .*

Blond, flattop haircut, Slavic features, small steely blue eyes, steroid muscles that made the swastikas on his biceps seem to breathe, Del Derbinsky was barreling the old Chevy pickup along the patchy gravel of Red Oak Road. He took the curves through the rolling hills at seventy miles an hour, his eyes flickering through the night-shrouded autumnal oaks and dogwoods on either side. An old mansion there, down that overgrown road on the right—if it was deserted he might use it to store some goods later. Bunch of mansions up here, once; several had burned down in the arsons, a few years ago. Of course that Wayne Manor was still out this way, another two miles on. Del had thought of doing an Operation there sometime—Bruce Wayne was pretty liberal, hired a lot of niggers and chinks and spics, gave money to the NAACP, had an African American college fund, a free rehabilitation program for ghetto drug addicts. Wayne was working against the Survival of the Fittest principle that made the world strong, in Del's view. Tempting place, Wayne Manor, lots of money in there, priceless antiques—but all kinds of security cameras, motion sensors, even rumors of an unmanned flying machine watching the place, a drone like they used in Iraq.

The time would come when they'd have the power to go in and drag a weak, decadent liberal like Bruce Wayne out of his velvet-lined rat hole.

But in the meantime it was all about building up money and guns—and making the first Operations Statement, this January.

Del had a lot of responsibility on his shoulders, and he knew it. White Eyes was counting on him to turn over the money they needed to arm the rest of the militias . . .

That Batman weirdo had screwed them out of more

than one lucrative deal; Gordon had gotten in their way, too. But the time would come when—

What was that?

A dark figure gliding through the trees near the rambling old three-story house they'd rented at the end of the road. Was that the shape of a vehicle, parked among the trees, where none should be?

Del cursed under his breath and flipped his cell phone out, pressed SPEED DIAL for the house. The house phone rang and rang. *Goddamn tweakers, answer the phone.*

At last the girl answered. "Hello?"

He felt a tightening in his groin at the sound of her voice. "Beth? Listen to me—get out of the building. Yell at Duck to get on the phone then you go out the side door, meet me by that old garage."

"What garage?"

"That building—the one that's leaning, like it's gonna fall over . . ."

"That's a garage? It's all—"

"Just do what I tell you! Now! There are enemies on the grounds! Call Duck to the—"

But she'd already hung up.

Batman was running through the fallen leaves, cape streaming behind him, under the slender red oaks and dogwoods—he could almost hear Alfred's voice, "*Yes,* Quercus borealis maxima, *Master Bruce. Whilst the dogwood that you see there is also . . .*"

Up ahead, the trees parted to show the rambling old house on the hilltop. A solarium on this side of the house caught the starlight; thrusting up on the southern side was an octagonal tower over a wide, ramshackle porch . . . and lights on in the kitchen.

He could already smell the acrid chemicals of the speed lab. Could be the finished goods were stored in that tower.

Jim Gordon had been crossing the line, and with a big stride, sending him up here—because the only way to involve the police, without a warrant, was to wreak havoc and attract them.

Okay, Gordon, Batman thought. *You're on. Havoc it is . . .*

He spotted someone moving away from the house, trotting toward that old garage outbuilding. Difficult to see from here. Maybe a sentry. He drew a Batarang from his belt to take the sentry out . . .

And then a roaring metal presence to his left made him spin and throw the Batarang in a different direction, right into the windshield of the truck that was suddenly trying to run him down.

The truck had come up so abruptly, cutting full-bore across the brown grass of the dead lawn, that Batman had to leap and do a forward tumble to escape getting run down.

The truck roared past just behind him, the Batarang stuck in its webbed glass, as Batman leapt to his feet— and a house window shattered outward overhead, broken out by a murderous strafe from an auto-shotgun, its blast missing him but ripping up the ground close beside him and making tatters of the end of his cape.

Batman ducked in close to the building, pressed between a hedge and the wall, sidled quickly along it, out of the gun's shooting angle. He emerged near the solarium and immediately jumped up onto the wooden lip around the bottom of the solarium windows, then dove through the glass, rolling for cover behind an old, warped grand piano set up between the pots of dead plants.

Someone once had come here to play the piano, surrounded by plants that'd loved the solarium sun. Now the plants were dead and the only notes heard were the discordance of .45 bullets striking the piano's guts, cutting wires that sang out before they snapped at the ceiling. It was pistol fire this time—and Batman saw the silhouette of a skinny, shaking woman in the doorway, emptying the pistol into the piano, with some ludicrous idea that the rounds would break through to him. "You die, you son of a bitch, you die, whoever you is, you die!" she shrieked.

He was up before she quite ran through her clip, one of her rounds deflecting from his chest armor. He snapped a Batarang at her, knocking her off her feet. He started toward the door that led to another hall and, he guessed, the kitchen where they were doing their "cooking," when he saw the wiry little thug with the auto-shotgun step over the fallen woman, swinging the gun his way.

Batman dove for a doorway on the right, tumbled through, came up running, circled down a narrow side hallway—an old servants' corridor—and burst out into the old-fashioned kitchen, almost immediately choking from the fumes. He plucked a suctioning rebreather from his belt, slapped it over his nose and mouth, then threw himself flat as gunfire erupted, loud as repeated cannon fire, from the doorway ahead.

The auto-shotgun missed Batman—and hit the pots on the stove.

Volatile chemicals were flung together from the shat-

tered vessels and reacted: the resultant fireball filled most
of the room. Grateful for his flameproof costume, Batman felt the flames wash over him—there and gone, for
the moment, as the fireball retracted to a blue-yellow
pillar of fire licking at the ceiling.

The man in the doorway wasn't flameproof—his
screams were piteous as he ran, flailing at himself, a figure of fire, down the farther hallway.

Batman jumped to his feet and rushed—trailing
smoke but not burning—from the heat-rippling room in
time to see that the woman had gotten up, was running
in a panic out the side door.

The flames in the kitchen crackled; another pot exploded . . . Batman looked at the ceiling, decided the
flames would take care of the "product" up in the attic.
He ran after the woman, thinking he could tie her to a
tree, leave her for Gordon to interrogate. Gordon had
said he'd wangle some chopper units into the area—and
the fire was visible for miles. They'd get here fast.

And he'd have caught her on the front lawn except
that she was shot to ribbons by a centrifugal gun fusillade fired from the pickup truck—driven by a blond
man with a flattop, a guy with a broad Russian face that
Batman didn't know. A scared-looking girl was huddled
in the cab beside the trucker. Maybe he could leap onto
the vehicle . . .

But the driver fired another sloppy fusillade, this time
at Batman, from the truck. Batman knew that weapon
well enough to respect it, and had to throw himself behind
a big oak. The bullets ripped into the oak, cutting two
thick branches down, spraying the air with splinters. He
heard the truck race away, watched it go as the flames
roared up over the house behind him, throwing attenu-

ated shadows, painting the trees in a ghastly blue-yellow light, making the pitiful body of the dead woman on the sere grass look like it was quivering.

He couldn't chase the truck in the Batmobile without the police getting involved. The cops would nail it on their own, wouldn't they?

The Gotham PD choppers came, but they hung around the burning house—an old wooden house that went up like a gas-soaked match. They speared the house and grounds with their spotlights, one of which fixed on his Batmobile, parked in the trees. A voice boomed from a loudspeaker, coming from on high.

"You down there—this is the Gotham Police Department. Do not attempt to leave the area . . . Put your hands over your head . . ."

The police searchlights probed the grounds, looking for Batman as he dodged through the shadows, kept under the trees, tapping his gauntlet to call the Batmobile to him.

"Not me, you idiots," Batman muttered, jumping into the Batmobile. The pickup truck . . . How did they miss it?

He had Gordon on the special line in minutes, as he drove cross-country—having to smash through a couple of fences and switch on his "digital paint job" camouflage to elude the choppers—and twice swerving to avoid running over someone's horses. "I don't know as they *did* miss it, Batman. Lieutenant Burkhart was with them . . ."

And the next morning the *Gotham Register* headline above the photo of the smoky wreckage, read,

**WHY DID "THE BAT" BURN DOWN
THIS HOUSE?**

7

One second it's too hot out here, Cormac thought as the sun beating off the Santa Monica boardwalk made sweat start on the back of his neck, *and the next moment the breeze is cool and sweet, right off the sea.* But he wished he'd left the suit jacket in the van.

Beat boxes thumped, rhythm for the motion of the crowd streaming by the open-air shops and street performers. The tourists droned and laughed, watching the magicians and jugglers. Small black kids did old-fashioned break-dancing spins on squares of cardboard. The air was redolent with pot smoke.

Most of Cormac's attention was engaged in sorting faces passing on the boardwalk: tourists mingled in with a good percentage of bored black teens, some Hispanics, and young Asians. The Asians looked like they were in a competition to get tougher looks on their faces than the obvious gangbangers, and lately the Asian gangs were some of the most hard-core.

But right now, on a fine sunny Saturday, there was an almost tangible feeling of mutual tolerance, mellow indifference. If somebody got enough drink into them, that could turn around, Cormac figured.

A blond, shirtless skateboarder snaked through the crowd, Cormac's eyes following his sinuous path. Gary used to skateboard, got pretty good at it for a while. But that wasn't him.

Not Gary. Not that kid, either, or that one, nor that one over there. Not Gary, not Gary. Nope, not that one, either. Not Gary.

The asphalt path took a turn toward the west. Squinting against the late-afternoon sun, he put on a pair of sunglasses. Everything was instantly slightly blue.

He passed yet another surf shop, yet another health-food smoothie shop, the fiftieth T-shirt shop. He came to a sandy verge, flecked with grass, where a guy juggled flaming brands, keeping one eye out for the fire marshal. Just past the sizzling, spinning torches, a group of black folks—and one albino guy in dreadlocks—were listening to an African Homeland street preacher telling them that Jesus was black and so were the pharaohs.

Maybe so, Cormac thought. *Who the Hell knows?*

His eyes sifted through the crowd, finding slender white figures, here and there. Not Gary, not Gary. None was Gary.

Secretive behavior. That's the first thing they'd noticed, him and Rose. Then Gary's grades plummeting at school. Then he'd run away after not getting enough credits to finish his junior year. Tired of his old man's lectures, his mom's hectoring. He'd been gone a month this time. He remembered taking Gary to the campground in Pennsylvania, trying to get to know him, a few years ago—it was like the kid wanted to tell him something, all the time, and never quite did.

Was that Gary, over there? That kid at the crêpes stand?

Cormac strode through the crowd, against the stream, indifferent to hard looks and muttered curses, stepped up to the kid, put a hand on his bony shoulder, spun him around.

"What? Get your hands off me, dude!"

Not Gary. Dirty-faced kid, maybe fourteen, could even be fifteen, with blinking, red-rimmed eyes, tattoo of a masked face on his right jawline—Cormac thought the tattoo related to a band that Gary liked, too: SLIP-KNOT. Band members wore masks on stage.

"Sorry, kid. Hey—you want to earn twenty bucks?" Trying out his best unassuming, harmless expression.

"Not into your pedophile shit."

"No, I'm a . . ." *What? Don't say bounty hunter.* ". . . a private detective. I'm looking for a kid . . . and some friends of this kid . . . no one's gonna get hurt. Kid won't go to jail. Here's a picture of him . . ."

"Piss off." The kid started to turn back to the crêpes stand.

Cormac dug in his pocket, put two folded twenties under the boy's nose, rubbed them together. "That's forty. I swear, I just want to talk to the kid. I won't, like, use force on him or anything."

No more than he had to . . .

Long shadows under Santa Monica Pier up ahead. Cormac walked along the edge of the water, feet crunching the sand as he approached the pier from below, trying to look like a guy who was just on his way down the beach. As if he weren't interested in what was under the pier.

He glanced up at the Ferris wheel turning hugely on the pier, which was as wide as a four-lane highway. A permanent carnival up there, the small amusement park that occupied Santa Monica Pier. Loud with music from the Tilt-A-Whirl, people shouting at one another from the rides.

Up above it was crowded with families. Down below, squatters and addicts, in deep shadow under the pier, right under the feet of the straight people from places like Orange County. He turned and headed under the boardwalk, trudged up the sandy slope toward the shadowy places. He wondered if they were watching him now. If they were armed. If they would just take off . . . Maybe he should have been more careful. But he just wanted to get in there and find his son. He trudged up, deeper into the shadows. It was almost dark here, where the sand came up to within ten feet of the smoky underside of the pier. Someone had a fire going . . .

They kept the fire small, so the park cops didn't hassle them about it, feeding it with little bits of driftwood, beer cartons, pieces of a cardboard box. The smoke gathered against the underside of the pier in a blue cloud, and gradually dispersed.

There were three teenagers and a guy, maybe forty, sitting around the fire. That'd be Moth. The older guy had his arm around the girl—she was a true gamine, in a man's dirty white shirt she was using as a dress, no more than fourteen, scratching in thatchy brown hair that was probably lousy. Across from her and Moth were two tattooed, much-pierced skinny boys in cutoffs. Cormac's eyes adjusted, and he looked at the boys closely.

Not Gary, and . . . not Gary. Neither was Gary.

Cormac felt relief and disappointment sumo-wrestling in him.

The older guy had carved his black, white-streaked beard down to two long spears extending a couple of feet from his chin, each strand made up of a braid ending in a point. His nose was pierced, his lower lip was pierced, his ears were pierced. His face was smeared with charcoal, on purpose, in a skull design. His head was shaved. His eyes were black and he was whip-lean, and dressed in a frayed black suit, like an undertaker. In Cormac's professional opinion, Moth probably didn't have a gun handy, but you could never be sure.

"You'd be Moth," Cormac said, stepping into the firelight.

Cormac heard a coughing and looked up into the shadows where the sand met the concrete wall under the beginning of the pier. There was someone else he couldn't make out there, huddled in the shadows to one side, working on a glass pipe: smokable meth, he figured; ice, some called it.

Moth tossed trash into the fire, pretending to ignore Cormac. "Don't burn out that pipe, little brother," Moth said, over one shoulder, to the kid in the shadows. "Ain't nothin left." His voice was sandpapery, but almost gentle.

Cormac sighed. "Moth, send these kids here—" He pointed at the three by the fire. "—send them away, down the beach. Safest for them."

He saw Moth stiffen, saw him reach for a long stick, one end burning in the fire. He used it to poke at the flames.

"You want to explain yourself, sir," said Moth. He

eased his left arm off the girl. "This is a private party. The police know we're here. We have an understanding with the Santa Monica PD."

"If you do, Santa Monica Internal Affairs is going to be interested. You're dealing meth. And you're groping an underage girl."

The girl shot Cormac a venomous look.

"I've got papers on you, Moth." Cormac patted his inside coat pocket, where the papers were folded up. "You skipped bail. Left somebody else with the debt. Your ex-wife, was it? Sister? Your mom? Some stupid female. You going to send these kids away?"

A moan came from the boy on the dark shelf of sand above them . . .

Cormac looked up there, felt a chill. Took a single step in that direction. Saw the pipe light up with one of those small handheld gas torches—

There was a flash of sparks and red cinders as Moth used the stick to slap some of the campfire up at Cormac's face. Cormac shouted without any definite words, eyes stinging, cheeks and forehead singeing, as Moth Gimby ran away, dodging between the posts.

Cormac almost let him go so he could see if the kid farther up the pier was Gary, but then he saw the skinny girl running after Moth, shouting for him to wait for her. He had that much grip on her.

"Shit," Cormac said. The son of a bitch needed to be in a cell.

He jumped over the two boys—twisting free of a pair of hands trying to trip him up, coming down stumbling but staying on his feet, pawing at his watering eyes, spitting ashes as he followed Moth. The guy was on speed and rail-thin and was probably going to outdistance him.

Cormac saw a chunk of wood, about the size of a football, sticking out of the sand. Probably once part of a small signpost, with a nail in it. He scooped it up. He'd been both lineman and, briefly, quarterback at UCLA. Nothing brilliant, but more than competent.

He sent the wood chunk spinning at the back of Moth's head. It caught him a little lower, between the shoulder blades, but it was enough, down he went, face-skidding in the sand.

He had the cuffs on his belt in back, under his coat, and with long practice got them on the squealing Moth in under two seconds, locking his wrists behind him.

"You should've been in rodeo, my friend," Moth laughed, surprising Cormac.

"You should've been a pimp, or maybe in child porn," Cormac said. "But maybe you are."

"Now you slander me," Moth said, spitting sand out of his mouth. "I'm just a sickly drug addict, in need of love."

"Oh, shut the hell up and come on."

Cormac dragged him back toward the pier. Taking Cormac for a cop, the two teenage boys were dragging the gamine away—staring, crying as she went. One of the boys was shouting at someone.

"Gary, run, it's the five-oh, dude!"

Gary was too stoned to process anything like a warning. Cormac found him sitting with his back to the world, against a post, shaky hands poking a wire into the glass pipe. "Whas goin' on," he mumbled as Cormac dragged Moth close.

"You got flannel in your ears, little brother," Moth said. "I've been arrested."

"What?"

The boy didn't even turn around. He was poking at the pipe, his hands making insectlike movements.

Cormac wanted to cry. He wouldn't, but he wanted to. The sounds of the carnival overhead seemed like a sick mockery. He looked away, shoving Moth facedown in the sand.

"Ow! You're hurting me, Officer!"

"I'm a skip tracer, not a cop," Cormac said. Digging a small cell phone from his pant pocket. Speed-dialing.

Finally something penetrated to Gary, and he turned, blinking, gaping, mouth twitching, to look at his father. "Dad?"

"Oh, my good Lord," Moth said.

"Darrel Cohen," said a voice on the phone, barely audible.

"Darrel? Sullivan," Cormac said. "I got your man Gimby here but I can't take him in. Come and get him, he's cuffed. Santa Monica Pier. You got to come around under the pier, right near the start of it, because I got my son here, and—"

"I can be there in . . . twenty-five minutes if we're lucky with traffic."

"Thanks." He put the cell phone away.

Without quite knowing that he was doing it, Gary was poking at the cylindrical glass pipe again with the wire.

Cormac slapped it from his hand. The pipe smashed on the concrete wall. Gary just stared at the fragments. Then he brought his knees up close against his chest, encircled them with his arms, and sat there, rocking and muttering. Cormac couldn't hear what he was saying.

It was a long twenty-five minutes.

Gary came some way out of it when Cormac was dragging him by the wrist up the stairs by the parking lot. Wailing, "Why are you *doing* this? I left and I'm not living there anymore so leave me *alone*!"

People were staring as he tugged Gary by the wrist up to the van, and Cormac knew cell phones would be in use. He didn't want to have to explain things to the SMPD.

He unlocked the van, thinking about the pitying look Darrel had given him when he'd seen Gary, then glanced up, hearing the crunch of approaching boots. A Santa Monica park patrolman was trotting up between a couple of SUVs.

"Sir?" A chubby Chicano patrolman, with a large black mustache. MUNEZ was incised into the black plastic tag under his badge.

"He's kidnapping me!" Gary howled, immediately.

The cop put his hand on his gun butt, was moving into a stance Cormac knew meant he was about to point the gun and demand that Cormac get down on the ground. But Cormac managed to get his private cop license out first.

"I'm on a skip trace, Officer Munez."

The guy stared at the ID, blinking, his gun about two inches out of the holster. Then he shoved it back down and relaxed a little, hooking his thumbs in his gun belt, frowning. "Wanna tell me what's going on?"

"Well, Officer, the kid was heavy into speed, working

for a speed dealer, probably helping him deal it on the beach, and—"

"He's a liar!" Gary shrieked, his face bright red, a mask of rigidity, flapping like a fish in Cormac's grip. His words running together: "He's kidnapping me, he's my dad but he's not, he's just some asshole who likes to kick people's asses and he blew us off and moved to Gotham City and I'm just trying to get to someplace peaceful and he's kidnapping my ass, are you gonna do something or not—"

Munez rocked back on his heels thoughtfully. "So he's your dad?"

"Technically, but so what, he's kidnapping me—"

The cop had already tuned Gary out. "You need some help, here, getting him into the van?"

"Actually, I wouldn't mind."

They manhandled Gary into the back and he collapsed facedown, almost magically stopped fighting once he was inside. Cormac thinking about how many times he'd forced people into cars, as a cop and a skip tracer. Only now it was his own son.

"You going to cuff him?"

"Oh, I think the fight's gone out of him," Cormac said.

"I don't think I'd turn my back on him," the cop said.

"You better not, either," Gary mumbled. But he was curling up on the folded-up tent and the sleeping bags Cormac had brought along for their trip into the mountains: sinking into something like sleep, the lethargy of someone who's been up on speed for several days. It wasn't exactly sleep—more like the trance of sheer exhaustion. But Cormac recognized it; he'd dealt with a lot of tweakers. Gary'd be all right for a while.

He waved to the cop, got in, drove away. Sensing that Munez was having second thoughts.

Don't drive away too fast, he told himself.

Minutes later he was on the freeway, heading for LAX. Get two tickets for Gotham.

Cormac had a plan. There was a place out in the northern Appalachians, a few hours from Gotham. Cormac had taken Gary up there once when the boy had come to visit him, before the dope. Kid had liked it, then. Maybe he could reconnect with him there.

"It's the Bat," Del said. "He just cost us at least a million dollars—and we lost our Operative for the congressional hit because of him, too . . ."

"Blaming failure on your enemies is not the way of the Brotherhood," White Eyes said. "The failure was yours. You should admire your enemy for winning—and then work twice as hard to destroy him."

"Yes sir," Del said, licking his lips. "I'll do that."

They were standing in the chill, foggy dawn on the edge of the cliff overlooking the foothills below Hatchet Mountain. The nearest hills, black and sparsely spotted with scrub, were artificial: slag from the strip mine that'd been here, a chunk of mountain torn away, squeezed of coal, and thrown down the cliff. Below the slag mounds, fog cloaked the forest and trailed from seams in the mountain's roots.

Del had never felt comfortable here. To his mind, Pennsylvania was too populated to make a good site for the compound. But White Eyes said they had to be closer to their targets out east. And the Zionist conspiracy would be looking for them somewhere in the West.

Though he wore a long trench coat, Del shivered and sniffled in the cold, looking down at the roiling fog below; trees poked up through the cottony mist here and there, and the dawn light turned it all silver and gold. The wind soughed and made his eyes sting.

White Eyes, of course, never seemed to feel the cold. He stood there bare-chested, doing alternating curls with the barbells, a hundred pounds in each hand, not even breathing hard as he gazed out over the hills below. "A glimpse of Valhalla," he said.

"Uh—of what, sir?"

"Valhalla, where you'll go when you die if you serve the true God as a true warrior. Not many of us know who the true God is, Dirbinsky."

"No. Not many do."

Del had almost decided not to come up to the Brotherhood compound. He hadn't been sure White Eyes wouldn't kill him. He'd blame him for losing all that crystal, all that PCP—all that money. And for running from Batman. It didn't sound like White Eyes planned to kill him, though. It sounded like he was going to give him another chance to "serve the true God as a true warrior." Of course, that could mean a suicide attack. Maybe he'd be the one to take on that congressional hit personally . . . He wondered if he could go through with it.

"You're wondering what I have in mind for you," White Eyes said matter-of-factly, continuing to pump the barbells, his arms swelling with blue veins.

Del swallowed, unnerved and impressed by White Eyes' ability to read his mind—or to guess what he was thinking. "Yes sir," Del said. "I just want a chance to serve.

But you know, our plan would've held together, what with our people in Gotham PD, if it weren't for Batman—he breaks all the damn rules and no one does anything about it. We do it, they're breathing down our necks."

"You're making excuses again," White Eyes said, pumping. "As for the Bat, of course they don't come down on him—he's a tool of the Zionist conspiracy. He's the government-sponsored vigilante. Where do you think he gets all that fancy equipment he uses? He has to get it from the government. They only pretend to disapprove of him." He was finally beginning to show some sweat at the temples; to slow his pumping a little. But he continued pistoning the dumbbells as he went on, "Must be this Batman's a CIA agent, Dirbinsky. He can do whatever he likes. Now—I want you to direct a series of money-raising operations. We'll do three simultaneously. First one tomorrow night in Gotham City. You'll send some of our Blitzkrieg Martyrs to rob the Gotham City First National Bank. It's Friday tomorrow—the bank is open till six. Hit it just as it closes. Take the entire staff hostage. Have the Martyrs send the money out the back."

Del stared. "Tomorrow, sir? I need time to plan—"

"I just gave you the plan. Add to it—work up a good decoy of some kind. Now you'd better leave to meet with our people in Gotham. They're already expecting an Operation tomorrow—they just don't know where. Inspiration arises from on High and we must act on it, you follow?"

"Uh—yes sir."

"We need that money for the revolution, Dirbinsky."

He tossed one of the dumbbells at Del, who barely

managed to catch it—though he was strong as a bull himself. He had to drop it almost immediately to catch the second one as White Eyes, laughing, walked back toward the circle of buildings—the Quonset huts like wagons circled against Indians, on the raw stone and dirt of the old strip mine. Within the circle was a cinder-block building where the guns were made, and the new chapel they'd built, of raw wood. There was a razor-wire fence around the whole fortresslike affair—and he knew there was an emergency escape tunnel that led out of the cinder-block building, to the side of the mountain, in case the feds should raid them.

White Eyes walked toward the fence, which whirred open when he was almost upon it. Without breaking stride, he walked through, under the protective gaze of the armed sentries in the four wooden guard towers. The whole thing was reminiscent of a concentration camp setup—close enough, anyway, to gladden a white supremacist's heart.

Grunting, Del picked up the dropped barbell and, carrying one in each hand, followed White Eyes back through the gate under the watchful eyes of the tower guards.

It was threatening to snow, that late afternoon in the Western Division—a part of Gotham City controlled by the Crips and the Bloods and, on certain blocks, the Golden Reapers. But Backwoods, so named for the cigars he favored, and his much larger homey Dimples, so named for his dimples, were feeling carefree. They'd both just quit their jobs at the furniture factory, because they'd finally gotten their territory from their boys and now they could start cashing up serious. "I'm gonna get those spinners, first thing, on my Town Car," Dimples was saying as they walked back to the crib from the liquor store. He was a heavyset guy about six-five, hadn't quite made the NFL draft but close; had that round baby face with those dimples, but Backwoods had once seen him break a guy's forearm with one hand.

Backwoods kicked at an empty plastic Bacardi bottle, sending it sailing over the weedy vacant lot. He was a rangy street soldier with a small carefully sculpted beard and cornrows. Like Dimples, he wore floppy clothes—except that Backwoods, a hockey fan, wore a satin New Jersey Devils jacket, deliberately two sizes too large.

"Screw that Lincoln shit," said Backwoods, who didn't have a car at all yet, " 'specially that old beat-up scraper of yours. We gotta get the Benz, dawg. I get a red one, you get the white one with gold trim."

"Yeah the . . ." Dimples' voice trailed off as they both stared at the dark blue SUV pulling up in the middle of the street, the four white skinheads inside sitting there leering at them. "What the Hell these wankstas doing here?"

Backwoods already had his beeper out, was sending out the call as the nearest skinhead, riding shotgun, rolled down his window.

"I think we're lost, nigger," the wanksta said.

Backwoods suddenly became very still, his voice icy. "What'd you say?"

Four of them, Dimples thought, *and they got guns, you can tell they're holdin' guns below the windows . . .*

Stall until his boys get here? Or just pull the gats? He had a niner under his coat in a shoulder holster, Backwoods had his in a waistband . . .

The skinhead went on, mock-innocently, "I said, *Nigger, I'm lost*—I can't find your mama's house and I need to get some crack-whore sugar, can you tell me where she's at?" The others laughed.

"I'm not going to wait," said Backwoods, talking low to Dimples. He was sensitive about his mother.

"All right, my brother," Dimples said, feeling a little choked up. He had a premonition about how this was going to end.

He and Backwoods pulled their guns at the same moment, flicking off the safeties with their thumbs and leveling the weapons, Backwoods firing a split second sooner. The leering skinhead's face exploded in red spouting, and the near-side windows flew apart under close-range nine-millimeter fire, and then the driver fired a .357 past the slumping shotgun rider and Dimples felt something kick him hard in the chest and he staggered back, fell on his ass . . .

A car screeched around the corner, that'd be their boys, a little too late, and Mac 10 bullets sprayed at the SUV, gunfire was returned, and then another SUV came around the corner, firing at the gangstas in the car, and another car after that, and Backwoods had thrown himself facedown, was lifting up to fire his gat with one hand and frantically tapping his beeper with the other and more cars were coming and . . .

But after that Dimples only heard the riot, couldn't see it, because he was lying on his back, staring at the first snowflakes spiraling down toward his eyes, how big and slow and fluffy they were . . . the gunfire was distant . . . sounded so far away . . . Sirens coming . . . more gunfire . . . Backwoods screaming . . .

It was all a long way away—and getting farther. Farther . . . So distant . . . So faint . . .

*   *   *

Batman didn't like going out in the daytime. *Bruce Wayne* didn't mind it, but Batman, like a bat, preferred to hunt in the cloaking darkness of the night.

It was barely dusk, this time, as he drove the Batmobile down side streets, through occasional fitful flurries of snowfall, changing direction twice to avoid the cops his aerial surveillance told him were on patrol nearby. He was responding to a text message from Captain Gordon:

> *Report BB op casing 1st National,*
> *O'Barr Str, PD diverted to*
> *G-fights w-div . . .*

BB, Batman knew, was their shorthand for the Bavarian Brotherhood; *G-fights* meant another of the recent street fights between skinhead gangs and black street gangs, in *W-div,* the Western Division, this time—Gordon believed the confrontations were purposely fomented by the Brotherhood. They amounted to riots, and it seemed likely that this one was a decoy to draw police attention away from the bank.

Batman had seriously cut into the Brotherhood's funding in the raid on the house at the end of Red Oak—now, he suspected, they had to replenish. Armed militias had used robberies to try to finance their cracker revolutions before this . . .

Feeling more tense and distracted than he should, Batman pulled up in the alley behind First National. He needed to be in the right state of mind to undertake a Mission—he should be in the pocket. But he was distracted, thinking about the people who'd died, recently, around him and this Mission. Skeev Skeven, murdered; three men blown to pieces in the old Y; a man burned to death, a woman shot to pieces at the end of Red Oak Road . . .

Getting out of the sleek black armored vehicle behind the Gotham City First National, Batman drew a deep breath and, taking the package of plastic explosives from the Batmobile's volatile-storage locker, pushed all that from his mind. He brought his attention back to the present moment, the task at hand. Distraction meant mistakes.

And Batman couldn't afford to make mistakes.

The three gunmen in their "Rebel flag" ski masks herded all seven bank employees into the open vault. To Trask, looking at his dulled, distorted reflection in the polished stainless steel of the massive bank vault door, it was as if the masks were cut from the Confederate flag. They were the neo-Confederate nation, come alive, he figured.

"Get your big ol' ass in there, nigger!" Harmon shouted, jabbing the black woman in the hip with the muzzle of his AR-15.

She turned furiously, her eyes flashing, looking like she wanted to tell him to go to Hell, but he raised the assault rifle to his shoulder and pointed it at her face from a foot away, and she turned and stepped into the vault with the other six. Four women, two of them black, and three men, two of them Asian.

Could be a good time to make an example, Trask reflected. Kill the so-called people of color, let the others live. Their faces were covered, after all, and the getaway should be almost at hand.

The chopper—a hijacked traffic chopper with a GOTHAM CITY CHANNEL 43 logo on it—would be approaching the roof of the building about now. It was an older building with a fire escape up the side. Harmon and Tegrif were already dumping half a mil in cash into the big duffel bags, and they'd take it up the fire escape.

They had come into the bank just at closing—there were no customers, as it happened—and taken over without a hitch. Front doors locked, nobody with a chance to set off an alarm. It had been that fast and efficient. But then Del had rehearsed them half the night. They had the lesson of Skeev, killed with impunity in his jail cell, to remind them what failure meant. Now with luck the decoys and their friends in the PD would—

What was that thump from the back door? Sounded like a muffled explosion. "I'm gonna check something out!" Trask said, turning toward the back. He walked around to the triple-reinforced back door—where the armored car guards would bring money in, or take it out—and stopped dead, staring into the hallway. The door was hanging on its hinges, smoking. Someone had broken into the rear of the bank . . . Were they trying to rob it at the same time?

He walked down the hallway, assault rifle ready to fire from the hip . . . then noticed a storeroom door on the left, standing open. He swung the rifle that way— and a black-booted leg struck out, the boot heel cracking into the side of his rifle, hard as a pile driver, so that he felt its muzzle crack and his hands stung with the transmitted impact, the gun flying from his hands to clatter against the wall. He turned to run and found he wasn't going anywhere. Someone had hold of his belt, from behind, effortlessly holding him back. And then came a chilling voice . . .

"*Sorry. One mask here at a time, one only . . .*"

Oh, no. It was him. The Bat—pulling Trask's mask off him. He felt himself spun around, like a child in the hands of an adult.

He was staring into those cold, angry eyes . . .

"Trask, isn't it?" Batman said. "The one who got away."

Trask drew the razor-sharp bayonet from the scabbard on his hip and stabbed at those eyes—but his hand was stopped halfway. He felt the bones of his wrist cracking in Batman's grip.

He dropped the knife, hoping that would end the pain in his wrist—it was ended by Batman's other fist filling his vision with black-sheathed knuckles.

Batman dropped the unconscious thug on the floor, looking up to see another flag-masked gunman stepping from the other side of the open bank vault's door. "Yo!" the man called, coming toward the center of the bank.

The Dark Knight was in a rough spot here—in a narrow hallway, with a gun pointed at him. If he ducked into the storeroom he'd be trapped in there, ineffective at best. He could see the gun was aimed at his chest—an ordinary assault rifle, AR-15 this time, maybe they'd lost too many of their Dreads, but this was close range—and he turned so the bullets would strike his chest armor at an angle, deflecting. The burst came, and he took it right, compensated for its impact then cartwheeled forward, out of the hallway, coming down on his feet, jumping to a counter, leaping from it at the gunman, diving at him just above a second burst, and, a bit unnervingly, feeling the near passage of the bullets right by his crotch. Those rounds came within a quarter inch of ending any hope Alfred might've had of seeing another generation of little Waynes running around the manor.

Batman struck the bank robber hard just above both ears, as if clapping his fists together to find the man's head between, the gunman shrieking with pain, falling to his knees as Batman continued over him, tumbling in the air to land on his feet, a Batarang in his hand snapping toward the other bank robber—but the man had stepped aside, was raising a weapon. That one was an auto-shotgun, Batman saw, preparing to jump aside. It'd be tricky at this range—

But there was a dull *clomp* sound and the man slumped, dropping the gun and clutching his head. The black woman bank clerk behind him was smiling, slapping one of her spike-heeled pumps in her hand like a blackjack. She hit him again and he fell face-forward, out cold.

"Nice arm, miss," Batman said, nodding to her as he turned to the man he'd struck to his knees. He kicked the racist thug's gun aside and dragged him to his feet, pulling off his mask.

"He's one ugly dude!" a young Asian woman said, staring at the thug without his mask. A real pug-face, like an inept boxer at the end of his career. "Like to see under *your* mask, one time . . . ," she added, looking at Batman. "I mean—in private."

"I'm uglier than he is, ma'am," Batman said, spinning the thug to face him.

"I doubt it," the young woman said, looking Batman over.

"Um-*hmm*," the black lady said, elbowing the Asian lady. "I doubt it, too."

Batman lifted the pug off his feet by the throat.

"Now, good-looking—we've got to talk. Where's White Eyes?"

"Dunno . . . ," the man choked out. "Dunno who you mean . . ."

"Looks like you were right," Burkhart said. He was a tall, slender, long-nosed man with a high forehead, receding hair, and arms so long his blazers always looked too small for him. He tended to keep his hands in his pockets, to stand around stooped, head shoved forward on his long neck, eyes darting this way and that. He gave Gordon the creeps.

"Yeah, there's something going down in there," Gordon said, raising the binoculars to his eyes again. The snowfall was thin, didn't block his view much, but the bank heist was going on mostly out of sight of the street, the way the bank was set up. He could just make out part of an open bank vault door with people milling back there—and was that Batman's cape? A flash of movement—yes, he recognized the style. That was Batman. So he was there already. Gordon hoped he'd made the right call, giving Batman a heads-up on this one. He suspected that if this was a Brotherhood heist, the hostages might well be killed—and Batman was the best person to put a stop to that. There was no indecisiveness about Batman. He remembered when LAPD had waited till the last possible second to take out a shooter holding a little girl hostage—and in their panic, as the guns started going off, they'd accidentally shot the little girl, too. He didn't want that to happen in Gotham City.

"There a sniper in place?" Burkhart asked.

"A sharpshooter?" Gordon lowered the binoculars to look at Burkhart. What was he up to? Just didn't trust the guy. For one thing, he'd seen him with Breen. And he was an extreme neo-con—Gordon had a pretty wide conservative streak himself, but some of the neo-cons had notions and affiliations that made him nervous. His uncle had told him too much about liberating Dachau . . .

"Sure, Captain—they've got hostages in there. They start to shoot them, we got to try and take the shooters out."

Burkhart had a point. "Go ahead, Lieutenant," Gordon said, "get the SWAT sharpshooter over here if you want."

"When I heard you were staking out the bank, I took the liberty, already, Captain. He's gearing up now . . . No, I tell a lie, he's ready—he's back there waving at me." Burkhart pointed at a nearby convenience store rooftop and nodded. The sharpshooter, moving awkwardly in his SWAT armor, was running toward the convenience store.

Gordon started to comment that Burkhart was jumping the gun, then turned to stare at the sky through the spitting snowfall, distracted by the sound of helicopter rotors close by. "What the hell is that television chopper doing over the bank?" Gordon asked. "How'd they find out already? And why are they so close in?"

"I don't know, I don't know!" the pug was saying.

"Let me hit him a few times!" said a fat white lady clerk, coming scowlingly from the bank vault.

"You folks move into the corner over there, under the

counter, and flatten down," Batman said with cool authority. They went.

Batman threw the pug-ugly against the wall. "Now—you were saying? How were you going to get out of here with the money?" If he could trace whatever the getaway was, he would eventually come to White Eyes.

The pug had taken one too many thumps. He looked dazed. "The roof . . . chopper . . ."

Batman glanced at the ceiling. In the back of his mind he'd noted the sound of a helicopter somewhere near.

"Where's the chopper going?"

The pug shook his head. "No. No way, Bats. No."

On the tarry roof of a convenience store across the street from the bank, Lieutenant Burkhart knelt beside the SWAT sharpshooter, Abel Perez, a young Puerto Rican fresh from the marines. Used to taking orders, Burkhart figured.

"You got three targets in there, that I can see," Burkhart said.

The sharpshooter was hunkered down, laying his rifle atop a metal ventilator chimney. He looked through his scope. "Sir, I don't see but two of them—the third one may be down already. Batman's in there—he might've knocked the guy out already . . . and he's got another two already down . . ."

"Batman is hijacking the bank robbery, we figure," Burkhart said. "Where do you think he gets the financing for his lunatic vigilante trip, Officer Perez? He goes after criminals so he can take what they've already stolen from other people. He's cowing those scumbags and he's going to take the money himself. Word is, it may already be in the Batmobile." Perez had no way of knowing that wasn't true. Burkhart could say it was a guess, later, if anyone called him on it.

"You want me to shoot *Batman*?"

"All three of them, including Batman. And the other guy, if there is one—we're not sure how many there are. But Batman first, then those two bank heisters. It's our one chance to stop the guy . . . and to save the hostages, all at the same time."

"Sir—Batman's not armed."

"He's got all kinds of weapons on him. Probably a bomb—he blew up three guys recently. Firebombed that house in the country . . ."

"Sir . . . I don't think I should . . . I mean, I can't shoot any of them, until I get official word . . ."

"You're new here." Burkhart didn't mention that he was new to Gotham PD himself. "You don't get it. This *is* the official word. I'll get in trouble—not you." Unless of course Burkhart could make it look like Perez had decided to do it on his own—and he would.

Perez bit his lower lip, shivering as a cold wind slashed a fresh flurry of snow at them. Then he set himself and looked through the scope. "Say when, sir . . ."

Both bank robbers near the vault were waking up now—Batman didn't think he was going to get anything more out of them about White Eyes. He couldn't actually torture them, and though they were scared of him, they were more scared of the Big White.

He grabbed both semiconscious men by the back of the collar, dragged them to their feet, spun them to face the counter; they just managed to stand, and he reached for the compressed cuffs in his utility belt. He'd leave these guys and the duffels of money for Gotham PD and go to check out that chopper . . .

The front windows shattered under high-powered rifle fire, burst apart in their entirety, all the glass falling at once so it looked like a waterfall, and both men were jerked back toward Batman—one of them jerked twice, taking two shots. Batman could feel the power of the bullets' impact in the reverberation of the two bodies as they slammed back against his hands.

Sharpshooter, he thought, letting go of the dead men and dropping below the counter. *And one of those rounds was probably intended for me.* "Everyone stay down!" he shouted over the screams of the hostages, and, hunched over, he moved quickly out of the sharpshooter's line of sight. Then he straightened up, vaulted over a counter gate. Three strides took him to the back hall—where he saw that Trask was gone. The chopper!

He rushed out the breached back door, stopped in the alley, looking up to see the chopper flying off, out of range of his grapple. Was that a traffic-watch chopper, up there? Sure looked like it. Hijacked, maybe. But there was a man dangling from it, climbing up a rope ladder, pulled inside.

"Trask . . . lost him again!" he muttered.

"Put your hands on your head, uh . . . sir!" came a quavering voice from one side. Batman turned to see two scared-looking uniformed cops, both with their guns out, pointed at him. A white one and a black one—both quite young.

"Gentlemen, you'll find two bank robbers inside, probably from the Bavarian Brotherhood, with all the money. The hostages are safe but the gunmen are dead. Your own sharpshooters—"

"I said put your hands on your head or . . . or you're going down!" the young white cop said. "You're under arrest for breaking into this bank and . . . and for . . . because you're a wanted man! Now put your hands up!"

Batman nodded gravely. "I understand," he said, starting calmly toward the Batmobile, not walking too quickly. "If you feel you've got to shoot me, you're just doing your job." He didn't want to Batarang these guys. Not good relations with the police department. Things were iffy enough. Besides, he might hurt one of them.

"Rusty—" the black cop said, holstering his pistol. "I'm gonna use a taser . . ."

"Or a taser," Batman said, nodding, almost in reach of his Batmobile. He touched the studs on the back of his gauntlet, in the exact right pattern—the Batmobile started itself and the driver's-side wing door opened. Sirens were approaching. More cops.

"Shoot him!" yelled a tall, skinny plainclothes cop from the mouth of the alley. Batman didn't know him but he could see the gold shield on the cop's belt—and the police-issue gun he was pulling. Could this be the Burkhart mentioned by Gordon?

A taser hook shot out from the uniformed black cop's taser gun, snagged in Batman's cape, delivered its voltage—sparks flew and arced, but the charge failed to penetrate his insulated costume.

Batman reached back, grabbed the wire, snapped it off, and got into the Batmobile just as the plainclothes cop fired. A bullet sang off the Batmobile, smashed a building window overhead, and then Batman was driving away, zero to sixty in three seconds, the two cops jumping aside, firing at him as he passed.

Bullets rebounded from the Batmobile's armor . . .

and then he was around the corner, whipping between police cars to break through a cordon of onrushing cruisers.

By the time the cruisers had gotten turned around to pursue, Batman had taken three turns already and switched on his street camouflage. He lost the cops easily.

He tried to pursue the helicopter on surface streets, but it angled away, passing as-the-crow-flies over buildings he had to drive around, and he soon lost sight of it. No police pursuit of the chopper, he noticed. Either they hadn't seen a man climb into it from the bank—or they'd seen it too late.

White Eyes and Trask had gotten clean away.

But then, from the Gotham City PD's point of view—so had Batman.

"I'm gone!" Trask hooted, shaking a fist toward the last place he'd seen the Batmobile, below and behind them. "I got away from Batman again!"

"Just dumb luck," Del observed, voice loud over the thumping helicopter rotors. He was in the back of the chopper, too, scowling at Trask.

"He can't touch me!" Trask shouted gleefully. "I'm slipperier than the Bat!"

"You're an *idiot*!" Del shouted. "Where's the damn money!"

Trask suddenly looked meek. "Uh—the Bat got it, Del, he took it, he—"

"The Bat! Oh, Lord. White Eyes is gonna be . . . He's gonna blame this on me . . ."

I can't go back to the compound, Del thought. *I gotta run. He'll kill me for sure this time.*

Then he remembered that White Eyes was away from

the compound, had gone that morning to a conference down in Georgia with the KKK, trying to get them on board. There was time to get Beth from Hatchet, get out of town . . .

White Eyes had been looking at the girl. But Del wanted her, too, young as she was—wanted her to be his woman.

Whether she wanted to be or not.

8

"I am not believing this shit," Gary said. "You hear what the man said on the radio? It's *snowing* out there, dude."

"Dad is spelled D-A-D, not D-U-D-E," Cormac said. "Don't be calling me dude. It'll be nippy up here, but so what? We'll build a big fire . . ."

They were driving the midsized rental truck up the mountainside, in the early evening, toward the campgrounds in the Hatchet area, where they'd stayed several years ago when Gary was out visiting his dad. Gary had almost admitted having a good time then. Cormac thought the trip to the same mountains might soften him a bit.

The kid had slept the whole plane trip—had walked onto the plane like a zombie when his dad had given him a choice between planes to Pennsylvania or piss tests and juvenile hall. He'd been so tired, coming down from the crystal, he'd hardly had it in him to object. But now, the next morning, Gary was wide awake, bristling with withdrawal and resentment and sullen with depression.

"A *big fire*?" Gary muttered. "You save me from camping under the boardwalk where it's warm and take me to the mountains where it's cold—to go camping?"

"I didn't pull you out of there to protect you from camping." He glanced at Gary, who was slumped in his seat, looking pale, almost too weak to sit up. "You hungry?"

"Don't know if I can eat . . . yet."

Cormac shook his head, taking another curve. "That stuff leaves you feeling like crap after you come down from it—and you pay money to feel that way?"

Gary changed the subject, going from defense to offense, something he'd learned from listening to his mom. "So how'd you enjoy beating the hell out of Moth?"

"I didn't beat the hell out of him."

"Come on, you kicked his ass. You like to kick ass—right, 'Dad'?"

"No more than I like to take out the garbage. Sometimes you just gotta take out the garbage, Gary."

"Tough guy. I'm so impressed. You should have stayed with the Gotham PD. You could have beaten the crap out of people real regular."

Cormac shook his head. "I never had a brutality beef at Gotham PD. Not one." He wasn't going to get into the skip trace beefs. Special conditions. "How come you told people I was beating you up? I never hit you in your life . . ."

Gary stared sullenly ahead.

Cormac watched the boy rub his sunken eyes with a trembling hand. "If your mom could see you—"

"Don't! Don't even talk about Mom!" Gary moaned to himself, squirming in the seat. "Why don't you just pull over and let me out. I'll hitch. I'll run my own life."

"Yeah, right. We tried it your way and it didn't work. I found you floating in a puddle of scum. I'm not letting you go back to it, Gary."

"This ain't even legal, dragging me off like this . . . You didn't ask Mom . . . Forcing me into the car back in Venice . . ."

Cormac smiled thinly. "It's a gray area. You aren't of legal age and you aren't emancipated. For now, your ass is mine, pal."

Gary swore at him. Cormac thought about telling the boy not to use profanity, but he figured he ought to pick his battles. One thing at a time. He glanced at Gary again and saw him nodding, the crash fatigue catching up with him again.

Cormac reached with one hand into the backseat, pulled out a wool blanket, and, when they came to a straight stretch, managed to get it over the boy's lap without stopping the car.

Together, one wide-awake and pensive, the other dozing fitfully, they climbed Hatchet Mountain in a rented Dodge pickup.

Alfred was frowning at the bow tie on Bruce Wayne's tuxedo. "Forgive me, sir, I must retie this . . . hold still, Master Bruce . . . How you can be so adept an aerialist, so exacting with the use of a Batarang, and remain unable to properly tie a bow tie . . ."

Bruce smiled distantly as Alfred repaired his bow tie. His mind was elsewhere. It was back in the bank; it was on Red Oak Road; it was looking at pieces of bodies in the smoking wreckage of an old swimming pool . . .

Alfred glanced at him. "You seem troubled, Master Bruce. I mean—unusually so."

Bruce sighed, turning to examine himself in the mirror of the walk-in closet attached to his bedroom. "All I know, Alfred, is that people are dying around me. Skeev Skeven murdered in the jail. Three men blown to smithereens at the old Y, a man and a woman killed at the dope lab. Then two more at the bank." He tugged discontentedly at his jacket. Nothing looked right.

"It was none of your doing, Master Bruce," Alfred said, picking lint off Bruce's sleeve. "You didn't bring that bomb along, you didn't open fire on volatile chemicals, and you certainly didn't shoot a woman down in cold blood to keep her quiet. Nor did you assassinate two men in the bank. I expect that too was done to keep secrets."

Bruce walked out of the closet to look broodingly out the window at the sparse snowfall. "It just . . . it feels like death stalks me lately—follows me around. When I beat the brush, the predators rush out—and lately it happens that they kill one another. And that's six dead in a short time. It's like I've become a magnet for death. As if . . ."

He didn't finish the thought aloud. *As if my own hunger to destroy criminals somehow climbs out of me . . . gets a murderous life of its own.*

And he seemed to see that dark, mocking figure in the Batcave again—the first Batman costume, walking around on its own, clothing only shadowy emptiness . . .

A chime sounded from the security system. The panel hiding the surveillance controls was already open, and Bruce glanced over at the monitor, seeing an image of the hired limo at the front gate. His heart lifted. "That would be her . . . Teia!"

He started briskly for the door, pausing only to tap

the OPEN button for the front gate. Alfred was hard-pressed to keep up as Bruce strode down the hall. "Master Bruce, youthful vitality is one thing, but I simply do not understand how after only three hours' sleep, and having worked out for hours, *and* having spent hours in the lab, you're now fresh as a daisy!"

"Because, Alfred, I'm now seeing Teia in my mind's eye. You have *seen* Teia, have you not? Or do you need new glasses?"

"I only wear glasses for reading, Master Bruce, I—oh, I see. Yes, she *is* a delightfully . . . *stimulating* young lady."

"I'll wait for her in the dining room."

When she walked in, elegant in her understated dress—a dress the color of a young girl's blush—the chandeliers seemed to Bruce to glow more brightly, the silver service to shine in response to her arrival. "Bruce!" she called, walking to him, putting out her hands. He took both Teia's small hands in his and gazed into her dark eyes—they were charged with the energy of life.

They ate fresh salmon from the new Wayne Enterprises fishery—Bruce had designed the aquatic farm himself to raise fish free of PCBs and mercury—and fresh produce he'd had flown in from the Wayne AgriCo organic farms in Mexico. Afterward there was music—reel-to-reel analog recordings of Teia's favorites, de Hartmann, Brahms, and Nepalese folk music—as they sat together on a red crushed-velvet antique sofa, by the fire, talking of their adventures in the mountains of the Far East, cozily aware of the snowfall outside. But a moment came when, snuggled against him, she looked up in a way that was very particular, very special. It was as if she'd been on a balcony, before, talking to him in the garden below, and now she'd opened the front door wide for him . . .

He kissed her, a kiss that went on and on, astonishing him with its permutations, its capacity to communicate, and then she climbed into his lap, and whispered something to him, and he caught her up in his arms—was caught up himself in the hot, unstoppable current of the moment—and carried her upstairs to the bedroom.

Cormac hadn't slept well and it felt good to be outside, in the crisp air, looking at a beautiful, clear morning on Hatchet Lake. Fish jumped in the shadows where trees overhung the water; a blue heron flapped through the soft, meditatively drifting early-morning mist, landing on a gray, weatherworn log thrusting from the shallows. Was that an eagle wheeling out over the deeper, bluer end of the lake?

And no people. That was the advantage of coming here off season. His breath was jetting visibly from his nostrils and his ears stung, so, yeah, it was a little cold. But there was almost no wind, and a pale sun shone on the mirrorlike water. When the boy woke, maybe the scene would touch him. Anything was possible.

Cormac turned and walked to the cabin, went through the creaking screen door. Gary was lying in bed, coughing softly, as Cormac opened a can of soup, put it in a pan on the camp stove, turned on the little tank of propane, and lit the ring, turning on the timer. He watched it heat up for a while, then turned to find Gary sitting up in his bunk, rubbing his face.

Cormac walked over to the bunk, watched as Gary wiped his mouth with the back of his hand—smearing it with black.

"That come out of your lungs?" Cormac asked, feeling sick himself, then.

Gary shrugged. "I guess. The pipe." He blinked. "Where the Hell are we?"

"The cabin. Same cabin we stayed in a few years back. Got all the comforts of home. Well, bathroom and shower's in another building. But I've got a camp stove set up. It's got a little timer on it and everything . . ."

It beeped then, as if to confirm that, and he laughed—but Gary didn't. He just stared at his knees. After a moment he sniffed and said, "Smells, like, all moldy in here." Cormac went to the stove, took out the steaming mug of beef vegetable soup, put it on a tray with the vitamins he'd set out, brought it over to Gary.

"There. Take those vitamins, drink that soup. Make you feel a lot better. You'd be surprised how the vitamins will help."

Gary snorted, taking the mug. "What do you know about it?"

"We had tweakers in Gotham jail—the county doctors gave them vitamins to get them ambulatory again."

"I'm not a tweaker."

"On your way to being one, then. Take the vitamins, drink the soup. Feel better."

Gary just glared at him.

"You feel like crap, right?" Cormac asked, matter-of-factly. "Every muscle aching, your skin crawling, head pounding, weak as a bastard, and real, real depressed?"

"You enjoying that?"

Cormac wanted to hit him. Instead he closed his eyes and took a deep breath. *Stay calm.* "No, Gary. I'm not enjoying that. It makes me feel as bad as you do. I'm your father. But uh . . . look what I got here."

He took a small bottle of pills from his shirt pocket. "Just over-the-counter stuff—ibuprofen."

"Big deal. That won't make it. Got any Vicodin?"

"You're not getting any narcotics. You'd be surprised how the ibuprofen will help, get you through the worst. Take the vitamins, drink the soup, then you get some ibuprofen."

Gary glared at him, looking like he wanted to say *No way, none of your nursemaid crap.* But he felt so bad— you could see it in his eyes—he was willing to try anything to feel better. And a pill, after all, even a vitamin pill, appeals to a drug user.

Gary scooped up the vitamins, swallowed them down, and drank the soup. Cormac gave him three ibuprofen.

"I'm gonna try to catch some fish for breakfast— brunch or something. You want to come?"

Gary shook his head.

"Okay, Gary. Rest some more if you want or go clean up. I've got the propane heater going for the shower water. There's clean clothes for you, laid out on that chair. I'll be out on the lake for maybe an hour, not much more . . ."

"I'm just saying, Grenoble, maybe we shouldn't of come here on an *I-think-I-know-that-guy,*" Egerson was saying as they walked down the old wooden sidewalks toward the Hatchet sheriff's office that brisk morning.

The sheriff's office was next to the post office, which was next to the frame building that was city hall, the Grange, and the Eagles Lodge. There were only eight other buildings, none bigger than two stories, on the main street of Hatchet. Around the town, Grenoble knew, having seen it from the air, was a strip of woods, then clear-cutting for a quarter mile, then a rocky area, gradually descending the mountain, where there were abandoned coal mines and a couple of old gold mines. Somewhere in the woods at the farther side of town was an RV park, a trailer park, a propane station, and a small state park.

"We got to find out where that ordnance is coming from. Tip said Hatchet, so up here I come and I see this guy I busted for gunrunning . . ."

"But Derbinsky hasn't got a warrant on him right now, far as I know. Did his time."

"Wanted on suspicion."

"You better hope he's got a dumb lawyer."

"What's up with these wooden sidewalks, these people never discover concrete?"

"It's probably one of those tourist things, get that 'old town' look. They're starting to get gold prospectors up here, too, man, at the gas station said."

"No shit? In these hills, at this late date? Here we are . . ."

He opened the front door for Egerson, making a comical *after-you* gesture with his hand, and followed him inside. A small place with oak paneling, bulletin boards with WANTED posters, a few desks and computers. It smelled like burned coffee and dusty paper, just like it was supposed to. They walked up to the counter and Grenoble stared, seeing the sheriff taking a wallet and keys from a manila envelope and handing them back to Del Derbinsky. Giving him back his property. Letting him go.

"Sheriff, I thought we had an understanding," Grenoble said.

Sheriff Whipple, a slump-shouldered man with deep-set, red-rimmed eyes and an obvious toupee completing the remains of his sandy hair, looked at Grenoble with a set to his jaw that he knew from thirty years of dealing with cracker cops. It was a *don't-give-me-orders-black-boy* look. It said that he knew he had to deal with black people as if they were equal, but he wanted you to know he didn't believe it, and you, colored boy, aren't going to get an inch of movement out of me I don't have to give you.

"Having an understanding don't keep a man in jail," the sheriff said. "No warrant, no reason to keep him."

"Federal government allows some detainment on the basis of suspicion until—"

"I *was* detained, Sambo," Derbinsky said. "Now I'm outta here. Come on, Beth. Let's make a move before he notices you and decides he wants some white girl."

"What the hell do you think you're doing," Egerson said, "talking to a federal agent that way? Sambo? I'll kick your redneck ass!"

Egerson started toward him—Grenoble put a hand up to block him. "Let him leave, Egs." Grenoble was looking at the skinny little white teenage girl with the brown hair and freckles whom Derbinsky was dragging along by the wrist. She looked like she wanted to say something.

"Say, miss," Grenoble said, "this man related to you? You going of your free will?"

"We checked, he's her guardian," Whipple said. And he opened the gate in the counter to let them pass through.

The girl opened her mouth, hesitated, then shut it and shook her head, her lips trembling. She let Derbinsky pull her from the office to the street. "Come on, they hardly gave us a damn thing to eat," Derbinsky was saying. "We're going to the café, get some breakfast, and then we're out of Dodge."

"That girl is scared," Egerson said.

Grenoble nodded. He glanced at Whipple, and decided to say nothing else in front of him. But he knew Derbinsky for a racist, Aryan Nations, which might mean militia—maybe Bavarian Brotherhood. And with those guns in his hands . . .

By the time Gary had showered and changed, he was feeling a little better. The vitamins and food and analgesics were helping. Wouldn't have picked a plaid shirt and blue jeans, too redneck for him, but it was good to be in clean clothes. He was still mad, though; still aching inside, with the crash from speed; still looking for a way to show his dad how he felt.

His dad, the tough guy. Knocking Moth around, manhandling him into the car. No way was Dad going to understand the one thing that he needed to understand about Gary . . .

Just get away. That's all. I got to . . . just go.

He found seven dollars in the cabin, lying beside a few groceries on the table Dad had bought along the way somewhere. He took the money and looked out the door—no sign of him. So Gary headed down the access road, trotting till he was out of breath.

Where am I going to go with seven dollars? I'm out in the middle of nowhere. Even if I get to a town, what then?

But he couldn't turn back. He had a point to make. He wasn't sure just what it was—but he had to make it anyway.

Less than a quarter mile along the gravel road took him to a narrow, two-lane highway. There was a camper truck stopped on the side of the road, a swag-bellied, red-faced man with puffy eyes and stained, grimy overalls tossing tools in the back, slamming the tailgate shut, cursing under his breath.

"Hi. You have a flat?" Gary asked, walking up.

The man looked sharply at him, glaring. "Tailgate popped open. Lost some tools."

"Work up here, somewhere?"

The man sniffed, belched beerily, looking Gary over. "Dredgin', pannin', like that."

"Panning? Like for gold?"

"Sure, there's a new deposit opened up, somewhere up the mountain, people've been—what's it to you anyway?"

"What? Nothing. You need some help finding your tools?"

"Hell no. What do you want?"

"Sure could use a ride to the nearest town." And he sure did hope this guy wasn't Old Joe the Rapist around here or something. "Almost anyplace but here. My old man's gone off on a drunk, so I'm on my own again. Wanna get some work in town maybe."

"Well. Climb in, you can ride to Hatchet. Just don't ask me nothin' 'bout the gold. I don't like to talk about my spots. People steal things around here."

"They do, huh?"

"Stole my other truck. This's the one I usually live in. Come on, stop yappin' and get in . . ."

*　　　*　　　*

The prospector dropped him off at Bedelia's Truck Stop on the edge of Hatchet. Two parked semitrucks cooled their hot radiators in the morning air. Gary was feeling tired again, his body still dragged out from the drugs. He waved to the old man who'd given him a ride, getting only a suspicious glare in return, and approached the greasy spoon. A chunky waitress with dyed-auburn hair that was shaped, in Gary's view, like a seashell, was standing outside, smoking a cigarette, and looking at Gary in irritation as he walked up. She'd just started the cigarette and here was another customer. "What you gonna have?" she asked. There was lipstick on her front teeth, he noticed. "I'll tell the cook soon's I smoke my Kool. Or . . ." She looked at him warningly. "Do you got to see a menu?"

"Um—pancakes and coffee." It was the first thing that came to his mind.

"Sure thing."

Gary went in, feeling alone, hating feeling alone and at the same time afraid his dad would roar up outside and drag him out of here in front of all these people. He knew he sort of, kind of, maybe wanted his dad to find him. But he didn't want to be dragged out of anyplace else.

He found an empty booth near a jukebox with an OUT OF ORDER sign on it. In the booth diagonal from his sat a girl just about his age, and a big muscular guy with a blond flattop, some tattoos—you'd be scared to get in a car with him if you were hitchhiking. Gary found himself admiring the guy's muscles, though.

He smiled at the girl. Something about her reassured

him. Made him feel like someone else was in the same boat. She was in the shadow of that big muscular guy, maybe brought here when she didn't want to be; something about the way she sat there, shrinking into her seat, avoiding the big man's eyes.

The girl looked at Gary for a long moment, then smiled back. A lost, haunted smile.

"Ain't you gonna eat your French toast, girl?" the big man asked her.

"You can have it."

"Wasteful." The guy pushed his empty plate aside, and pulled hers to him.

"We got to go back to the . . ."

He shot her a glare as if to shut her up.

She finished, lamely, ". . . to that place?"

"I don't know. I'm trying to see what he . . . if it's good to go back there. Hand me the syrup."

"I'd rather stay with my cousin—"

"You can forget it. You stay with me or you go back."

Gary watched the parking lot, half expecting to see his dad pull in. A truck pulled out; no one came . . .

In a few minutes his pancakes came, though, and he ate those, just inhaled them, and drank some coffee. By the time he was done he'd decided to try calling his mom, see if he could get her to wire him some money somewhere. Maybe the next big town. If he stayed in Hatchet to wait for the money, Dad would find him.

He got up, went to the back of the truck stop. He could see a pay phone back there. But when he tried to get a dial tone, an operator, nothing. It didn't work.

He went into the men's room, and he was just done peeing into the urinal when a girl's voice sounded right behind him.

"Listen, could you—"

"Whoa!" he burst out, hastily tucking himself back into his pants. A few drops ran down his leg as he zipped up.

"I'm sorry," the girl said. It was the girl from the booth across from his, he saw, turning. "I didn't mean to—"

"That's definitely a urinal there so—I'm not in the ladies' room. That'd be next door."

"I know. They'd look for me there. I just need you to give me a boost to the window here so I can climb out."

He blinked at her, felt a chill of excitement—and fear. "Why? Who's . . . who are you . . . Oh, that big dude?"

"Yes. And some others. Look, I gotta hurry. Will you do it or what?"

"Um—sure."

They went to the window—it was partly opened. He linked his hands to boost her; she stepped in his hands and jumped up. She was heavier than he'd thought but he managed to boost her so that she got hold of the window frame, wriggled herself through.

Gary stared after her for a moment, then returned to the café, paid his bill, and went outside, noticing that Del was staring at the hall to the bathroom.

Gary found the girl around the back, a few steps from the bathroom window, standing up to her knees in weeds, looking like a startled doe—like she might run in any direction.

"So—where you going to go?" he asked.

"I don't know—what's down that path?"

"Uh—I don't know. I was here a few years ago with my dad but it's not like I know the place. I think it probably goes to the state park—it's that way. I think."

"Then I'm going that way."

"Not much down there but woods."

"I know. I figure he'll find me on the road."

"I'm . . ." He glanced at the highway. Half disappointed his dad hadn't shown up, half relieved. "I'm running from someone, too. My dad."

"I know how that is. Not that Del—that guy I was with—not that he's my dad. He's just some asshole I got stuck with. But I had to run from my dad more than once. Especially when he got stoned."

"Those truckers out there'd give you a ride."

"I don't trust 'em. My dad was a trucker."

She started along the path that led through the weeds, past rusty debris, to a broken-down hurricane fence and then into a shadowy pine woods. "My name's Gary," he called after her.

She paused, glanced back at him. " 'Kay. I'm Beth. Thanks, Gary. I'm gonna go. If there's a state park I can get a ride with some of those RV people. Somebody's grandma."

He started after her. "Look, I gotta find some other way to travel, too. My dad's . . ." He didn't want to tell her about his dad being a cop and a bounty hunter. "He'll find me on the road. RV grandmas sound good to me."

"Then come on and be quiet. People are looking for me and you don't want to be found with me."

"Either you're crazy paranoid or you're in deep shit . . ."

"Could be both, you ever think of that?"

"*Beth!*" came a deep-throated shout from the front of the building. Del was out there, looking for her.

"Come on!" she hissed and they ran down the path, over the bent-down fence, into the woods.

Seconds later, out in front of the building, Del was stalking over to his truck when the screech of tires made him turn to see two dark green SUVs pulling up. Ford Explorers. He knew the men inside.

One of them, riding shotgun, was White Eyes. "Going someplace, Del?"

"Yeah—I was . . . just going back to the . . ." He walked over to the SUV as if he weren't worried that White Eyes was going to kill him for trying to get away from the compound.

That goddamn sheriff, supposed to be on our side, holding me overnight. "I got to make it look good for the feds or they'll crawl up my ass," Whipple says. Traitorous bastard. Probably has Jew blood.

"—yes sir I was going to the compound," Del finished, his voice low, as he came to stand by the Explorer.

"Why'd you take the girl out of the compound?"

"Just—to be . . . to give her a break from the place. Hard for a teenager there. I was just coming into town, get a few personal supplies—the feds were snooping around. They got Whipple to put me in jail overnight."

"Whipple did that?"

"Said it was for appearances. There's a nigger from the ATF and some other goop with him."

"The ATF." White Eyes looked like he was carved from ice, in that moment. Amazingly inert. "They got a whole crew up here?"

"Impression I got, it's just them two snooping around."

"Is it. Maybe you were followed here from Gotham City."

"No way, sir. But you know there's a lot of us up here—somebody got loose-lipped. Maybe Whipple."

"Next time you don't move anybody from the compound without my permission."

Del swallowed. And nodded.

"Bad enough," White Eyes went on, his voice a rumble, "that you lost the bank money. We needed that."

"I wasn't there on-site—you told me to supervise from a distance. It was that idiot Harmon—and Breen, Burkhart, those guys. They should've kept a better watch. They did manage to shut those boys up, but the Bat was . . . well, if the Bat hadn't come . . ."

His voice trailed off. There'd been no obvious change in White Eyes, but something warned him not to mention the Bat again.

"Eventually," White Eyes said slowly, "I'll figure out who the Bat is, and I'll go to his house and I'll find everyone associated with him and I'll hold them till he comes and then I'll make him kill them just to put them out of their misery. And then I'll kill him with my bare hands."

Del could only rasp, "Yeah. That'd . . . that's right . . ."

"Where's the girl?"

"The . . ." How was he going to tell him? He knew that White Eyes wanted the girl for himself. "Beth's . . . I can't find her. She . . . wandered off."

"She wandered off."

"Yeah, I'm sure she's . . . just looking around."

"Or talking to those feds. We're going to find her, Del, and we're going to find those feds, and we're going to put them all in my little bag of marbles till I'm ready to play. You got me?"

"I . . . yes sir."

"Get in. Next Operation, you're going out on point."

Del got in the SUV, wishing he had the guts to run. But that'd only make it worse. They'd catch him and use him for training . . .

He'd have to wait his chance.

A pickup truck pulled into the lot, behind them. A big, dark man got out. "Gary!" the man shouted, looking around.

I wonder what that's all about, Del thought as the SUV drove off.

Despite being dragged out from coming down off drugs, Gary felt a muted exhilaration, tramping through the woods with this girl. It was an adventure. It was like a video game where you had to elude someone.

They passed through a copse of pines, into maple trees, half barren, their remaining leaves like fletching on a half-plucked bird. Sunbeams shot through the branches, illuminating Beth's hair. The spicy smell of the woods seemed as vivid as a woman's perfume.

"How come you didn't stay with your dad?" Beth asked suddenly.

"Um—well, how come he didn't stay with me and my mom? I don't know. He argued with my mom. He split, went to Gotham City . . . she had some problems but he was a workaholic . . ."

"*Work*aholic? I wish my dad was just a workaholic. Your dad do any time? Maybe he met my dad on the inside."

"Time? Oh . . . no. He was . . ." He sighed. Had to tell

her sooner or later. "He was a cop. And a bounty hunter, other times. He put people inside."

She stopped and stared at him openmouthed. "You're yankin' my chain."

"No. I'm not."

"A cop. Well, maybe he's still okay. Did he beat you much?"

"What? He never beat me."

"He never? Ever? Really?"

"Not really. Well, when he . . . he was kind of rough when he kidnapped me. Taking me away from the bad street people."

She looked steadily at him, baffled. "And—you ran from that?"

"He did it against my will. That tough-love bullshit."

"That kind of kidnapping—if I had a dad who . . ." She swallowed and looked away. "Let's go that way—I can smell food cooking down there. I didn't eat nothing yet."

"How'd you get hung up with that guy at the café?"

"He was my . . . not exactly my stepdad. For a while he was living with my mom, after my dad got ten to twenty. But she wandered off on the street one day, on crank, and never came back. So he took me up to this house where he was . . . he had business there. And then some guy broke in, some weird . . . some guy in a mask . . ."

"Like a ski mask?" he asked as they went on down the trail. He could see trailers up ahead, between the trees.

"Not exactly. I didn't see him good. Del won't talk about who it was. The cops came and we came up here to the compound . . ."

"The what?"

"The militia compound. They're all into that political shit about the Jews and the niggers and all that."

He was a little shocked by her casual use of the N-word, but they had come to the RV campground now, to an enormous recreational vehicle set off from the other campground sites. There was a bumper sticker on it that said, DON'T HONK AT ME, I'M LISTENING TO RUSH, and an NRA sticker in the windshield.

An old woman in a pink polyester pantsuit was barbecuing steaks to go with eggs, in front of the RV, and singing to herself, "Strangers in the night . . . exchanging glances . . ."

"There," Beth whispered as they approached her, "I told you, follow the cooking smells . . . and there's a perfect grandma."

"But what are we going to say?"

"Hi!" Beth called out, making the old lady gasp and step back in alarm. "Boy, it's, like really nice out, isn't it? Say, are you guys going to be traveling anytime soon, because . . ."

She was backing away and calling out, in a choked voice, "Lance! La-a-a-ance!"

Her husband came bounding out of the RV with a shotgun in his hand. "Get outta here, you two!"

"Whoa, dude!" Gary said, instinctively stepping in front of Beth. "Look, we were just—"

He pumped the shotgun. "Get out! Now!"

And he fired at a park garbage can in front of them—trash flew, and Beth and Gary were turning, sprinting so fast they didn't see the garbage hit the ground.

"Shit!" they said, both at once.

"Get on the CB, call the park rangers, Ellen!" the old man shouted as Gary and Beth dodged into the brush.

Cormac saw his son coming out of a side path onto the main access road of the state park, along with a girl he hadn't seen before, both of them out of breath and—were they laughing? What had they been up to?

The laughter faded from Gary's face when Cormac pulled the truck up in front of him. He looked like he was thinking about running.

Getting out, Cormac put on a smiling, relaxed face, as if the boy had only been out on an errand. "Who's your friend, Gary?"

"This is Beth. Look, Dad, I don't want to go with you, I just want . . . I don't know, if you could give us a ride somewhere and some bus fare, I'll take care of myself . . ."

Beth was staring at him kind of wistfully. "Hi. You're Mr. Sullivan, huh? Gary's dad?"

"I am. Call me Cormac, Beth. You had your breakfast?"

"No sir. I could use some."

"Beth—" Gary began. "I really don't want to—"

"Gary," Cormac said, "let's get her some breakfast, and figure things out. Maybe you could stay in someplace separate from me. Maybe I'll give you bus fare. We need to talk about it—that's all."

Gary stared at him. "This supposed to be psychology?"

Cormac shrugged. "You prefer the other method?"

"Oh, come on, Gary—" Beth began, then she broke off, staring at the green SUVs pulling up, one on either side of the truck. And behind the Explorers, a sheriff's black-and-white, pulling over. "Oh, shit. And that Sheriff Whipple, too . . ." She lowered her voice to a whisper. "Don't tell 'em anything about your dad."

Some instinct had told Cormac to bring a gun along, and he was already reaching under his coat, a hand on his .45. He'd recognized White Eyes from police artist sketches and descriptions—hard to mis-ID a guy who looked like that. Like an ice sculpture that could move around and talk.

"Del! I'm coming with you!" Beth said. " 'Bye, Gary . . ."

"Um—'bye."

"You tell that kid anything?" Del demanded, getting out, grabbing her arm.

"Hey, yo, take it easy, dude!" Gary said, trying to pull her away.

"No, I didn't tell him!"

"She's been with him too long, she told him about our . . . campground," White Eyes said. "He'll have to come along. As for this one . . ."

He turned toward Cormac only to see the .45 jumping into view. "Get away from the kids. They're going with me. Or I nail you first."

"Hey!" Whipple shouted, stepping up from Cormac's right. He turned—just in time to see a rifle butt slamming toward his face.

There was crunching pain and a flash of white and his limbs went rubbery.

"Dad!" Gary shouted, from a long way away.

Someone took the gun from his hand and he was on his knees, blinking. "I'm . . . I'm a . . ."

But then he thought, *Maybe I shouldn't tell them I was a cop.*

He tried to get to his feet, but someone kicked him in the gut, and he doubled over.

He heard Gary shouting, from somewhere, but couldn't make out what he was saying through the thickening haze in his head . . .

He heard the sheriff clearly enough, though. "I'll take this one, I don't see a license for this gun on him."

Left the gun license in the cabin, Cormac tried to say. *In the gun case.* But he couldn't speak.

". . . And me and him have old business," the sheriff went on. "You take the kids, I don't wanna deal with 'em . . ."

"You're taking this one? What if those ATF guys see him, Whipple? Suppose he talks to them . . . or someone else."

Cormac felt a boot pressed onto his throat. "Hey," Whipple said. "You listenin' down there? We run into any other badges, you keep your mouth shut. The feds or anyone else shows up lookin' for these kids, the teeny-boppers get it first."

Whipple. Didn't he know that name? He tried to get up . . . and someone kicked him in the head.

He never quite lost consciousness. It was all a gray churning in-between, and the next thing he knew clearly, someone was throwing him headlong into a jail cell.

9

Bruce Wayne woke up late that morning, after a long, luxurious sleep—an experience that was almost unknown to him.

He sat up on the edge of the bed, looking at Teia, who was just beginning to stir in the silken bedclothes. *Damn, she looks good.*

He shook his head. What was he doing? He should have been up training by now. Even worse, he hadn't gone out on patrol the night before.

A wave of guilt washed bitterly over him. Instead of the Mission, he'd had sex with this woman half the night and just . . . just *lain* there with her afterward, basking in afterglow, and sleeping. Sleeping! He'd been self-indulgent, useless—while who-knew-what was going on in the city. While people were being killed . . .

He had intended a nice dinner with Teia, a little dalliance maybe, then—he had *thought*—he would say good night to her, send her back to her hotel in the limo.

But somehow, once more, he'd lost himself in her. No, that wasn't exactly right. It was more like he'd let himself go—and somehow she'd confirmed his manhood, the full range of his humanity. It was a feeling that was hard to let go of. Somehow . . .

"Bruce?"

He turned to look at her. " 'Morning."

She sat up, smiling. "I'm famished! What's there to eat! If you don't have anything but rice in your poor little hovel, I'll eat that! And somehow I'll repay you for it!"

He had to laugh. Maybe one night, now and then, wasn't so bad . . .

No. He had let Gotham City down. He had let his parents down.

"Bruce? Anything wrong?"

"No, I just . . ." Maybe he should simply tell her.

"Sir?" Alfred's voice on the intercom. *"I have this on one-way. I just wanted you to know that you got a call from . . . the main office."*

Bruce touched the intercom TALK button. "Just tell my secretary to—"

"No sir—from Mr. *Gordon's* office. He left a message on your *other* phone."

"Oh! I'll uh, call him back on . . . the office phone. Can you find some breakfast for the lady?"

"Certainly, sir. Anything she likes."

"When he says anything, Teia . . ." He bent to kiss her quickly on the lips. "He means pretty much anything. But if you want fresh yak-milk curds it may take an hour or so to fly it in. Think about what you'd like and touch the intercom button there, I've got to make this call . . ."

Bruce put on a silk bathrobe, went down the hallway to his upstairs den. He closed the door behind him, locked it, and strode to the floor-to-ceiling bookshelf.

He found *The Adventures of Zorro*, pulled it out, and pressed the knothole behind it. As he drew his hand back the shelves slid away, revealing the elevator already rising to meet him.

In less than a minute he was in the Batcave, on the special phone to Gordon. "I miss anything?" he asked, in Batman's voice, when Gordon answered.

"Not a real eventful night for us," Gordon answered, to Batman's enormous relief.

He wasn't in costume—but in his mind he was already Batman. He'd have Alfred take Teia back to her hotel. Send some flowers later in apology. A roomful of orchids.

"But this morning," Gordon went on, "I got a call from Hatchet. It's up in the Pennsylvania hills—where they had those gold strikes. Cormac Sullivan gave me the *howling-at-the-moon* code. Said he was there in Hatchet, in jail. He didn't think it was safe to call anyone else in. The sheriff's in with them, he said, and there were threats to the kids, if the feds showed up, and I said, 'In with who and what kids'—and then I heard someone shouting and the cell phone went dead. I figure he'd had it on him and they missed it—they make them small now. But when they saw him making a call . . ."

"Sounds that way," Batman said.

"You really going out there?" Gordon asked. "I think I ought to call in some help. It's not my territory, Lord knows, but I've got friends in that state . . ."

"No. If there's someone threatening Sullivan's kid . . ." He broke off, thinking. "Did you say gold strikes?"

"Yeah, I was reading about it in the paper. You think an area's mined out, but—"

"*Hatchet.* Gordon, there was gold-mining equipment

in that truck—the one the auto-shotguns came in. And samples of the right kind of soil for gold mining."

"I'd better get the feds up there."

"Not yet. That kind of forensic connection is going to be too thin for them. And, Gordon—I gave him my word. Sullivan has good judgment. If he called for me specifically, he had a reason. Let me look into it first."

Gordon hesitated. Finally, the reluctance heavy in his voice, he said, "Suit yourself . . . But stay in touch."

"Suit myself—is exactly what I'm going to do, Captain." He hung up and went to take a shower and put on his costume.

Time to suit up.

"You don't remember me, do you, boy?" the sheriff said, grinning at him from the other side of the bars.

Cormac shrugged carelessly, though in fact he remembered Whipple. He just didn't want the sheriff to feel like he mattered to Cormac.

Cormac was sitting quietly on his bunk, wondering if he'd gotten enough information out to Gordon before the sheriff had seen him with the cell phone; he'd taken it away and crushed it under his boot, tossing the fragments back to him.

"How long ago was it, 'Officer Sullivan'?" Whipple said, making a joke of reminiscing with an old friend. "Gosh, must be four, five years? You were out here with some brat kid, and I was a deputy at the time patrolling that cabin campground and I found a nigger spookin' around up there, I got his ass in cuffs and you didn't like seeing one of your nigger home-bros in custody . . ."

"*Home-bros?*" Cormac said. "Good to keep up on the latest black English."

". . . and you come over and says how you're a Gotham cop and I say how this here is Pennsylvania, not Gotham, and you say something about federal laws and how I'm abusing a prisoner and it might be a hate crime and you keep me talking till that highway patrolman shows up—and later I find out you called the highway patrol in—and he lets the guy go . . ."

"You had no warrant on the man," Cormac said matter-of-factly, rubbing the puffy side of his face, "you cuffed him and beat him up because he told you to stop searching his car illegally."

"I'll tell you what really happened. You interfered with a policeman doing his duty—acting like I was low-down, all *supercilious* with me . . ."

"*Supercilious?* Good usage. New vocabulary word in the *Reader's Digest,* was it?" All the time that he was prodding the guy, Cormac was thinking anxiously of his son. Was Gary even alive?

". . . and I said to myself, if I come across that high-yaller nigger again I'm gonna drop his ass down one of them old mine shafts. And you won't be the only nigger we dropped down a mine shaft around here, boy. We got a revolution coming, and the day approaches when your Jew masters are going to be thrown down from their thrones and you with 'em, you'll all be piled up down in that mine shaft, and you can kiss Jew ass really good down there—"

"That's a colorful image. You should have been a poet, Sheriff. You can work on it in federal lockup after I have the local mine shafts searched."

"You can search one of them yourself, high-yaller. I'll see to it."

"You're not native to Pennsylvania, Sheriff. Your dialect says, what—southern Arkansas?"

The sheriff looked a little startled.

"Don't be surprised, Sheriff," Cormac said. "I'm just like Henry Higgins."

The sheriff blinked at him in momentary confusion. Then he went back to familiar territory. "I'm gonna beat your ass, when I get my deputy in here."

"Why wait? You saying you can't take me when you have a gun and a club and me all bruised up and dizzy?" Cormac asked, standing up. "Come and get it, big boy."

"Hell, I can take you out of there feetfirst, boy." He reached for his keys and his gun—but then a noise came from the sheriff's office, beyond the locked hall door of the holding cell.

"Sheriff?" someone called from the office.

"Maybe tonight'd be better," Whipple said, turning away.

Disappointed, Cormac watched him go through the door. He was pretty sure he could have disarmed the son of a bitch, if he came at him alone. It'd be harder after this. Unless he had help, himself . . .

"And in other news, a UFO has been reported over eastern Pennsylvania this evening. Some have described it as being like the triangular UFOs reported over Belgium a few years ago, but smaller . . ."

"Whoa, Bud! We're getting mini flying saucers around here?"

"Report says the UFO's about the size of a fighter jet, Lou!"

"And it doesn't occur to anyone it might *be* a fighter

jet? Hel-*lo-oh*! Gimme a break, here, Bud—I know it's a slow news day but spotting jet fighters . . ."

"Oh, you can laugh, my friend, but this one is all black, including the windows, has no markings except it's got wings shaped like the wings on bats—"

"Like the wings on a bat? It's flapping around up there, is it, Bud?"

"No no, the wings don't flap—at least the report here doesn't say they flap. Doesn't say if it eats fruit or bugs, either. But we've got eight reports of a low-flying vehicle with bat wings, making hardly a sound, and one time stopping in midair and going straight up—and it ain't a chopper . . ."

"Stopping in midair and going straight up? Right. And I'd like to report that the Playmate of the Month is sitting on my lap right now—but that, too, is all in my mind."

"What's on *my* mind is our sponsors. Geico, my friends, has a message for you and yours . . . We'll be back with more of *Noon Nonsense with Bud and Lou* right after this . . ."

Stealth technology isn't perfect, and Batman's cockpit indicators had informed him that radar had picked up the Batplane twice, though briefly, since he'd entered Pennsylvania airspace. Another check showed he'd dropped off their radar screens, but he still found himself wishing he'd equipped the hull of the jet with digital camouflage. Only, he hadn't found a way to do that and make the stealth tech work, too. It was a choice between eluding radar and quasi-invisibility. It'd been hard enough—over a million dollars in bribes alone—to get the Batplane built without anyone knowing who it was for. He'd had to do the wings separately—the bat scalloping was a telltale.

The jet was buffeted in a sudden updraft and Batman struggled for a moment with the pitch trim, to stabilize it. He wasn't quite confident of his control of the Batplane yet, this early in his career, though he'd checked out on a prototype of the jet.

The sky was hitting back at Batman just now—rough early-winter weather out here.

Alfred's voice—recorded to be used by the plane's computer—announced, *"A military aircraft appears to be following this vehicle. It is paralleling your course at two o'clock at a horizontal distance of about four thousand feet."*

Batman turned in the cockpit and looked out through the polarized glass—he could see it, just a fleck from here, but it could be on him in seconds.

Another voice, crackling through the radio, came over his headset. *"Unauthorized aircraft, identify yourself, over . . ."*

Batman had only taken the Batplane up for short test flights before now—he'd wondered what he'd do at a moment like this. He could simply elude the pilot—but in the current law-enforcement atmosphere that was a dangerous thing to do. He could get half the eastern seaboard scrambled and looking for him if he didn't explain himself. Since he had no flight clearance, he would still be breaking FAA rules, but it might be enough to keep them from assuming a terrorist attack.

Better decide. The military aircraft was coming closer . . .

"This is Batman," he said, into the radio. "I'm flying

out of Gotham City. I expect to be out of your airspace soon. Over."

There was a pause, and then: " *'Batman' is not a recognized flight authorization,"* the air force pilot said, the dryness in his voice coming through even on the radio connection. *"I'm closing with you. I'm almost right on your tail . . . I'm going to escort you to an airstrip where you will land, or I'll be forced to open fire. Coordinates are—"*

"Sorry," Batman interrupted. "No can do. But keep up the good work, my friend."

With that, Batman engaged the VVIF mode: vertical vector in flight. The Batplane slowed to cut the inertia; then its jets swiveled to vertical, and the Batplane—a VTOL "jump jet" as well as a stealth fighter—went straight upward, so that the pursuing plane shot by underneath, rocketing far ahead while Batman, moving horizontally again, was rolling off to starboard, already a thousand feet above, angling into the dark cloud cover . . .

"Oh, Hell," the pilot said, on the radio, "I lost him. You won't believe that maneuver . . . I swear that was a stealth plane with vertical vector capability . . . we don't have anything like that, both stealth and VTOL, do we?"

"If we do," came another voice from the AF base, "it's classified . . . You think that was the Batman or is *Bat Man* some kind of CIA code we haven't been briefed on?"

"I'll be damned if I know . . ."

Batman changed course again, remaining in the cloud cover till he was over his destination: Hatchet Mountain, Pennsylvania.

Then he descended, slowing till he spotted a gently

sloping, deserted clear-cut in an area otherwise forested, about a mile from town. A tall spur of granite over-looked the site; it would make a good landmark. He switched again to VVIF and set the Batplane down, landing vertically like a helicopter—or like a rocketship from an old science-fiction story, coming down on retro-jets in a great plume of dust and exhaust smoke.

Seven minutes later, with the Batplane locked up and set for automatic self-defense, and the black Ninja-style motorcycle lowered from its hold in the plane's belly, Batman was ready to explore the dark side of the mountains of northeastern Pennsylvania.

Standing beside the low, black racing motorcycle—bat-wing scallops, of course, on its frame cover and rear fender—Batman looked over the hills and valleys below him. He took in the streaming cloud cover, the treetops whipping in the same wind that snapped his black cape. He felt a kind of disorientation; a momentary loss of confidence. This wasn't Gotham City. It wasn't even New York or Metropolis. He'd developed his methods for an urban setting . . . He felt strange here. He remem-bered that moment with Skeev, on the docks. Who was he, after all, to wear this costume—to take this job on himself? Who—or *what* was he?

He thought he heard a mocking whisper, the words not quite intelligible, coming from behind him; he turned and in the shadows under a tumble of boulders, thought he made out the shape of his old costume staring sight-lessly back at him—just as it had in the Batcave. He took a few steps toward it—and it seemed to melt away.

He shook his head. He *was* going through something. But what?

He didn't have time to wonder. Someone in Hatchet

needed his help—and he suspected that before this case was over, the whole country was going to need him.

Reaching inwardly for determination, he returned to the motorcycle and climbed on. It started at the touch of a switch and, long black cape streaming behind him, Batman rode the racing bike along a deer path, jumping obstacles, till he came to a dirt road that turned toward the town of Hatchet . . .

"You think they're going to let us out of here anytime soon?" Gary asked, without much hope. They were in the chilly "nig brig," as Del had called it: two locked, boxlike rooms across from each other in a metal-walled Quonset hut. Gary was cold and hungry and scared and he felt like talking just so he could stop wondering what was going to happen to him. "I mean—like, after they finish punishing you for running off . . ."

"I don't know," Beth said tonelessly, leaning against the floor-to-ceiling padlocked hurricane-fence gate that replaced a door on her little cell. "I don't think they're going to just . . . let us go."

"So what do they . . . you know . . . plan to . . ."

"They're all, like, into a revolution up here. They've got a militia. They want to start a race war or something. And I think White Eyes wants to use me to . . . he said something about me being breeding stock. And he was going to be doing the breeding himself."

"You're yokin' me."

"No, I'm not." Was it despair in her voice? No. It was the voice of someone who'd never had anything good to despair of.

"That's sick, to call it that. Breeding stock."

"I guess he didn't want to call it rape. But I don't

know if he'll be able to do it, unless he takes that Viagra shit. He's on some kind of weird steroids—his own formula he got from MachineHead."

"From who?"

"It's this guy from South America—I think his name is Esperanza, really—who works for White Eyes. He's a crazy guy, most of the time locked up over in the Workshop. That's what they call it—I kept my ears and eyes open when they had me here before. That's where they make guns and stuff. They got a lab there, too. They make stuff to explode, steroids, all kindsa stuff. Machine-Head, he does it. Del told me he's some kind of speed-freak half-German half-Argentinian dude who used to be a scientist but he got kicked out of the big college place he was working for, down there. Whatever that capital city is for Argentina."

"Buenos Aires?"

"I think that was it. He makes this stuff for White Eyes called the Aryan Formula that he says wakes up some, like, Aryan white-guy superpower in his genes but it's just like he's another 'roid head far as I can tell . . . Anyway, steroid shit makes it so you can't get it up. That's what I'm hopin' for."

"I thought steroids made 'em more manly and horny and stuff."

"Only at first. After a while, what I hear, they get all limp and they shrink. But that's good, he'll have a tough time raping me . . ."

Gary said nothing, but he was thinking that, from what his dad had told him about criminals, not being able to get it up wouldn't stop them from raping anyone. They'd just do it with a knife. It was all about violence anyway.

"So how do they get away with this bullshit? I can't believe that cop just slammed my dad down and let these freaks haul me away . . ."

"That sheriff is in it with them. He's one of them—he's one of the reasons they picked this area. His deputy's in it, too. I guess this spot doesn't have planes flying over it much—stuff like that."

"Where are we, anyway? I was here years ago with my dad but this time when we came I was . . . asleep. Somewhere in Pennsylvania . . ."

"Hatchet Mountain—in between the Poconos and the Blue Ridge Mountains, I guess." She leaned her head on the fence material, hard, so that her skin was marked by the rings of metal. She pressed harder, squeezing her eyes shut.

"So if they want to start a race war, they're hard-core racists. And . . . I guess I'm about one-eighth black . . ."

"You don't look much like it. Just don't, like, say that shit around them, anyway. Say you're Italian or something. Or they'll put you in the hunting grounds for sure."

"Am I going to be sorry if you tell me what the hunting grounds are?"

"Probably be sorry, yeah. You don't want to know. Or about the mine."

Gary opened his mouth to ask her about the mine—and then shut it again. He had enough to process now. Where was his dad? Was he bringing the feds here? The state cops?

Was his father dead? Had that knock on the head killed him?

His stomach twisted and he turned away from the

locked gate, afraid he was going to throw up in front of
Beth.

He felt sick, thinking about it. His dad had been trying to help him. Now he might be dead. And he never
had told him . . .

Gary went to the bunk in the farther corner, away
from the doorway, in case he started to cry. He wasn't
sure if he could keep himself from it, and he didn't want
Beth to hear. For her, at least, he had to try to be an example of courage.

That's what his dad would've wanted him to do . . .

"What the Hell kind of road is this anyway?" Grenoble asked.

"It's a dirt road, Bill."

"I know it's a goddamn dirt road. That's not what I
mean. Who put it here?"

"I saw a sign about North Atlantic Coal. Old mining
access road, I think . . ."

"Somebody's been using it. Nothing's grown up on
it . . ."

"You know how much trackless land there is up
here?" Egerson said, sucking at the dregs of the espresso
drink he'd bought from the hollow-eyed, bearded man
at Hatchet Espresso Drive-thru. Grenoble was driving
them around the mountain in their dark blue government-
issue sedan, beginning to feel like they were on a wild-
goose chase. They'd been driving a good hour, trying to
get a sense of where somebody could hide an illegal gun
factory up here—and they realized now it could be hundreds of places.

"No, Egs, you tell me, how much trackless land is
there up here?"

"A big butt load of trackless land, that's how much. You think that sprawl and development is eating up the land, then you get up here."

"We're not all that far from those resorts in the Poconos."

"Far enough. I don't see anything but trees, for a good half hour now. We're wasting our damn time."

Grenoble sighed, wishing he'd gotten some coffee, whatever his doctor said. "We should've followed that Derbinsky character."

"Like somebody couldn't see you following them up here . . . We'd have spooked him. Which you probably did anyway. By now maybe they've already moved house."

"Looks like it might rain—or snow."

"Sleet, more like . . . Hey. Bill?"

"Yeah?"

"If we decide we don't try to follow them, it'd be kinda funny if they were following us, right?"

"Kinda funny? You call that funny? I don't call that—" He broke off, realizing Egerson was staring in the rearview. He turned in his seat and saw two dark green Ford Explorers five car-lengths behind them and accelerating fast. "Oh, crap. Is that Derbinsky driving?"

"I think it is, yeah. You pull over someplace, I'll get into a firing position."

"Where the hell am I supposed to pull over *at*? There's no shoulder here. Get on the cell phone, call for help."

Egerson already had the phone out. He was tapping at it, shaking his head. "No go. No service here. Just pull over."

"I told you—I can stop in the road, but there's no place to pull over, man." To the right was a drop-off—

not quite a cliff but a steep hillside, mostly tree stumps, with young trees growing up between them. Not a place you could drive a car without flipping it over.

To the left was mountainside, studded with pines and thick brush. There was no margin to pull over in. And up ahead . . .

Up ahead was a rusty old Mack truck without a trailer, bumping toward them in a cloud of dust, blocking the way completely. It pulled up short and they had to stop, too.

"Oh, shit," Egerson said.

"That about expresses it," Grenoble said, pulling his pistol and opening the car door. "Maybe the guy in the semitruck's with mining security. Maybe . . ."

But he already saw that the guy in the truck, jumping down from the cab, had an auto-shotgun in his hands.

Grenoble turned and saw that Egerson was aiming his pistol over the top of his open door at six, maybe eight militia types, including Derbinsky, approaching with a variety of weapons. His ATF-trained mind automatically logged in several AR-15s, a double-barreled shotgun, a pump 12-gauge, two Beretta .45s, and a weapon he hadn't seen before with a round chamber on top. Maybe had seen one—in a drawing. Could that be a *Dread*?

"Bill," Egerson said, in a hoarse, trembling whisper. "You get my back—then we'll head down the hill."

"Sure, Egs," Grenoble said, figuring they wouldn't get two steps.

He turned toward the guy in the truck, but that guy was already lifting his auto-shotgun to his shoulder—just like the one he and Egerson had taken apart in headquarters—

and he had a look on his face Grenoble knew, having looked at more than a few guys about to open fire.

Grenoble threw himself flat, firing his pistol as he went, clipping the auto-shotgunner in the shoulder, but the guy got off a burst, and Grenoble rolled onto his back to see Egerson cut right in half by the auto-shotgun, just like a chain saw had ripped him in two. Cut in half by the weapon he'd been puzzling over not long ago.

Then Derbinsky was there, pointing a gun at his head from four feet away.

Grenoble dropped his gun and sat up, raising his hands over his head, watching the life drain from his partner's eyes . . .

10

The sheriff's department paddy wagon rumbled out into the gathering night.

Cormac knew they were going to take him out into the woods and execute him. Shoot him dead and throw his body down an old mine shaft. Or cripple him and throw him in to die slowly.

He had never understood people who let themselves be cowed into just submitting to an execution. On death row, sure. What else was there? But out in the world—with a psycho stalking through a McDonald's, or even outnumbered on some lonely road on the edge of Baghdad, hey, *go for it*. Try to grab the bastard's gun. Kick somebody in the groin. Sure, they'd probably cut you down. So? They were going to do it anyway. Go down fighting.

Which is what Cormac intended to do. They had his hands cuffed behind his back, but right before they took him out of the paddy wagon, he'd worm around, get his knees up, push his feet through the circle of his arms, get the cuffs in front. It'd be hard, he might dislocate something, but he thought he could do it. He'd known GCPD prisoners to manage. When these two rednecks opened the doors, he'd go for them. Who knows, he might manage to blind Whipple, or break that goopy-looking deputy's neck.

Funny to think that this morning he'd been happily fishing, just glad he knew, at least, where his son *was;* looking forward to getting back into some kind of relationship with him. To helping him get clean. Show him the world in a new way.

Then they'd fallen into a nest of racist militia lunatics, and, chances were, Gary was either dead already or as doomed as he was himself. It was like a serrated blade, twisting in his heart, thinking of Gary in White Eyes' hands.

Who knows, he told himself. *Maybe they'll let him go. Maybe he'll escape. He's a bright kid. Don't underestimate him.*

He got up from the bench, swaying as he stood in the back of the paddy wagon, to look out the small, wire-mesh window in the locked back doors, see where they were, decide if it was time to start working on getting his hands in front. Hard to tell in the darkness but he was pretty sure they were driving off the highway now, onto some old logging road. Yeah—it was time.

But there was something else turning off the highway, behind them. Something following them.

It was a dark oval shape on the road, maybe a motorcycle—hard to tell exactly, without its headlight on. But it passed through a ray of moonlight and he made out a racing motorcycle and a rider: a chilling silhouette, what looked like horns on the rider's head, something flowing along behind . . .

Then it was gone, dropped back as they went around a curve. Following, but not wanting to be seen.

Cormac grinned to himself. Who else could it be . . . but *him*? Must have followed from the jail.

I've got to be ready to help him, he thought as he got down on the floor of the paddy wagon, squirming to move the cuffs around to the front. Hell, this was harder than it looked. The cuffs were tight and he was a big guy—his own muscles were in the way . . .

Uh-uh. No good. Batman would have to handle this on his own.

"Quite a few of these old mines here. Gold, silver, tin, copper . . . I think this one was copper," Whipple said conversationally as he and Deputy Donaldson shoved Cormac Sullivan toward the gaping, partly blocked hole in the mountainside.

"Yeah, it was copper—I think, or . . . or, uh . . . ," said Donaldson. He was a sallow, stocky man with receding hair, receding chin, and all his statements seemed to recede before they were quite finished. "Lot of 'em out here, and people startin' to mine again, but this one's, it's . . . it's . . . "

"They could mine nigger bones out of this one, I expect," said Whipple as he shoved his pistol's muzzle against Cormac's spine.

Batman was crouching behind an old, lichenous pile of slag just thirty feet from the three men, his fingers automatically readying several Batarangs.

Cormac and the dirty cops were two steps from the shaft. A few dry-rotting timbers remained, crumbling at the entrance; the irregular edges of the dark shaft were angular as teeth. How many other people had they dropped down there, Batman wondered. Was there a pile of human bones at the bottom?

With his left hand he took a set of UV goggles from his utility belt, opened it without looking, fixed it to his cowl—it stuck there without a strap.

The scene before him jumped into sharper relief, in reds and blues and grays. Cormac—hands cuffed behind him—was turning to face Whipple, bracing himself, his face defiant, looking like he was going to try to body-slam him. Donaldson was gaping around, as if he wondered if they were really alone. He had a shotgun in his hands; Whipple had brought along an extra-big hand-gun for this one: a .357 Desert Eagle. In Batman's experience, the bigger the handgun, the smaller the man's confidence in his own manhood.

"This here," Whipple was saying, "is what they call a winze shaft. Goes down to the crosscut. Entrance to the crosscut was filled in by an avalanche so this's the only way in or out. And it's straight down to a stope: a widened place down there. So there's no crawling back up, even if your bones wasn't broken by the fall. And they will be. Besides, I intend to blow a hole in you. I was thinking of giving it to you in the gizzard . . ."

"Just tell me one thing," Cormac said. "Of you two, you and the deputy here, which one's the top and which one's the bottom? I'm thinking you're the bottom. But you'd know best."

"That's all for you, nigger—" Whipple snarled, cocking the gun.

The two Batarangs zipped through the air at Whipple's gun hand . . .

And missed.

Batman suppressed his astonishment at missing—he *never* missed—and vaulted over the slag, shouting, "Sheriff!"

As Batman had hoped, Whipple spun in startlement, turning the Desert Eagle his way—away from Cormac.

Whipple fired at the dark figure rushing him—a black shape like a giant bat with red eyes. Batman had spread his cape so he seemed enormous, and Whipple couldn't see him clearly in the darkness: the bullet cut through Batman's cape near his left side. The big .357's recoil made the spindly Whipple stagger and at the same instant Cormac rushed Donaldson, head-butting him so that his shotgun fired wildly, its load peppering the timbers around the shaft.

Whipple got his balance and was cocking the handgun but Batman whipped a Batarang at the sheriff, ordering himself not to miss, and this time the missile flew true, cracking hard into the Desert Eagle. Whipple shouted in pain and dropped the gun, looking up in horror to see Batman looming over him.

Shrieking, Whipple ran blindly—into the mine shaft. His scream echoed up to them as he fell 113 feet onto a pile of bones—one of them an arm sticking up, and though all but the index finger had crumbled away it was as if the bony arm were eternally reaching for the upper world, so that Whipple was impaled first by the finger, then the ulna and radius bones, then the humerus . . . ramming through his gut like an ivory spike.

At the surface, Donaldson had struggled away from Cormac—who couldn't use his hands—and was pumping the shotgun, turning it toward the place he'd last seen Batman, babbling, "You killed the . . . he was . . . he was the sheriff and he . . . you'd better . . . better not . . . you . . ."

Then he looked around, swinging the shotgun left and right, searching for the big dark shape that had assaulted them—and couldn't see him. The man—was it a man?—was gone.

He felt a rush of relief, for a moment, which evaporated when he felt a brooding presence behind him; heard the creak of leather, the cracking of knuckles.

He turned slowly to see the fulsome, caped figure of the Batman standing inches from him, a foot taller, leaning over him—staring down with eyes like holes through the night sky . . .

Donaldson opened his mouth to scream and couldn't, somehow, remember how to fire the shotgun. But it didn't matter because the big dark shape was pulling it effortlessly from his hands. Then a black, gauntleted fist flashed . . .

And hit him so hard and fast he didn't feel a thing before he was out cold.

"Good thing the sheriff's office has a back door," Cormac remarked, emerging into the road behind the office, where Batman was waiting beside the motorcycle and Cormac's pickup—towed here by the sheriff. "Wouldn't want people to see you lounging about the front." Cormac put a shotgun and a Kevlar vest, taken from the sheriff's office, into the back of his truck, stuck a pistol in his belt.

Batman glanced at him. "Don't get jumpy with those weapons."

"I'm a professional, Batman."

"With your son involved—it's not a professional situation."

Batman had tilted the bike's seat up on hinges, and now he bent to gaze down at a glowing square of light: a small computer monitor and keyboard in a compartment under the seat. On the hand-sized screen was a digital map—Cormac could see HATCHET there, and a topography of the local mountains and foothills, designations for mines and forest roads.

"What else you got in that thing?" Cormac asked, rubbing his wrists where the cuffs had bruised them. "Kitchenette?"

"There *is* something else . . ."

Cormac watched in fascination as Batman opened a leather saddlebag hidden under the scalloped fenders, bringing out what looked like a mechanical bat about the size of a pigeon. He tapped the back of his gauntlet, then touched the head of the bat, twisting a ring around its neck. There was a faint humming sound and the "bat" began to flap its wings, fluttered up into the sky.

"A damn robot bat," Cormac marveled, staring up after it.

"Surveillance. Appreciate if you didn't tell anyone about them," Batman said. "No one."

"You got it, man. Anything. You saved my life—and I'm gonna owe you a lot more: You've got to help me get my son away from those scumbags. We can't just send the feds in there—they'll kill him and the girl if they see anyone coming in."

Batman nodded. "I'll find them. You secure Donaldson?"

"Locked in his own cell. I put the SHERIFF'S OUT OF TOWN, CALL HIGHWAY PATROL sign on the door and the same message on the answering machine. Donaldson's got water and a little food in there, and a toilet. No gun, no phone, no windows. I figure if anybody hears him yelling they'll think it's some wino in the drunk tank. We can get him out in a day or two—we'll need him to testify after we take White Eyes down."

"He tell you where they took the boy?"

"Claims not to know. But he's keeping something back. He seemed scared of you—you might pound it out of him quicker than I could. Break a few fingers . . ."

Batman shook his head. "I'll pressure people. Sometimes I get a bit rough. But I don't use torture."

"But that guy's gotta know where Gary is. I just don't think Donaldson's going to talk any other way."

"I'll find your son my way. You can ask some questions around town. After that—you'd better leave it to me."

Cormac cleared his throat. "I have to go with you. That's my son . . . I . . . wasn't always there for the kid. I have to make sure he's all right. I can't rest till I get him out of there. I want to see the kid grow up, Batman. I don't know if you can understand . . ."

Batman didn't answer. His voice was softer than usual when he responded, at last, "Oh, yes. I can understand that."

It seemed to Cormac there was something personal behind the response.

"All right," Batman said, "you take your truck, I'll take the bike. Lead the way to wherever you saw them last. You might be the better man to interview witnesses."

"You got it." Cormac started toward the truck, silently praying as he went.

Just let my son live a little longer, God. I won't let him down again.

"Don't matter it's the middle of the night," Spud said as he marched Gary toward the hillside that loomed over the compound. Gary's hands were bound behind him with disposable plastic cuffs. "No night or day where you're going. You'll forget all about night or day . . ."

He chuckled. He was several inches shorter than Gary but outweighed him by sixty pounds, at least, all of it muscle. He had shoulders that looked way too broad for his bald head, and a lumpy face knobbed with blemishes on an oval head, hence his nickname. He wore a sleeveless Levi's jacket, his exposed arms showing prison tattoos— some of the swastikas were backward—and greasy jeans, cowboy boots with high heels. But mostly Gary was hyperaware of the big gun in Spud's hand. It was some kind of cross between a machine gun and a shotgun, looked like, and he didn't want to see it demonstrated.

They were crossing to a back gate in the compound under the watchful gaze of the men in the wooden guard towers. One of them had a searchlight turned on them and Spud—Gary had heard Del call him Spud—put one hand up to block the light. "Dammit, take that light out of my eyes! The Big White don't want you to use them unless you need 'em!"

The light switched off. Gary noticed Beth—who'd been taken out of her cage half an hour before he'd come out of his—being marched by two armed men to a building, looked like some kind of barracks. He nodded to her. She just stared back. Too far away for him to read her expression. But he knew. She had given up. He noticed that they'd changed her clothing. She was wearing a pink dress and a pink sweater, like something you'd see on a little girl in about 1962. As he watched, they took her into the barracks building.

"What's going to happen to Beth?" Gary asked.

"None of your goddamn business and I don't know anyhow."

"You guys oughta consider something—my old man's a cop." *Close enough to a cop, anyway,* he thought. "And you can't just run off with the son of a cop and expect to get away with it."

"Son of a bitch, you mean. Hell, boy, I heard what happened. They didn't find no badge on that man and it don't matter no how. The sheriff took his ass out to the mountainside. He could see the man was a Descendant of Cain."

"A what?"

"One of Cain's children! Cain slew Abel and the Lord marked him by making him black! All them African Americans is Descendants of Cain. That's why they're suitable for slaves. And they're crossbred with monkeys, too—leastwise that's what I think."

"What do you mean, took him out to the mountainside?"

"The sheriff is one of us, boy. You can just say goodbye to your pop. Ain't no one going to see him alive again. You want to stay alive a little longer yourself, you'll work hard and do as you're told."

Ain't no one going to see him alive again.

Gary felt broken inside, thinking about it. Was his father really dead? Had they already murdered him out in the countryside? Was his father's body right this second lying cold and still under the soil of this same mountain?

No! He refused to believe it. His father had been alive when he'd last seen him. Cormac Sullivan was tough. He'd have found a way out. His dad was still alive. His dad would come and get him out of here. He was tough enough to . . .

Tough? He'd mocked him for being tough. Now his dad's toughness was his only hope.

They'd reached the gate, and Spud made Gary kneel as he unlocked the gate, then he gestured with the gun and Gary got up—harder to do than he thought it'd be, with his arms cuffed behind him—and walked ahead of Spud away from the lights of the compound.

They circled the cliff beetling over the compound, Gary looking for an opportunity to run. As if reading his mind, Spud said, "And don't think about running. First off, I'd shoot you dead—this here gun'll cut you in half. Even if somehow you was to get away, you wouldn't get far with your hands like that in the woods. Then we'd have to punish you bad. Cut off your nuts or something. MachineHead might have a use for those little pink nuts of yours. Make some kind of steroid potion out of 'em. He just might want to do an experiment on you anyway. He likes to experiment on people sometimes. Boy, you sure got yourself a big ol' adventure up here, didn't you?" His laughter was like the creaking of a rusty hand pump.

They walked through deep, cold, damp shadows now, and then out into thin moonlight, along a path that turned to follow the curve of the bluff. There was a light up ahead, next to an outbuilding. When they reached it Gary saw a pile of old tailings, with a thatch of weeds growing from it, next to a ramshackle building—a series of linked-up sheds, really, containing ore-processing equipment, he supposed, for the mine nearby. A battered, rusty camper-truck was parked beside the outbuilding. It was only a few strides more to a tunnel entrance recently shored up with new timbers, Coleman battery-powered lanterns hanging on either side.

A padlocked gate, much like the one on the cell Gary had been in, secured the tunnel a few steps inside the

entrance. Leaning against the gate, an auto-shotgun cra-
dled in his arms and a nine-millimeter pistol in his hip
holster, was a tall, jut-jawed man with a scar from a
badly sewn-up slash across his lips and right eye; that
eye was entirely pale, the other brown. His hair was cut
short, like most of the militiamen, and he wore camouflage military togs with the pants tucked in his boots.

"This is Peepers Johnson," Spud said. "He's your new
daddy."

Peepers grinned, showing green teeth. "He belonga
me now, huh?"

"Peepers here's from Albania. Lots of us from over
there. We got yer Russians, Albanians, Serbs, some
French, Germans—"

"Hey, you better shut-a the mouth, you, Spud," Peepers said.

"Oh, yeah, well . . . unlock it and take him."

Maybe I should run now. Maybe . . .

"Talk too much, you, Spud, always you do," Peepers
said, unlocking the gate. He swung it back and gestured
for Gary to enter.

Gary hesitated, looking into the stony tunnel, the
darkness of its gullet. If he went in there, he might never
see the surface world again. He might never come out.

Spud got tired of waiting and shoved him hard, with
a hand between his shoulder blades, so that he stumbled
through the adit forward into the mine, falling on his face
on the sandy floor, feeling skin rip from his cheekbone
as he slid to a stop. Hearing the clang of the gate shutting; hearing the click of the lock closing behind him.

11

Batman watched from the shadows of the trees as Cormac approached the homeless camp. The bounty hunter stood outside the encampment's ring of light for a minute or so, watching. Batman had known that the homeless sometimes camped around state parks, but he was surprised to see them on this chilly mountain, at this time of year, with so few resources around. There weren't many— a few camper-trailers without the trucks, four or five tents, lit from within like glowing fungi, and several campfires. A gray-bearded old man stood warming his hands at a rusty oil barrel.

As he waited, Batman reached into one of the motorcycle compartments, found the headset comm that would communicate through the subsystem hidden in one of the Wayne Enterprises satellites. He put it on, pressed the activation button. He heard a crackling, and then Alfred's voice. *"Yes sir? You haven't crashed the plane, have you?"*

"You of little faith. I managed very well with it."

"You seem to have generated some UFO reports, sir."

"Let them think that. Was the lady upset, Alfred, when I didn't come back?"

"*She is a Buddhist, I believe, sir. She took it with equanimity. What shall I tell her when she calls?*"

"That I'll be in touch—I'll try to get back before she leaves town."

"*Is everything all right, sir? I'm rather surprised at this call—you are not prone to checking in.*"

Batman hesitated. "Another man died near me, Alfred. Ran from me into a mine shaft."

"*You're quite sure he's dead, Master Bruce?*"

"I shined a light down there—he's quite dead. Did the lady say anything about . . . Did she give you any warning for me?"

"*No sir. It's not like you to seek supernatural warnings. Have you seen the, ah, manifestation again?*"

"Yes. It's . . . just an irritant. I hope. What's the status of Gotham?"

"*Status quo, sir. No emergencies. Will you be all right? You're on unfamiliar territory.*"

"I'll hold my own, Alfred. I have a job to do." He broke the connection, watching as Cormac walked up to the old man . . .

Long practice at talking to the homeless, a useful source of information to a bounty hunter, made Cormac choose the old man at the flickering oil barrel. The old rummy had a pocked tomato of a nose above a flowing white spade of a beard, a pink face flecked with purple veins. He had taken a mud flap from a truck, hanging it around his neck on a string so it dangled in front of him like a sandwich board; on it, in luminous paint, the manufacturer had printed: TRUST IN JESUS.

Mudflap, as Cormac mentally christened him, glanced

at the stranger and looked back into the fire. "So you got away from the sheriff, hey."

"You saw that?"

"Sure. Saw them kids runnin' from a shotgun, too. Shouldn'ta got near them old tourists, they is Hell on wheels, hey."

There was a commotion from a trash can nearby. They both looked over to see a black bear, not much bigger than a large dog, standing on its hind legs poking its snout in a large plastic peanut butter jar.

"Get away from there, you, hey!" Mudflap yelled, and tossed a chunk of wood at the creature. It loped off, and Mudflap ambled over, took its place at the trash can, sticking his fingers in the peanut butter jar, licking them. "Damn bears, makin' a mess out here."

Cormac strolled up, reaching into his pocket. "Any interest in these energy bar things?" He passed the old man a Clif Bar.

"Hain't seen one before." He stuck it in a pocket. "For later."

Cormac took a step closer, raised a hand to gesture— but Mudflap took it wrong and backed suddenly away, his eyes flaring with fear. "What I do? I didn't do nothin' to you."

"Whoa, hold on, pard, you're not in trouble with me. I just thought maybe you could help me. You probably keep a close eye on this park . . ."

The old man licked his lips; his eyes darted left and right. "Only way to dodge them rangers, hey."

"That's what I figure. What I'd do, too, I was you. If you saw those kids, maybe you got some idea where they are now?"

Mudflap stared at him. Sucked overgrown mustache hair into his mouth and chewed.

"I got a twenty here," Cormac said. "I could pay one of these other guys but I thought you'd know what goes down around here better. Nothing gets past a man like you."

Mudflap hesitated—then put out his hand. Cormac laid a twenty on it; the bill instantly disappeared into the folds of the derelict's shapeless clothing. "Those jarheads are from the compound," Mudflap said. "Took him to the compound, hey."

"The compound. Where's that?"

"Not many knows about it. You get close, you don't come back. I used to live up there, in that woods by the compound. They chased me out. They shot my dog, too. He was a schnauzer, hey. Well, part schnauzer. I didn't have no papers on him. But he was. He was part schnauzer."

"Hell of a thing when they shoot a man's dog. You show me where this compound is, I'll pay you some more."

"I don't have much chance to spend money. They don't let me in the store. You got a tarp, maybe a flashlight, too?"

"I'll give you a tarp and a flashlight—Hell, I'll give you a whole goddamn tent. Got it in my car. Bought it on the way up the mountain, hasn't even been used. I was staying in a cabin but I thought . . ." *If the weather stays clear, Gary, we can stay outdoors, in a tent by the lake.* He'd imagined saying that, while he was fishing that morning, and Gary saying, *Yeah okay,* and then they'd have a great time setting up the camp and . . .

And Gary'd run away. And they'd taken his boy.

Mudflap took a step back. "You look like you gonna hit somebody."

"I was just thinking about those guys who killed your dog. They're the ones I'm going to hit. They've got my son."

"They wouldn't like that I told you. Wouldn't like it, hey."

"They won't find out from me. I'll make up a story if they catch me."

"They'll come after me . . ."

"They shot your dog. Don't forget that."

"They sure as Hell did. Shot my damn dog. Hell, they did, too."

"Half schnauzer, too," Cormac prompted. He was good at saying something like that without sounding like he was making fun.

"That's right. Okay. I'll point you that way. But I gotta have that tent and flashlight first, hey."

The small chamber off the main tunnel was chiseled from the naked rock, its curved walls crudely beveled and incised. The only light was from two battery-powered Coleman lanterns, hanging from the support timbers, and one of those was flickering, threatening to go out. "You stretch out there, on that blanket. Work starts in four hours," Peepers said, shoving Gary into the chamber. "If you don't work hard, you going to be training bait. Dead in an hour." He closed a second gate behind them, locked it, and stalked off toward the entrance.

Gary made out six other men in the pocket chamber—a man who looked like he might be from India or Pakistan, an Asian, two miserable-looking white men who might be there as some kind of punishment, and two black men, stretched out on blankets, on the floor, shivering in the chill—all but the Asian, who sat up, hugging himself, rocking in place.

"Another one—a white boy this time," said the Asian, with a slight accent. He was a plump man—or *had* been plump, Gary guessed, a certain gauntness beginning to show; he had a high forehead, intelligent, sardonic eyes, the tattered remains of Hush Puppies and slacks, and a button-up Arrow shirt that still contained a pocket protector with a few pens.

"Actually I'm part African American," Gary said, sitting on the blanket, almost choking from the smell in here. The reek was not only of unwashed men, but of excrement.

"I figure," Gary said, after a couple of minutes of listening to the other men cough—one of them sobbing quietly to himself between coughs, "I figure these guys are totally bluffing. They're not serious about all this shit. They're going to ask for ransoms maybe, but . . ."

"No ransoms, kid," said one of the white men, a toothless, bearded man with white hair and a hooked nose. "Hell, that man next to you there, the other new guy, he's a federal agent. ATF."

"I still say it's all . . ."

The tall, chunky black man lying beside Gary, his back turned, rolled over to face him. In the thin light Gary made out quite clearly that he'd been beaten almost beyond making out the lineaments of his natural face.

And his left eye was gone—they'd gouged it out.

". . . it's all a bluff . . . ," Gary heard himself finish—wincing even as he said it. They'd beaten this man half to death; they had put out his eye. "Sorry. I guess they're . . . they're pretty damn serious."

" 'S'okay, kid," the black ATF agent said. Gary had the impression he was talking to take his mind off the pain. "Name's Bill Grenoble. ATF."

"I'm Gary Sullivan. Listen—aren't your people going to look for you?"

"Yeah. But they covered their tracks pretty good, getting me here. They figure to make their move pretty soon—before the ATF really starts combing the area for me. They think there'll be a revolution . . . they figure they'll be 'occupying' Washington, D.C." He closed his remaining eye, quivering with pain.

"Deluded lunatics," the Asian said, cheerfully. "Of course, many will die before they realize their lunacy."

"Maybe he'll win," said a white man, his voice dull; his eyes hopeless. "You don't know. Guy has a vision."

"Based on a lie," the other black man said softly.

Gary shifted on the blanket, trying to turn away from the worst of the smell.

"I can see you wrinkling your nose up," the Asian man went on, chuckling. "There's a small room back there, carved into the walls—there's a crack in the floor, going down a long way. That's our bathroom. Also, I'm afraid—that crack in the floor is our morgue."

The flickering lamp went out completely; the room got darker, everyone's eyes becoming like skull sockets. Gary shook his head. "No way. You're not telling me they put bodies down there."

"Pieces of bodies. My name is Kyu, by the way. I was a professor, in Davis, out in California. Traveling through Hatchet. One of the men insulted me, and I insulted him back, and they followed me, and here I am."

"Q? Your name is Q?"

"Kyu, K-Y-U. There's some water there, in a plastic jar, if you want some."

"Better conserve that," said the black man across from Gary, his voice listless. "They don't refill it but once every two days." A truly gaunt man, his arms stick-like. He noticed Gary staring at him. "Yeah. I been in here a long time. I don't know how long . . . Maybe six, eight months. The others were here longer—they used 'em for training and cut 'em up and put 'em down there and . . ." His voice trailed away. "They give us no choice."

"They make you . . . go to the bathroom on . . . ?"

Kyu nodded. "On the remains of people you've met, talked to, tried to comfort. Yes. We all said we'd never do it but there's no place else to go . . ."

"What the Hell are they mining in here?"

"Ask Harold here," Kyu said, indicating the starving black man. "He was a mining engineer."

Harold chuckled. "They think there's gold in here. There was once, but it wasn't much of a vein, and it was mined out. White Eyes says he had a vision that there's gold waiting for us to hit it down here. But he's delusional about that, just like everything else. So we wear ourselves to a nub, digging . . . digging . . . deeper and deeper . . . a grave seven hundred feet deep . . ."

"You better get some sleep, kid," Grenoble said. "We start in a few hours."

Gary opened his mouth to tell them that his father would get him out—but he was afraid that Peepers might be listening. So he just lay down and hugged himself and tried to sleep.

The hours passed. Not a damn wink. Then just before

dawn, Peepers came and took the two white men away. They wept as they went.

Beth sat on a bed, fully dressed, not sure what time it was; not sure if it was still night, or dawn. It was an ordinary-looking bedroom, in a lot of ways, but there was no window. There was a vent, and a ceiling fixture, which she left turned on, and a dresser, and a throw rug, and a little bathroom. And there was a door—which she watched, and watched, afraid to take her eyes off it.

She had a wooden chair—the room's only chair— propped against the door handle. Afraid of Aaron— whom the others called White Eyes. He had told her his first name, himself. Said she was allowed to use it. Said this as he caressed her head. Said he'd be back to see her later. Said . . .

The door handle was turning, from the outside.

The door started to open but stuck against the chair before fully opening.

She pulled off one of her shoes and held it in her white-knuckled hands like a club.

"Beth!" White Eyes called, through the door. "I just wanted to let you know—that friend of yours? We're going to let him go free this morning. I just wanted you to relax about that."

He meant Gary, she supposed. It would make her feel better, true, if they let him go. Only, she knew they wouldn't. She knew White Eyes was lying. Wanting to soften her up. Not wanting to have to force her, maybe.

"And Beth—I'll be along to see you a little later, we'll be alone, and we'll get to know each other. I have to exercise—I have work to do . . . But I'll be along."

He paused, then went on, still talking through the gap of the door, open only an inch or two. "Destiny is a funny thing, Beth. Sometimes you don't see it for what it is, at first. The Lord speaks to me, Beth. He tells me who is destined to live; who to die—who to love. When I come to you—I'll show you what I mean. You're going to feel different then. Believe that."

She started breathing again—realizing only at that moment that she'd been holding her breath—when he backed off the door, letting it shut.

Then there was a squeak of boards, and the door smashed inward, straight-armed by White Eyes, the chair bursting into splinters under the impact.

Beth let out a shriek, then bit her knuckle to keep quiet, so she didn't make him mad, scrambling backward on the bed, clutching the shoe, knowing it was useless and unable to let go of it.

She swallowed and managed, "Please . . . Aaron . . . Don't!"

White Eyes just stood there in the door, smiling at her, with his head tilted. "Can't have the door blocked off." His smile broadened. "There could be a fire."

He turned away and closed the door. She heard the rattle of a chain; the click of a padlock.

"Maybe Mudflap gave us a bum steer," Sullivan said.

"Maybe not," said Batman thoughtfully, peering at the digital map in the hidden compartment of his motorcycle.

They were standing in the shine of the pickup's headlights in a forest of autumn-orange mountain laurel. They'd spent hours on these dirt roads, it seemed to Sullivan, looking fruitlessly for the compound. So far the surveillance bat had found nothing. Batman had mentioned the possibility of help from satellite surveillance—but the cloud cover was heavy, and there was some kind of problem with moving another "special surveillance device" from its orbit over Gotham City to this spot.

"Mudflap gave us a general direction," Sullivan reflected, aloud. "An area, a road number—but the road splits up into all kinds of others, and some unmarked roads . . . we've covered less than a quarter of the area that we figured it for . . ."

"Here," Batman said, stabbing a black-gloved finger at the glowing map. "Where it says AGM." Sullivan came to look. Batman went on, "My uplink just came in with the details. *AGM* stands for 'abandoned gold mine.' It's the only one in the area. I've got reason to believe they've been mining gold—or they're close to some kind of gold-mining operation."

"There are placer mines, people panning, all that sort of thing all over this area," Sullivan said. "But as for actual mines . . ."

Batman tapped the map once more and closed the compartment. "That's it. We're going to recon that area. But there are probably a lot of them and they're heavily armed. You sure about this? I'm armored, Sullivan. You're not."

"I took two guns out of that sheriff's office—and I've got a Kevlar vest in the truck. They've got my son, Batman. And as far as I'm concerned—this is war."

12

"You heard me, Del. I'm moving up the timetable," said White Eyes, cutting up the four-inch-thick slab of raw steak with a butcher knife. He nodded toward a newspaper, fetched from Hatchet, folded on the table beside him. "Something announced there just begging to be targeted. We'll hit them as soon as we can get the delivery systems in place. Perhaps as soon as thirty-two hours from now—we will attack every significant infrastructural and political weak point in the United States of America. Chemicals plants, Congress—even the White House. We'll use Professor Esperanza's new ordnance . . . We will have twenty shells, that should be enough, exactly used, to destabilize the country." He cut off another piece of bloody Angus and bit it off the end of his knife, chewing so vigorously that beef blood squirted from the corners of his mouth.

Hands clasped behind his back in stand-down fashion, Del shifted uncomfortably, wishing White Eyes would let him sit at the table. He'd been supervising a training session, and he was tired. But still he remained standing, by the big oaken table near the crackling flames of the stone fireplace in the dining room of the lodge, one of the few compound structures that was not a "hardened" Quonset hut. "Sir—about the girl . . ."

White Eyes glanced at the ceiling—telling Del, without intending to, that she was upstairs. "What about her?"

"I . . . would like to ask permission to marry her."

White Eyes looked at him in surprise, snowy eyebrows lofted. "Really! Well—you shall have her. When I'm done with her. But I'll be raising the child myself, once she has it."

Del swallowed hard. So White Eyes had made up his mind that the girl was a suitable "breeder." Suddenly Del wanted to take that butcher knife from White Eyes' hands, ram it into his smug face. But he knew he wouldn't live through the attempt—this man was faster, more deadly than he could ever be. This man had almost killed the Batman, after all. That was closer than anyone else had come.

And Del had felt awe for the Bat since that night at the house on Red Oak. The guy had broken into the house—and moments later it was in flames, along with his assistant, and he'd been forced to shoot Bev. It was as if Batman pulled destruction along behind him, in the slipstream of his cape.

"You have a problem with that, Del? The girl's going to take my seed. I will see that she carries my child within her—it may take many attempts but I will place the seed in her." He stabbed the knife deeply into the steak. "I can sense it about her—she has the right genes."

"It's just—I don't know as I'll make it back from the Operation. We can do a lot of damage. But if they have to, they'll drop a bomb to stop us. The US military isn't going to play games once we start firing those things—"

"You're too pessimistic, Del!" White Eyes said, tearing off another piece of red meat. "You'll make it back. I'll see to it there's a backup chopper just to take you out of there, once you see that the weapons have done their work, of course. Not until then, Del. You understand."

Backup chopper? Liar! Del wanted to scream. *You are sending me out to die, as punishment for failing to pull off the bank job—and for trying to get away from here.*

But Del said nothing aloud. He knew better. He kept his face impassive.

Still, something must've showed, because White Eyes spat out a piece of gristle and said casually, "Some of my most loyal soldiers will be along with you, Del. With specific instructions to . . . watch your back. Don't think to turn that back on the Operation. Don't try to run."

"I'd never desert in action, sir," Del said. "Never."

"Not in action? Maybe just wait for . . . a time of inaction?"

"No sir—that's not what I meant—"

"MachineHead's got the gear set up, sir," said Spud, coming in, his voice hushed with veneration in the presence of the great man.

"Don't call him by that nickname when he can hear you," White Eyes chuckled, "or Dr. Esperanza will use you for one of his little experiments . . ."

Spud gaped wide-eyed at that. Even Del had to smile at Spud's expression.

White Eyes took an unmarked brown glass medicine bottle from the table, unscrewed the top, drinking deeply to wash the steak down, and to take his latest dose of the Aryan Formula: a mix of designer amphetamines and a whole new family of synthetic steroids.

Del had seen another man take a swig from the bottle, before anyone could stop him—the man had died two minutes later. White Eyes, drinking far more, seemed only to swell, to slightly tumesce as he absorbed the Formula into his system. Sweat beaded his forehead; his eyes glistened . . .

"Now," White Eyes said huskily, "let's see the demonstration. Let us see . . . our *power*!"

"*¡Que hermosura!*" Esperanza enthused, polishing the steel launcher with an oily rag. "What beauty! How it shines in the first light of *alba*!"

To Del it seemed pointless to shine up the handheld missile launcher. But that was what Esperanza was like: fetishistic. Esperanza was a short, intense Latino—said to be half German, actually, his father the son of an escaped Nazi, and his blue eyes suggested there was some truth to this. He wore a headset connected to a pair of glasses with a small digital heads-up display visible only to him; he boasted he could adjust them for infrared or ultraviolet. Esperanza had a strikingly pointed nose, its tip constantly moving when he spoke, as if there were an invisible wire from his nose to his lips. Impossible not to watch it in fascination.

It wasn't quite dawn in the center of the compound, but predawn was beginning to shine on the outlines of the MAN-PADS launcher—*MAN-PADS* for "man-portable air defense system"—which Esperanza had set up on a special recoil-adapted tripod. Essentially it was a modified Stinger surface-to-air launcher, similar to the ones used by the mujahideen in Afghanistan against Soviet choppers. It was the miniature missile itself that was special.

White Eyes had summoned everyone but the sentries: sleepy, grumpy-looking Brethren, dragged out of bed moments ago, from the bunkers and the bunkhouses and the Lodge, to stand in ragged lines, carrying flashlights, nearly two hundred strong, outside the launchtest strip Esperanza's assistants had marked out by yellow tape on wooden stakes.

At the other end of the test strip a six-foot-by-six-foot wall of brick, shored up by timbers, had been set up with two steel sheets, three inches thick, leaning against it. A bearded, ragged, half-naked man, wearing a blindfold, stood trembling against this improvised wall—one of the white men from the mine. Another white man, snowy-haired and bearded and toothless, his fellow from the mine, was tied to a stake on the other side of the wall, facing it. They hadn't bothered to blindfold him and he stared aghast at the wall, likely thinking that this barrier would be the last thing he'd ever see.

Del was moved, seeing them there—he had worked with these men, Gerry Smith and old Dunc LaTrelle, on two Operations. Had known Dunc from prison. But La-Trelle and Smith had tried to get out of the compound, together, when White Eyes had assigned them to an Operation that was thought to be a suicide mission, and one of them was suspected of trying to contact the feds. A punishment of months in hard labor with almost no rations, no comforts, and numerous beatings wasn't enough for White Eyes. He was going to test weapons on them.

Got to stay with the big picture, Del thought. *The Brotherhood'll need that kind of ruthlessness to win the war against the Zionist puppets of the Antichrist . . .*

It was getting harder and harder to believe that story.

"Now," boomed White Eyes, "most of you have seen us practice with Stingers. The IR launchers are effective—the Afghan rag-heads used 'em to bring down two hundred and sixty-nine Soviet aircraft. Well, now we've got a new version—it's all in the payload. Doctor?"

"*Sí,* thank you, my leader!" said Esperanza, his fluting voice carrying over the compund. "One of our people infiltrated the US Navy's warfare center in Virginia—he stole the plans and I developed and enhanced them. Our shop has built twenty-one of the shells now. Today we test one of those precious weapons! It contains a mixture of aluminum polytetrafluoroethylene and perchlorate oxidizer. It is molded into an aerodynamic shape and contained in Teflon coating. When it strikes, the impact acts as a catalyst . . . forcing the two chemicals together in a hot—oh, a *gloriously hot* reaction! The projectile will become so very hot so very fast it will *burn* its way through armor plating without exploding—it will only explode within the target! There is little that it cannot penetrate—and destroy from within! To enhance the effect, we have impregnated the shells with tiny balls containing virus pustules taken from Ebola patients under the 'care'. . . heh, to think they call it care, since they quite deliberately gave these Negroes the disease—"

There was general laughter at that.

"—under the care of our associates in the Congo. This particular shell does not contain the Ebola—do not worry, amigos! Today we test only the penetrating power of these missiles!" He turned ceremoniously to White Eyes and bowed. "Shall we, my leader?"

"In one moment, Doctor." He turned to the assemblage and his voice boomed to echo from the cliff over the compound. "Men—my Bavarian Brethren—I have heard rumblings from some of you that we're starting a war we cannot win. But I know—I and God know—that tens of thousands of like-minded free-republic Aryans will rise up and join us when we launch our multiple, simultaneous attacks across the country! We will avenge the martyrs burned at Waco! We will avenge Timothy McVeigh—*and we will avenge Adolf Hitler!*"

They cheered at that. He raised his hands for quiet, smiling indulgently, and went on, "Some of you will be engaged in helping to launch those attacks—your risk will be great, your glory will be greater! Your reward will be in this world if you live—each of you ruling over a portion of the former United States. If you don't make it, your reward will be all that much greater in the next world! As surely as the sun rises on this weapon—our sun rises to burn the mud-races from the world!"

The men roared in response, and fists shot up to shake at the sky.

"And as for these two traitors," White Eyes went on, "today we show them our mercy! Because they betrayed us they deserve to die slowly . . . today we'll show them just how quick justice can be! Doctor—fire away!"

"*Jahwohl* and *sí,* my leader!" And Esperanza pressed the button on his remote control. There was a hesitation of exactly one second before the launcher quivered— and fired. The projectile flashed in a burst of hot gases from the launch tube and rocketed straight for the screaming men at the end of the test strip.

It went so hard, fast, and hot that it penetrated the man in front like a pencil punched through a ripe pear, so that for a split second he looked down in horror at a seven-inch, perfectly round hole in his chest, just under his sternum—before he exploded.

The man behind him screamed as the projectile sizzled through the steel and brick and wood, blowing him into wet gobbets that spun to catch the first rays of dawn in spiraling sprays of blood . . .

There was a moment of shocked silence. The wind rose and blew the smoke away—and they could see a hole punched right through the steel armor. Burned through.

Spud, standing next to Del, burst out in amazement, "Like a hot knife through cheese!"

The men reacted to that with laughter and cheers and they crowded around Esperanza to congratulate him. His face fell and he backed away from them, mumbling thanks, but turning, finally, to trot hastily toward his machine shop.

Seeing his discomfort, the crowd went to inspect the remains of the targets. White Eyes turned to follow Esperanza. He had some technical questions to ask. Del trailed along, thinking about the two men he'd known so well—blown to pieces to make a point. But still—he was lucky, the way things had been going, that it wasn't him out there standing against that wall.

Dr. Esperanza stopped, staring at the sky. He adjusted his glasses to infrared. White Eyes and Del caught up and looked at him—then both looked at the sky. Was Esperanza thinking about the weather? "Looks like a storm—rain or sleet maybe," Del remarked.

White Eyes shook his head impatiently. "What is it, Doctor?" White Eyes asked. "Did you see a chopper?"

"I . . . no, my leader. I saw something else. Merely . . . merely a bat."

"A bat? So? Lots of bats around here."

"It was a *strange* bat. Something about the way it moved. And I thought its eyes . . . were made of glass."

White Eyes and Del looked at him, wondering if the veneer of control had cracked; if Esperanza had finally let his inward madness show on the outside.

Then a thought struck Del. "Did you say—a bat?"

"Yes. Just . . . a bat. Perhaps."

A bat. They studied the sky, seeing nothing but gathering clouds. And Del shuddered.

It couldn't be a sign that he is near. It couldn't be him. Could it?

"Let me play that back," Batman muttered.

As Cormac watched, the Dark Knight touched the controls of the small computer set up in the hidden compartment of his motorcycle. They had found the compound, were in the woods near it; when it became clear there was an assembly going on, they'd sent the bat to recon.

The footage recorded by the robot surveillance bat whipped by, backward, on the small screen. Batman stopped it, and hit PLAY. Shot from above, jittery with the bat's movements, the digital footage unfolded . . . He tapped the controls to slow it down this time.

Cormac and Batman watched the odd little man with the gear on his head point a remote-control device at what looked like a Stinger MAN-PADS on a tripod. They watched the weapon firing. The slow-motion image jerkily showing the projectile passing through the air, penetrating the man at the target, penetrating the wall, penetrating the man behind it . . . a slow-motion explosion, a blossoming disintegration of human flesh . . .

"Oh, Lord," Cormac breathed. "So much for those poor bastards. And Batman—that looked like steel plating . . . Look at that hole!"

"It was thick metal of some kind. The missiles just burned right through before exploding. I've seen research on them—they're called hot-impact missiles. They could use that against hardened targets. Like chemical storage."

"Or the Pentagon," Cormac mused.

"*Air Force One,*" Batman said.

Cormac looked at him. "Nuclear power plants!"

Batman nodded. "We can't count on them waiting till next month. We have to stop them now. Today."

Cormac swallowed. And nodded. "We'll have to call in federal agents. But that means Gary . . ."

"I'll have Gordon call them in. But before they get here, we'll try to get Gary out. I'm going to transmit this to—" He almost said *to Alfred.* "—to an associate. He'll send it to Gordon. It should be enough to get them here."

"Then let's get Gary out of there—now!"

Batman looked at the sky. "Looks like a storm moving in."

"What's that? It sounded like another explosion—but closer!" Gary said, pausing in hammering at the chisel he was using on the mine-shaft wall.

"It was thunder, I believe," said Kyu, coughing as his pickax raised mineral dust. "A storm."

"Could be this is the time," whispered Grenoble as he chipped at his own section of wall. "Might have a better chance of getting away in a storm."

"I didn't survive this long by taking chances, here," Harold said, doggedly chipping.

"You call this surviving?" Grenoble growled. "You may as well be dead. Worth dying just for dignity, Harold."

Harold turned to stare at him, his face especially cadaverous in the yellow lamplight.

"What is it, this jabber-jabber, you?" shouted Peepers, coming into the gallery, the big gun in his right hand, flashlight in the left.

"Just wishing we had some power tools, make this go faster, might actually find you some gold," said the man from India, Jedda.

"You want to have breakfast, work another hour, then maybe!" Peepers declared.

"I'll breakfast on your liver, you bastard," Grenoble muttered.

"What you say?"

"He said breakfast is what he lives for!" Gary interjected.

Peepers snorted. "Maybe he lives—if he works . . . !" He turned away and went to talk to Spud and another Bavarian Brother, at the entrance.

Grenoble stared after them with his one good eye.

"You must be in pain, my friend," said Jedda, looking at Grenoble's festering eye socket, his bruised face, his contused arms.

Grenoble shrugged. He continued to look after the militiamen, hefting his pickax.

Dabney "Dim" Muggles hated Periphery Duty. That's what he was thinking about as he paced along the edge of the woods, about fifty yards from the mine, nursing his last blunt. Hoping no one smelled it—he'd get in big trouble, smoking a doob on duty.

"Hee-hee, *doob on duty,*" Dim muttered. "Doob on duty . . . dooby duty do . . ."

He stopped chuckling, thinking: If they caught him . . .

But he was far enough from the others, he'd get away with it. They'd put him out here as far as you could get from the compound and still be on duty.

He looked around, seeing shapes squirm at the corners of his vision. Hella lonely out here. Smoking weed was supposed to make him chill but it wasn't working today.

Here he was outside the inner perimeter of the compound, outside the fences, outside the protection of the sentries in the guard towers, where anything could happen. It was the wilderness, after all. There were bears out here, he reflected, inhaling the last of his dope. And if the feds came after the Brethren, which "brethren" would they come upon first? And consequently, who'd they shoot first? Him, that's who.

Plus, Bigfoot could be up here. He'd seen a special about Bigfoot on the Fox channel. The damn things were tromping around all over the country, Bigfoot and the Mothman . . .

Dim shivered, thinking about the Mothman. Like a giant flying insect but part of his body like a man. That's what they said.

And those homeless weirdos were wandering around up here, some of them could be psychokillers, for all he knew, and . . .

A crack of lightning in the distance made him spin around, finger tightening on the trigger of his auto-shotgun. The rain was coming from that direction, brooms of rain sweeping toward him, like showers of coal dust against the early-morning light. As he watched, the light started to mute, as the rain and the clouds dimmed the sun. Darker and darker.

Dim had an impulse to go and hide himself in the processing shed, get out of the rain. But if he did that and White Eyes found out, what then? He felt sick, thinking about *what then*. He'd known Smith for a while, had bunked with him, and to see him blown to Hell like that just to make an example . . .

Better just stand here under the trees, as much out of the rain as possible.

Dim moved under a laurel, still thick with golden leaves, just as the rain struck, filling the world with its *rat-a-tat*. Leaves spiraled down, knocked loose by wind and rain. It was getting so dark out—yet it was daylight. Didn't seem natural. It made him want to . . .

"They send you out here, all alone?" came a deep, chilling voice from behind. "Alone . . ."

Heart hammering, Dim spun, raising the weapon—but a cable was whipping around its barrel from above and before he could squeeze the trigger the gun was jerked from his hand: a black metallic-looking cable jerked the gun up into the tree. He looked up into the branches, blinking away the raindrops that filtered through, to see a winged man shape standing above him in the shadowy foliage, his boots on a branch about six feet over Dim's head; perched there as confidently as Tarzan, arms folded across his chest.

Difficult to see his face—Dim could make out a square jaw, a firm mouth, and above it the face seemed to go all black, the nose a wedge of black, the eyes gleaming in dark hollows, the head crowned with hornlike spikes. Or were those ears? And the wings—like a bat's wings. Or . . . was it a moth's? Was this the Mothman? Had

Mothman taken Dim's gun with a long prehensile metal tongue?

"Oh no, oh shit, " Dim said, voice quavering, "don't take me to your world, moth guy."

"Why shouldn't I?" the dark figure asked.

"I'm . . . I'm . . ." Dim was quaking so much it was hard to speak.

Lightning crashed, briefly illuminating the demonic face; the predatory silhouette hunched over him, ready to fall like a hawk on a mouse.

"Yes?" it demanded. "Speak!"

"I'm . . . just trying to do something here, that—my dad wanted me to do this, he said it was good to do, that White Eyes, that he . . ."

"White Eyes has something that belongs to me. Another human like you. Tell me where he is and I'll take him instead."

"I . . . what?"

"A young man. Taken prisoner with a girl."

"That kid? He's in the mine there, with the niggers and like that—the girl's in that big building in the compound. Don't tell nobody that I—that I told you, they'll, they'll just take me and—"

Something cracked against Dim's head, then he fell into the wet fallen leaves, and it was lights-out. He didn't wake up till that night, when it was all over.

13

Rain dripped from Batman's cowl, beaded off his water-proof cape, ran from its hem like a silver fringe; rain-water pattered irregularly through the branches overhead as he rejoined Cormac at the motorcycle under the big pine. Lightning flashed over the cliffs; the following thunder seemed to issue from within Hatchet Mountain itself, as if the mountain were rumbling in anger.

"You read that guy right?" Cormac asked.

"Yes. Smoking dope and scared. Easy to play him."

"What'd you do with his weapon?"

"Tossed it. Too dangerous to someone not checked out on it. You could end up shooting people you're try-ing to rescue."

Cormac nodded reluctantly as Batman went on: "Your son's in that old mine—the girl's in the compound, the main building."

"The mine's outside the compound! That's great news!"

"Except for the three armed guards I spotted at the entrance, right now, eating breakfast from trays—and all three of them are armed with the new weapons."

"If we don't do it right, they'll turn 'em on the prisoners. We've got to make sure the guards move away from the mine. For long enough."

"I'll decoy them—you move in and get between them and your boy."

"How you going to get their attention?" Cormac asked, looking toward the mine. They were on the edge of the woods; beyond it was a barren stretch, maybe seventy-five yards across a crumbling, ancient volcanic flow. It was wide open, no cover.

"Leave it to me. Set off fast, right toward the mine—take these." Batman drew two small capsules from his utility belt and passed them over. "Smoke. It'll give you cover if you need it. And this." He handed Cormac a lipstick-sized tube with a metal piece like a car key sticking out one end. "Put that in the ignition, it'll start any vehicle. Get your boy out of here as fast as you can. I'll try to get the girl out."

"Batman . . ."

"Go! Get north of the mine entrance—move in to the south. Hurry!"

Cormac checked the load on the 12-gauge, nodded, and set off, jogging fast across the rocky expanse, squinting against the stinging rain.

Watching Cormac go, Batman slung himself over the motorcycle, waited till the thunder rolled through the mountains. But he just sat there, gently gunning the engine, glad for the miniaturized hydrogen fuel cell—he wouldn't need fuel anytime soon—and waited for his moment.

The big pine swayed in the wind, its shadows shifting, merging and drawing apart with the dancing of its limbs, and he turned his head, glimpsing a shape, his old Batman costume forming and disintegrating.

I'm nearly as spooked as that sentry, he thought.

He had to pull it together. Sullivan and his son were depending on him. The whole country was depending on him. There was no guarantee Gordon would be able to get the notoriously badly organized DHS to move in soon enough. This was no time to brood about hallucinations; about dead men.

About a man found hanging in a jail cell; men blowing up, burning to death, falling into a pit to be pierced by a skeletal arm . . .

Why? Why so much death around him?

Just do your job. You've got a Mission to finish. You swore an oath.

Cormac was almost in place, north of the mine entrance. Batman shifted gears on the motorcycle. It was time.

But he knew he wasn't in the pocket—he wasn't as confident, as controlled, as cool as he needed to be for the job ahead. Maybe the hardest job he'd ever had to do. He remembered missing when he'd thrown the Batarangs at Sheriff Whipple.

Still stiff from those chest wounds, maybe.

Excuses. There was no reason to miss under those conditions. There was no excuse for it.

Only—something had stood between him and Whipple. Not visibly. But there anyway. His old costume—empty—yet standing there, staring at him . . .

"What do you want from me?" Batman muttered.

The thunder rumbled in response.

"Then that's what you'll get . . . ," he said between grating teeth, twisting the throttle on the motorcycle, making the bike leap out into the driving rain. ". . . the thunder's coming . . ."

Spud, Peepers, and Conroy were smoking cigarettes and staring out into the rain. Conroy, an ex-marine wearing his marine combat uniform, sans its insignia—the uniform looked incongruous with the red bandanna tied over his head—was scowling at the rain, finger-tapping the trigger guard of his centrifugal machine gun to some anxious inner rhythm. "This weather's weird—it's so dark. Full daylight but dark. Like the day they nailed Jesus up."

"Don't say shit like that, Conroy—not today," Spud said. "Seeing those guys blow up—"

"They deserved it. They were—What the Hell is that?"

He turned at a roaring sound from the left, saw a dark figure in a cape skidding, fishtailing, but coming right at them through the rainy murk on a motorcycle. The headlight of the motorcycle suddenly switched on—and there was a silhouette painted on the headlight glass: *a bat.*

Conroy raised his gun to take aim but suddenly the motorcycle changed direction, veering behind the ore-processing shed.

The three sentries fired a second too late, the rounds chewing up the shed, biting ragged chunks from its wooden walls, making the roof collapse. Then a curtain of driving rain came down hard, obscuring their vision. Conroy ran out into the rain toward the sound of the motorcycle, shouting, "It's the goddamn Bat! Call head-quarters, fast!"

Peepers screamed and Spud, fumbling for his walkie-talkie, turned to see a small bat-shaped blade, a throwing star, stuck bloodily deep in the Albanian's gun hand. Peepers had dropped the gun so he could pluck out the shuriken and the auto-shotgun's muzzle was choked with mud.

"Shit!" Spud burst out, then yelled into the walkie-talkie, "We're under attack out here!" He backed into the mine.

"Hey—Mr. Potato Head!" said someone behind him. He turned to see the big one-eyed black man swinging a pickax. It was the last thing he ever saw.

Conroy rushed back to the entrance of the tunnel, shouting, "Spud, Peepers, let's go, I need you to fan out with me, he's trying to draw me out there, every time I think I see him he . . . Yo! Where are you guys—" He broke off, staring, seeing a dead man lying in the lantern light about ten feet inside, his forehead broken open like a crushed melon rind.

Pickax! he thought. *Where's Peepers gone? They get him, too?*

He spun to the left, sensing someone in a dark alcove of rock—that big black fed, coming right at him—

"Gotcha!" Conroy said, grinning, popping his weapon to his shoulder. The black man was still two long strides off, no way he was getting to him in time.

"Toldaegarri saekkiya!" screamed someone just too close on Conroy's right. He turned to see the far smaller Asian—the half-mad professor, in his tattered slacks and Hush Puppies—rushing at him with a pickax in his hand, yowling something in Korean, face contorted in kill-fury.

Conroy swung the gun around, shouting, "Suck this, gook!" But the word *gook* coincided exactly with the *chunk* sound of the Korean's pickax sinking five inches into Conroy's chest, right next to his heart. Conroy squeezed the machine gun's trigger convulsively, all the while amazed that he had been taken down by this . . . this . . . *academic.*

The Korean guy was flying apart under the impact of the centrifugal gun's outpouring of silvery rounds, body shredding to pieces like a gull sucked into a jet engine. Conroy went to his knees, the pickax still stuck in his chest, two hands, severed from their arms, still gripping it. The bullets from the centrifugal machine gun ricocheted through the tunnel, tearing into two other men a step behind the Asian—the little dude from India and the tall skinny spade.

Probably got the damn kid, too, Conroy thought. *That's something anyway.*

But he saw silver flash from the left, looked to see the big black man swinging the pickax down at him.

Forgot about—

Conroy never finished the thought. The pickax dashed his brains—all his memory and personality and hopes and illusions—out of his skull and into the air.

And he fell forward with a splash into what was left of the Korean guy.

Cormac Sullivan almost ran headlong into Peepers, who was running full-tilt north, in a panic, thinking he was headed for the compound and going the wrong way. Cormac raised the shotgun but the man was too close and grabbed the barrel, pushing it aside, shouting for help. Cormac sidestepped, trying to let him rush past, but he kept his grip on the shotgun so that they were both pulled off their feet, rolling, struggling for control of the weapon, rain pounding at their faces, splashing around them in the grit. Cormac gave a great heave, throwing all his weight into it, got the other man under him, let go of the shotgun, knowing he had a couple of seconds before it could be deployed. He slammed two hard punches down into the jutting chin, feeling bone break under the second punch—the sentry quivered and went limp. Cormac pulled the shotgun away, got to his feet, and ran through the rain for the entrance to the mine.

When he got there he saw three figures. One was a big black man with a bloodied face, leaning wearily against the timbers supporting the entrance as he used cloth torn from his shirt to bandage the tall, gaunt black man's wounded shoulder; the third was his son—Cormac's own boy, Gary—looking out into the rain with a stunned expression. And then Cormac saw Gary's eyes light up . . .

His eyes lighting up because he saw his father coming to get him out of here.

"Dad!"

Reaching a corner in the base of the bluff overlooking the compound, just outside the scope of the searchlights, Batman spun the bike around, expecting to see the sentries in pursuit.

But the one who'd come after him was gone—must have realized he was being drawn off.

Another misstep, he thought. *Got to get back to Sullivan.*

Then gunfire strafed the rock close over his head. He turned to see a surplus military truck with a machine gun on a tripod in its bed, coming out the gate of the compound—right for him. Two more vehicles were behind it, SUVs filled with gunmen, and others were coming on foot behind the motorcade. Batman throttled up fast, so that the motorcycle wheelied for a moment, spinning up gravel and mud before it caught traction and squealed off to the left. Bullets stitched the air near his cowl; a couple of them struck glancingly off his chest and back armor before he maneuvered, weaving, out of their cone of fire—and Batman was thinking hard all the time.

He knew he'd disarmed one of the guys at the mine. Sullivan would have the drop on the other two. White Eyes' men had to be stopped on this front so that Sullivan and his son could get away.

Batman gunned the motorcycle toward the fallen shed and the camper-truck beside it—and at exactly that moment the camper started to drive away with Cormac at the wheel, Gary and two men with him.

Got to make sure they get away.

One foot out to help him with the sharp turn, Batman rode behind the fallen outbuilding, bullets strafing up behind him from the machine gun on the back of the truck. He reached the temporary cover of the fallen shed, turned the bike, and looked at his prospects.

The rain was thinning but the slanted fallen roof, tilting up between him and the oncoming militia, was wet and slippery. The angle wasn't all he could hope for. But he had to stop them short, and decisively, and this was the only way offered in the seconds remaining.

No mistakes. Not this time. Focus.

Batman looked past the ruins of the shed at the truck, gauging his angle. Then he gunned the motorcycle at the shed roof, getting up to speed.

Hope the roof'll hold.

At full power, the bike roared up onto the makeshift

ramp—and off, Batman taking to the air like a circus act, cape streaming behind him as he rocketed to thump down onto the roof of the truck, exactly as he'd envisioned it, bouncing onward to smash into the swiveling tripod machine gun, his wheels slamming the muzzle down so that its spurt of gunfire went into the bed of the truck, striking the gas tank. Batman had already flipped himself free of the wrecked motorcycle, but with the truck moving he fell awkwardly, forced to come down on his shoulder and upper arm, bruising himself but unbroken as he rolled out of the way of an onrushing SUV.

He continued the roll to get his feet under him, rose to a crouch in time to see the truck exploding from the bullets sparking its fuel tank, the Bavarian Brethren aboard it leaping to safety just ahead of a red-orange ball of fire that consumed both the truck and the wreck of his bike.

As rain hissed into the fiery wreckage, Batman felt a momentary regret at losing the motorcycle—it had cost him about four hundred thousand dollars to build, plus another hundred grand to ensure secrecy, and more to integrate it into the belly of the plane—and then he was throwing a Batarang and shuriken, one to a hand, at the gunmen swinging their vehicles around to run him down.

Where's White Eyes? he wondered as one of the gunmen howled in pain, dropping his weapon, his wrist transfixed by a shuriken. The Batarang struck another man hard enough to stun him, then rebounded, whirled to come back to him.

Batman sensed another SUV almost upon him, heard the zipping of bullets beside his cowl, turned to see the SUV angling his way; a grinning, tattooed Aryan had pushed the Explorer's door open, was braced inside—without his seat belt—firing out the door. The bouncing of the vehicle had so far made the firing inaccurate.

Batman ran at him, throwing a Batarang directly at the man's face. It struck between his target's eyes; they crossed and he sagged forward. Reflexively catching the rebounding Batarang, Batman leapt onto the frame of the open door, peeled the sagging man away from it, and slammed the driver in the face with his boot. The driver was out cold before the bewildered men in the backseat could fire their weapons and the Explorer was swerving out of control as Batman pulled himself onto the roof and rode it like a runaway rodeo bull as it roared toward the gate of the compound—where Batman fired his grapple at the roof of the guard tower. The grapple caught as the SUV crashed through the gate. He leapt free, triggered the grapple, and was pulled up to the startled sentry in the tower who scarcely got off a single wild shot before Batman's boot connected with the point of his jaw. He went down, Batman jerked his grapple loose, ducked down—

—he was *almost* in the pocket now, his heart racing, his senses going even faster, in that place where other people seemed to be in slow motion—

—as bullets strafed his new position from the opposite guard tower, ripping at the wood around him. Batman looked through a hole torn by one of the bullets, carefully assessing the structure of the opposite guard tower, then grabbed the machine gun from the fallen tower sentry, jumping up with the weapon in hand—

"Look at that—the Bat's using a gun!" Del said wonderingly as he ran back toward the compound . . . with the men he'd led out of it minutes before. In the back of his mind thinking: *We went out after the Batman—now he's gone completely around us, back in behind us, and we're running back in after him. He's got us running in circles like we're a goddamn joke.*

—Batman fired at the exact right spot, a join on the substructure of the opposite guard tower, near the ground: the tower collapsed, crumbling under its own weight, the man inside the cabin up top shouting in fear, leaping free, wailing as he broke his legs.

Batman was firing the gun at the tires of an intact SUV, coming toward him—the tires exploded, the car spun out and rolled. Before its occupants were out, Batman dropped on a cable from the tower and sprinted behind the nearest Quonset hut. Two solid-looking skinheads were just coming out, both turning toward him with pistols in their hands. Batman took them out in one second and one fist apiece, spinning on his heel between them, his whirling cape disorienting them, his fists whipping around to slam into their heads. He didn't stay to watch them fall, kept going past the corner of the building, really pumped now, toward the big central structure—designed to resemble a German hunting lodge, he guessed.

Two sentries at the front door of the lodge, beside a parked Humvee, were looking toward the men shouting from the gate; they were half blinded by the rain slashing down around them, the crack of lightning, turning toward Del Derbinsky, who was coming into the compound shouting angry orders; they didn't see the Batman till he was sending shuriken into their gun hands. His Batarang smacked into their foreheads, thrown so it glanced from one to strike the other, then spun back to him. Both men fell back against the wooden outer wall of the lodge, stunned. Batman paused to glance at the Humvee—noting that the keys were in it, wondering if it could be useful. Then he scooped up the throwing stars and ran inside the lodge to the stairs . . .

Where he paused, listening.

"Why'd we have to go this way?" Harold asked through the back window of the old Chevy camper, wincing with pain and clutching at the wounds in his shoulder as the truck bounced on the ruts in the gravel road.

"The only other way went right to the compound—swarming with sons of bitches," Cormac said.

"Man's right—couldn't go that way," Grenoble said. He was hunched on the metal bench across from Harold, holding the pistol that Cormac had given him—holding it almost lovingly.

Gary was riding shotgun beside his dad—literally holding his dad's 12-gauge pump shotgun pointed at the ceiling, its butt on the floor. The boy peered through the rain-washed windshield. "At least it's a road. Looks like the militia nuts use it for something."

Cormac sighed, shaking his head. "I just don't feel right about leaving Batman to deal with all those . . . they're idiots, but they're armed idiots. They're trained. And White Eyes is there somewhere . . ."

"And so is Beth," Gary pointed out. "I don't think we should leave her. But I don't know how we can get through to her, either."

"We'll get to help and we'll bring it back," Grenoble said. "It's all we can do."

"We sent for help, already," Cormac said. "We transmitted something that ought to bring them. But hard to say how long it'll take."

"I'd die before I'd go back there," Harold said.

"You really came here with the Batman, Dad?" Gary said. "I read about him somewhere. I thought it was made up."

"He's real, all right," Cormac said musingly. "I used to think I was pretty good at what I do." He shook his head. "Not compared with that guy."

"Kind of crazy, though, isn't he?" Grenoble said.

"The kind of crazy I want on my side," Cormac said. "Looks like the rain's stopped. For now anyway."

"What the Hell is that?" Grenoble asked, pointing.

They all looked out ahead of the truck to see the road passing between two high boulders into a narrow valley, a kind of box canyon, with a few trees, and a great many craters, edged with singe marks, that appeared to be from explosions; sheer stone cliffs loomed starkly to the right and left.

"Hey," Gary said, peering through the side window at the ground behind them. "We just crossed something like . . . like train tracks, Dad. Railings. Only there was only one rail."

"I saw 'em. I'm not sure what that's about."

"Look over there!" Gary said, putting one hand to his mouth as if he was about to be sick.

They looked—and saw the human skulls nailed to the trunks of trees, human bones, fastened beneath them, arranged in swastika shapes.

"Dad?"

"I'm turning around . . ."

Cormac swung the truck around, accelerated back toward the high, roughly rectangular boulders that stood

like Neolithic stones on either side of the entrance of the
ravine.

Moments before they would've passed through, a
steel wall slid into place, coming out on a rail that ran
from the brush, closing off the road between the slick
featureless stones, trapping them in the ravine.

14

"There's things going on outside," Beth said, moving to keep the bed between her and White Eyes. "You notice?" He seemed utterly stoned, swaying in place, his eyes pinpoints, pupils barely visible at all in the whites; his hands trembling, his mouth slack. He was on something for sure, she decided. "People shooting out there, Aaron. Don't you think you ought to see what they're up to?"

"I've got a whole army working on it," White Eyes said. "Esperanza gave me something to . . . enhance the reproductive experience. I can't waste it. Might be weeks before I get another chance. And this won't take long. Then you're coming with me. We're going on a little mission together . . ." He peeled off his shirt. "Now take your clothes off."

"That won't be necessary," Batman said, stepping through the doorway.

Beth gasped, seeing him, and White Eyes turned, snarling, hands fisted.

"Young lady—get behind me, then head toward the door," Batman said, edging quickly to her side of the bed.

But she cowered back, afraid of them both, trying to make herself small in the corner of the room. Batman moved to put himself between White Eyes and the girl—as White Eyes bellowed, *"I've had enough of you!"* And with a single swipe of his hands he threw the entire bed, frame and all, to the left, so that nothing was between him and the Batman, in the process knocking over a floor lamp and a glass of water on a table. The frame of the lamp shade was crushed out of shape by the impact with the floor, and water splashed on the shade, darkening it—but the bulb, switched on, remained intact, and it projected a strange shadow on the wall through the distorted lampshade. A figure that in Batman's mind—or perhaps in objective reality—squirmed into the shape of another Batman, his old costume, empty, with its arms spread, as if asking *Why, why are you what you are? Why?*

And then White Eyes charged. Distracted by the shadow apparition, Batman misjudged White Eyes' speed and failed to sidestep fast enough. White Eyes caught him up in his outspread arms—outspread just like that shadow figure—and slammed him into the wall with freight-train force so that the wall cracked and burst outward.

They crashed through the wall, the two of them, through shattering plasterboard and planks and studs, locked together, flying in a slipstream of debris through the air. As he went Batman saw the girl, startled, staring after them from the ragged eight-foot-wide hole in the wall.

"Run!" he shouted—and then they crashed to the muddy ground—at Del Derbinsky's feet.

Del and thirty-seven other militia stood in a semicircle

gaping at the two momentarily stunned combatants, Batman trapped under White Eyes—only his chest armor had protected him from being crushed. The carapace had creaked, but held.

Batman looked up into White Eyes' face, seamed with rage and as pale as permafrost, seeing him rear back, raise his arm high, the enormous fist poised over him like a medieval mace, ready to come down and crush the Dark Knight's face.

"Kill him, Big White!" Del shouted. The others took up the shout, chanting it.

"Kill him, Big White! Kill him, Big White! Kill him!"

But Batman did a sit-up, too close to be struck by that fist, and head-butted White Eyes hard in the jaw, so that the big man grunted and shook his head, dazed for a moment. Batman threw all his weight to the left, tilting White Eyes just enough so he could bend his right leg, get his foot braced, using it to push off—flipping the militia leader onto his back.

But Big White had recovered enough to roll with the push, and the two men thrashed through the mud in a mutual bear hug, ending with Batman on top—but trapped by the crush of his adversary's viselike arms. The pressure made Batman picture a car being crushed in a junkyard compactor. He felt his ribs beginning to crack—and knew he couldn't exert quite as much pressure through White Eyes' layers of steroid-thickened muscle.

So Batman let go of White Eyes' body and instead ground his thumbs into his eyes. Not quite hard enough to gouge them out, but hard enough that it felt that way to White Eyes.

White Eyes screamed and his grip loosened, and Batman twisted free, got his feet under him. The mud fell away from his costume—it had been treated so that dirt didn't cling to it—and he braced to take White Eyes' next charge, aware that heavily armed Bavarian Brethren were standing to one side, ready to pound him with bullets if White Eyes should go down. Batman glanced up at the hole where they'd crashed through the wall. The girl was nowhere to be seen. Hopefully she'd taken advantage of their distraction to run.

"Let *me* kill him!" White Eyes ordered the others, seeing them start to move in.

"You should let them help you," Batman said, one hand at his utility belt. "You can't do it alone." He wasn't at all sure that was true, but he managed to sound as if he believed it. Sometimes—especially with a personality like White Eyes'—taunts were weapons, too. "I doubt you can do it even with help."

Then he heard the rumble of a big car engine, saw the Humvee screeching around the corner of the Lodge, coming right at them—and the girl was at the wheel. She looked tiny in the big vehicle but she was driving with frowning determination, heading right for White Eyes. Batman could see she was straining to reach the pedals.

"Look out!" Del shouted, firing at the Humvee.

The bullets smashed the side windows in back—and White Eyes leapt aside as the Humvee rammed toward him. "Come on!" the girl shouted to Batman, slowing a little as she came abreast of them. Batman was already throwing the smoke capsules he'd plucked from his belt, one at White Eyes' face, one at his boots. They exploded into dark red smoke, making Big White yell incoherently, clawing at his eyes, choking in the fumes. Batman rushed through the expanding cloud and leapt onto the moving Humvee, vaulting onto the roof, holding on to the rim over the windshield.

"Go!" he shouted. "Accelerate!"

She floored it even as bullets sang past them, and veered to the right, around the edge of the lodge, fishtailing, sending up sprays of mud behind their wheels. The Humvee roared across the compound, through the broken gate, and onto the road that led past the mine.

"I don't know where to go!" the girl yelled.

"Keep going! There's a road up there!"

"I don't think we should go there!"

He started to ask her what she meant but then he heard a whistling sound that had a sinister familiarity to it and turned his head to see a projectile flashing toward them, fired by the man with the equipment on his head he'd seen in the video—standing just outside the gate.

If it was one of those shells, flying low—

"Swerve the car!" he shouted.

She obeyed—and he lost his grip, rolling off the roof as the shell struck a mound of volcanic rock just behind the Humvee.

The back wheels exploded; the Humvee jolted and bucked and spun around Batman. He landed on his feet, skidding, then turned to see the Humvee spinning to a stop just out of the toxic cloud rising from the crater behind them.

The girl was already climbing out of the car, running away from the compound, sobbing as she ran. Batman quickly overtook her, swept her up in his arms without breaking stride, ran around the corner of the bluff near the mine, then angled across the open ground toward the line of trees. A spare track of road curved through the open ground, paralleling the woods before entering another copse of trees about 150 yards on.

She looked up at him in startled wonder. "Um—thanks . . . for the ride."

"Thank *you*—for the one you gave me." He had to get his breath, jogging along with her in his arms, before going on, "That was brave, you bringing that big vehicle around."

She shrugged. "It surprised me, too. But . . . you got between me—and him. On purpose. To help me. No one ever tried to . . . protect me. It made me feel . . ." She shook her head, unable to articulate the feeling, and looked at him curiously. "What's your name, big guy?"

"You know who I am." He could hear men coming around the bluff. He heard the crack of gunfire. The hiss of a bullet passing near.

She decided not to argue. "Okay. We'll say you're Batman. I'm Beth. Not 'Beth-woman.' Just Beth. Where's Gary?"

"I figure they went down that road."

"We shouldn't go there. It's some kind of . . . some kind of training place for them—they trap people in there!"

That might mean Cormac and the others are trapped there, Batman thought.

"We have to go someplace else," she said, her lips buckling. "Someplace . . . I don't know where . . . the other direction."

"We can't go toward the main road. There's a hundred men or so back there with guns."

"We can cut through the woods!" she suggested as he ran into the screen of trees.

"Your friend's somewhere down this road," Batman

said, weaving between trees, trying to keep his speed up. "He's going to need our help!"

She swallowed. But after a moment, she nodded. "This is new to me. Helping people. It was always safer just to . . ."

"I understand." He paused to take in air. "You had to keep your head down . . ."

Bullets cracked through the trees behind them. She winced at the sound, biting her lip. By now, Batman figured, the Brethren would be organizing some kind of vehicle. They couldn't all be wrecked or stolen. They'd catch up one way or another.

Batman leapt over a fallen log, following a game trail that paralleled the gravel road Cormac had to have gone down. They passed between laurels and mountain ash, arcing blackberry vines, a few pine trees; everything still dripping. The storm had moved on, rumbling in the distance, but the sky was still boiling with charcoal-colored clouds. Batman was breathing hard now; his heart was pounding. But he knew he could carry her a long way at this speed.

"You can put me down," she said. "I can walk now!"

"Faster this way, I think. I've got longer legs." They ran into a small clearing where a deer looked over, startled, and bounded away.

She reached up and touched his jaw. He pretended not to notice. "You're sweating. You're breathing hard. You're just a human being."

He said nothing. But he had to smile. He thought about Teia. *Just a human being.* He wondered how much human being was left in him. Teia had found it. But maybe he should bury it deeper . . .

Then the woods ended at a wall, a daunting wall of

riveted iron; his expert eye judged it just over thirty-three feet high. About forty yards to the left the road ran into a kind of natural gateway between two tall blocky standing stones. There was a closed gate there, just a piece of it visible at this angle.

"This must be it," she said as Batman set her down on her feet. He glanced behind him; they were still looking for him in the woods. Would they expect him to go into their "training" area?

They hurried up to the wall, and Batman drew out his grapple. She watched, blinking, as he fired it at the top of the wall, tugged to make it grip.

Then he gestured to Beth. "Come on."

"Doesn't make sense to go in there."

He smiled reassuringly. "Not exactly. But it's the best we've got—till I can find them."

She nodded, swallowing visibly, and stepped in close. He slung her onto his back, and she clung to him piggyback as he triggered the grapple.

She gasped as it pulled them up. "Whoa!"

Beth on his back, he climbed onto the top of the wall, glanced around inside, reversed the grapple, and used it to lower them. Then, as he popped it back into its launcher and reaffixed it to his belt, she asked, "How do you get enough power in that little thing to lift two people up?"

He looked at her. "That was an intelligent question."

"And that's such a big-ass surprise? Well? You going to answer it?"

"New kind of battery." He looked around at the odd, blasted, straitjacketed landscape of the ravine, noting it ran roughly north–south. Trees and rocky outcroppings and distance hid the farther end. "Trade secret."

"You should, like, market it to computer companies and stuff—you could make a million dollars."

"Good suggestion. Come on . . ."

"Just another wall at this end," Cormac observed as they pulled up at the end of the ravine. "Wish we had some way to get over it . . ."

Harold hadn't said anything since they'd come here—he was just clutching his hands against his chest, breathing hard, his eyes welling with tears. "This is . . . it's not fair . . . I was out . . . and then this! This is where they would have taken me! This is where they kill them! This is where they kill them all!"

Gary looked at him, frightened—Cormac put his arm around his son, and, after a certain stiffness in his shoulders, Gary relaxed, and let him hug him for a moment.

"You said Batman sent word to his contact at Gotham PD?" Grenoble said.

"Gordon," Cormac said. "A good man. He'll get the feds in here somehow."

"Then we've got to hide till then . . ." He pawed at his mangled eye, then hastily drew his hand away from it as he felt fresh blood trickling.

"Dad . . . ," Gary said. "I was just . . . remembering what happened to Kyu and . . . I feel all . . ."

Suddenly he jerked at the truck's door, shoved it open, lurched out just in time to vomit into the turf.

"*A very impressive performance!*" It was a sardonic voice, amplified from somewhere above. "*But I don't think that is going to help you, young man! If you want to live a few minutes longer, you must do something other than to vomit, sí?*" And then it tittered with laughter that echoed across the narrow valley like the repetitive trill of a tropical bird.

"Gary—get back in!" Cormac shouted.

Gary jumped hastily back in and Cormac put the camper-truck in reverse, backing away from the wall. Thirty, forty, fifty feet back and then they could see a crudely bolted metal tower, with a zigzagging stairway rising up on the other side of the wall. On the top platform, at a panel fitted with levers, was the man Cormac had seen in the film taken by Batman's robot drone.

"Esperanza!" Harold cried despairingly.

"You will forgive the crudeness of my controls," came Esperanza's reedy, sardonic voice. *"But until recently we had only a few mines and the walls, for training—I insisted on new equipment. It will be needed for the new death camps. And now . . ."*

Now an explosion pitched the camper-truck over on its back, Cormac throwing himself over his son to protect him, holding him in place; the truck ending up like a flipped turtle, one tire blown to shreds and the others spinning in the air, flames starting to lick up from the ruptured gas line.

"You had better come out before the truck explodes . . . ," Esperanza called out, chuckling.

They were already crawling free, Gary on all fours turning to help his dad out, handing him the shotgun.

"Thanks, son," said Cormac, a little surprised by the look of deep concern on Gary's face.

Grenoble was pulling Harold out—and the two men, supporting each other, hobbled over to Cormac and Gary as they backed away from the truck. "Let's try going back the way we came. Maybe we can find a way out . . ."

Gary looked at the two black men. "You guys get hurt when the truck flipped?"

Grenoble shrugged. "I got so many dings in me already I can't tell. Nothing broken."

"Nothing broken," Harold said, parrotlike, staring.

"We got lucky," Cormac said.

They started toward the other end of the narrow valley, Cormac carrying the shotgun and scanning the granite cliffs to see if there was a way up. Nothing on the right; to his left was a sudden rise, an artificial hill, where boulders had been piled up, dirt heaped around them, the whole rising about sixty feet above the floor of the valley. There was a palisade of vertical logs set up at its crown, broken open in places. Obviously some kind of training structure. He could see that the palisade ran only partway across the valley to the mountainside. There was no way to climb from the top of the artificial hill to get onto the cliffs. Once on that hill, they'd be trapped.

Cormac and his companions had gotten thirty steps when the truck exploded. They felt the heat; a clap on their backs of shock wave, like a bully shoving them from behind, and they all staggered at once.

"Jeez," Gary muttered. "This is all too . . . just . . ."

"Son," Cormac said, softly, "it's probably going to get worse before it gets better. You got to take it one step at a time. Moment to moment. And we'll get through . . ."

Gary glanced at him, and his gaze lingered. His expression suggested he was seeing his father for the first time.

Behind them flames crackled, dark smoke twisted into the sky . . .

They got another ten steps—

The ground erupted in front of them, about twenty feet away. Cormac threw Gary to the ground, covering him; dirt pattered down over them.

"*No, you won't be going that way!*" Esperanza's amplified voice announced.

"Anybody hurt?" Cormac asked.

The others responded in the negative. They got to their feet—then clutched at one another in startled reaction as two more explosions were set off between them and the way they'd come in.

"*You can't get out that way. I simply have someplace else I want you to go . . . from here I can set off explosions all around you—or directly under you if I choose to!*"

Cormac doubted there were as many explosives as that planted here—or that each blast would set off many others. But he wasn't willing to gamble on just how many remote-control land mines Esperanza had.

Another blast cracked the air, about fifty feet to their right, geysering dirt into the air. They covered their eyes. Dirt and rocks rained down; smoke drifted.

"*You see? Not that way either—to your left! Toward that rise you see halfway to the cliff!*"

"We'll be trapped there!" Harold said, his eyes flicking desperately about.

Cormac nodded. "But it seems like our only option— and we might surprise them." He hefted the shotgun meaningfully.

"If we can hold them off long enough," Grenoble muttered, glancing at the sky. Looking for help that might never come.

15

"Where are we going, sir?" Del asked from the driver's seat as White Eyes got into the black SUV beside him. Smoke rose from the overturned, burning vehicles near the Lodge. Vehicles smoldered all over the property; thudding detonations were echoing from the training area, about a third of a mile away. Esperanza had taken one of the intact vehicles to the training center, Del knew—hopefully he was causing those explosions, not on the receiving end of them.

"We're going where I tell you to go, Del," White Eyes growled. "First, pull up over at the munitions bunker . . ."

Del drove across the compound and parked in front of the cement hump that was the entrance to the bunker. White Eyes jumped out, went down the stairs. Del glanced in the backseat—there was an auto-shotgun and a centrifugal machine gun, loaded, lying on the floor. He found himself staring at them—but looked quickly away when White Eyes came back a minute later carrying a crate about seven feet by three feet. He carried it as easily as a bag boy would hoist groceries, though it must've weighed at least two hundred pounds—if it contained what Del guessed.

White Eyes opened the tailgate, shoved the crate in, slammed the gate, and hurried to get in beside Del, watching the skies as he came. "Go!" he shouted. "Head down the mountain to road six."

"We expecting 'company'?" Del asked. The wind was rising again; rain was hitting the windshield, just enough so he had to turn on the wipers.

"First that black ATF agent, then Batman—what do you think?"

"But—what about the men?"

"They're a relatively small contingent of *Schutzstaffel*—and do they deserve that term? It means 'protective echelon,' and have they protected me, their *Reichsführer*? They have allowed us to be penetrated by my greatest enemy! They know nothing of my greatest secrets, nothing of my real plans—it doesn't matter if the feds mop them up. If any survive and escape, I will contact them through our Internet intermediaries. They will have shown their worthiness by coming through this . . . this test of fire, after all. They will be winnowed out, the herd thinned, by the federal agents."

Del was stunned. The son of a bitch was abandoning his men . . .

"I have many others to draw on, around the world—there are estimated to be up to half a million white supremacists in Russia! I have barely begun to draw on that pool. And we have plans to work with al Qaeda!" He chuckled, seeing the expression on Del's face. "Why so surprised? Because they're towel-headed camel jockeys? What of it? What do you think Hitler really thought of Tojo—of the Japanese? But he allied with them for a time. Eventually, if not for the treachery of the Zionist conspiracy, he would have won the war—and then turned on his allies, enslaved Japan. Eventually *we* will enslave the Muslims—but in the meantime the jihadists will be our allies. They hate the Jews, you see—we have that in common. The Jewish conspiracy will continue to move its puppets into place, and the Zionist conspiracy to elevate the Antichrist will come closer to bearing fruit—and at just the right moment we will be there to stop it!"

Till now, White Eyes' political vision had made some kind of sense to Del. Sitting in a jail cell reading his pamphlets, looking for an outlet for a seething rage, it had all seemed to make sense. Now, in the wake of all that had happened, especially his leader's blithe justification for abandoning his men, it sounded like ranting—like he was falsely connecting what was disconnected to justify his own agenda.

They had driven out of the compound—the remaining guards in the front towers had opened the gates for them, staring forlornly after them as they drove away—and now they had reached the side road that led off to the right. A small airstrip waited at the end of that road, Del knew. A Piper Cub. Escape.

What about the girl? The others would kill her . . .

He was glad she'd gotten away from White Eyes. If he couldn't have her, White Eyes shouldn't, either. Just to think of Big White touching her made him shudder.

"My father, you know, was a lawyer, a follower of the great Leo Strauss," said White Eyes musingly. "He was an adviser to Pinochet for a time—of course he was the CIA's man then, too. He felt the CIA was weak—when Carter came in, it became much weaker. He stopped working with them, came back to the United States and made a lot of money in Florida—he wanted to take over through the neo-conservative movement. But they stop short—they do not embrace the Aryan agenda. Fascism? Yes, perhaps. But racial miscegenation is perfectly acceptable to them. They elevated that mud-race half-breed to secretary of state! Oh yes, my plutocrat father educated me to be one of the neo-cons—called me a little weakling whenever I stumbled. Whipped me when I failed a class or failed to do the calisthenics he'd set for me. He did those good things for me and I'm grateful. But he did not go far enough, Del. Today—we will go all the way. You will see . . ."

What are they doing to Beth now? Del wondered. *Is she still alive?*

They were almost to the end of the side road, so overgrown that tree branches brushed squeakily across the hood of the car.

"We going to hit that nuclear power plant? The one upwind from New York City?" Del asked, as calmly as a man asking if they were going golfing.

White Eyes looked at him with narrowed eyes. "Should I trust you with the information, now? You failed me in Gotham City—twice. But the reason you're still alive is—I have seen something in you. More intelligence than I have been able to find in the others. Let's face it—most of my followers are not the sharpest knives in the drawer. They have had their native intelligence suppressed by the Zionists. But you—you have something, Del. I want you there with me today . . . to strike for me."

He's going to make me do the job—and he's going to

desert me like he did the others, Del thought. *Maybe even shoot me in the back if it looks like I'll get out alive. Too many secrets . . . All this personal chatter is to get me to trust him again . . .*

For whatever reason, White Eyes seemed in a talkative mood. Impulsively, Del asked, "You've said you get directions from God—you must know who the Antichrist is. Shouldn't we be targeting him first?"

"The Antichrist is whoever I say it is. Perhaps it will be useful to say it is the secretary general of the UN—perhaps the pope. I haven't decided," said White Eyes breezily. He chuckled, glancing at Del. "Again you look shocked! It doesn't matter if there's a *real* Antichrist, Del! All that matters is that people believe in him—and we use that symbol to bring down our enemies. The path to power requires the creation of myths—great, splendid, glorious myths! But of course—you must never repeat to anyone what I've told you today . . ."

Then they drove into the clearing and stopped the SUV. It was a long, narrow runway, cut like a terrace into the hillside, hardened with a strip of concrete. At the nearer end was a small plane, covered by camouflage netting. They got out and White Eyes and Del, clambering up onto the wings, began to remove the netting.

"It takes a good pilot to use an airstrip like this," White Eyes said as he worked. "—and I am that good pilot. My father loved planes. He flew them when they 'disappeared' some of those people in the Pinochet glory days—dropped them alive from the plane into the Pacific." He smiled fondly and added, "He loved to tell that story." The netting removed, he glanced at the sky again—then stared into the distance. "There—at the horizon. Do you see them?"

Del shielded his eyes and looked. Black specks. Moving. "Something. Not sure what."

"Looks to me like a group of helicopter gunships—not going to fly this way, I shouldn't think. But eventually they may well come to the compound . . . Let's get the weapons and the goods."

"What about Esperanza?" Del asked suddenly as they loaded the crate on the plane.

"I told him to leave, to go to one of our safe houses in Texas. If he doesn't, he's a fool. But you know how obsessive he is. He has new toys. I suppose he thinks he has time. I doubt he does. He is . . . perhaps a little too mad to be of much more use."

Not sane like you, Del thought, picking up the auto-shotgun.

White Eyes strode to the cockpit of the Piper Cub, the centrifugal machine gun in one hand. He opened it and got in—then looked back at Del. "Well? Get in!"

Del felt paralyzed. Almost physically paralyzed. The auto-shotgun was a weight at the end of his arm.

Finally he said, "I can't do it. I can't leave them. They're not the sharpest knives in the drawer. But they're the only comrades I ever had."

"It's that girl, isn't it," White Eyes snorted, almost imperceptibly turning in his seat, getting a better grip on the machine gun.

"Partly. I just . . . can't do it."

"Then, Del—you can't be trusted to live." And he brought the machine gun around, squeezed the trigger.

The impact of the bullets strafing across Del's chest

made him think, as he fell backward: *Must be how a jackhammer would feel, hitting a man.*

He was lying on his back, staring at the dark, fleeting clouds in the sky—breaking up now. The sky was starting to clear. The clouds changing shape—moving on.

They're so temporary, clouds, he realized. *They look big and substantial but if you really look at them they're just vapor that takes a shape for a moment and moves on. That's a man's life . . .*

The plane was starting, was taxiing. It was getting dark . . . Funny how little pain he felt . . .

But it hurt, when he made himself sit up. He felt like he was lifting the weight of the whole planet—and it hurt to lift so much. Still, there he was sitting up, raising the auto-shotgun—

Firing it at the taxiing Piper Cub, just as the plane took off. The range wasn't ideal, but he saw big holes appear in the rear of the plane's fuselage. Was that fuel slopping out? Maybe not a big leak.

But maybe enough. Maybe that fuel leak . . .

The weight of the world was too much, then, and it bore him back, onto the ground. What a relief to let go of it.

Batman was keeping to the shadows under the cliff overhang, where low boulders projected from the dirt. He jumped from rock to rock, when he could, conscious of the possibility of mines—he wanted to hurry more, hearing the explosions, but with Beth puffing along behind him, insisting she wanted to carry her own weight, it was taking longer than he would have liked. Then they came around a boulder, and they saw the little artificial hill about fifty yards up ahead—and the palisade.

And beyond them, the gate was opening—and militiamen were coming through, with ax handles in hand.

Esperanza's voice came echoing across the narrow valley. *"You see? Ax handles! A classic expression of American culture! There are one hundred of them! And they know you have a couple of guns—yet still they advance! Muy valiente they are! They know you will quickly use up your bullets—they show their valor this way, but I have asked that they stop the beating of the Negroes before they kill . . . We have a special tree for them . . ."*

Esperanza pulled another lever and a leafless "tree" rose into view at the top of the palisade mound; it was made of plaster over metal rebar, like something in one of the more worn-out areas of Disneyland. But the three nooses dangling from its three branches looked authentic enough.

"We have a noose for someone extra! Perhaps for the half-breed man! Perhaps for the 'bat' man! Perhaps it would be exciting to see the teenage boy kicking in the noose! Who will win the lottery? Advance, men, and let your ax handles decide!"

Batman was within thirty yards of the artificial hill when he saw that the three steel rails, running parallel about ten feet apart, bisected the valley. He heard a clacking sound, turned to see cylindrical metal devices, one at each end of the three rails, emerging from niches in the base of the cliff. Something Esperanza used to keep his victims trapped in the vicinity of the artificial hill—and maybe to test weapons. There were centrifugal guns atop the cylinders, which moved in tandem along the rails, back and forth, each about seven feet off the ground. When activated, the guns swiveled and tilted, prompted by cameras that sought out motion specifically south of the hill. When one of them ran to the east, another ran to the west, so that the territory was always being covered.

"*Batman, of course, must not be allowed to interfere with the training exercise . . . ,*" Esperanza boomed. "*I have released the perimeter drones . . . They are quite new, and only a little tested—you see what is left of the two red Indians we caught hunting on our property . . .*"

Batman saw them then: the partly decayed, eyeless remains of two men, lying near each other, arms akimbo, half covered in mud. The guns were swiveling his way . . .

"Beth!" Batman shouted. "Get down—behind that boulder . . . now!" He was already flinging Batarangs at the nearest cameras of the rail-driven drones—the machines moved about five miles per hour, neither very fast nor very slow. Their motion sensors were drawn to his projectiles, firing two bursts so that the Batarangs were shattered in midair.

But Batman had already seen the weakness of the drones. Their relationship to one another as they trundled back and forth on their rails, going in varying directions.

The one on the farthest rail was swiveling, lining up on him—he threw himself aside, cartwheeling then rolling into a ball, plucking at his utility belt as bullets strafed near him. The nearest drone was swiveling toward him now—he was throwing smoke capsules directly at the camera. They burst in dark red and orange, blanking out the camera's view of him for a moment—and the strafe stopped as the camera searched for him.

He wasn't hard to find—he was leaping directly for it, grabbing the top of the drone, making a leapfrog motion to bring himself atop it, tightening his knees against his chest, straightening, and then he was balanced atop it, nearly falling off as it jerked along its rail. The others were swiveling toward him, but they fired too low—designed to aim at a man's chest, not so high they'd strike one another's cameras. The two inner drones were converging as one came from the right and one from the left, and he fired his grapple so it flashed out to one side, the drone running into the extended cable, snapping its grapple back so it whipped around it; he sent a booster signal to the grapple to fire its secondary impulse and it hissed forward, whipping around the other drone.

All the time Batman poised atop the first drone as it moved back and forth on the rail, balancing delicately as he controlled the grapple.

With the grapple cable wrapped around both drones going in opposite directions on their contiguous rails, they pulled at one another, stuck in place, the cable creaking, and then the drones snapped off their support poles, falling to the ground.

Batman kicked down hard, twice, performing his delicate balancing act on his left foot while his right cracked into the top of the centrifugal gun under him, finally breaking its barrel so it jammed and fell silent.

"Come on, Beth!" he yelled, jumping down, going to unhook his grappler. It was going to take time to get it unlocked from the fallen drones . . . but it might be their only hope.

*　　　*　　　*

"You see him use that smoke?" Cormac asked, taking the smoke capsules Batman had given him from his pocket.

Gary nodded. "That what those are?"

"Take 'em. Just throw them at something hard enough—like the heads of these militia peabrains. A rock nearby. Then I'll step up and take care of him—and you get a couple of ax handles. You got it?"

Gary grinned. "I got it, Dad."

"Here they come . . . you ready, Bill?"

"Ready to make these sombitches pay for my eye, just for starters," Grenoble growled, peering Cyclopically through a gap in the wooden wall with his good eye.

Harold was sitting with his back to the wooden palisade, hugging himself. Cormac could see he wasn't going to be of much use. The guy's mind had snapped—Cormac couldn't blame him.

"Take your position, Gary!" Cormac said. Hoping he had planned this right. He needed to buy Batman some time . . .

Gary ran down through the dirt paths—felt a chill seeing a line of big men with ax handles in their hands coming up at him, forty feet away. He darted to the right, pressed himself to a low boulder, and, heart pounding, waited till he heard the foremost thug, breathing hard, coming up close. He threw the first smoke capsule at the opposite boulder so it'd strike near the man's face. It exploded into a gratifying outburst of smoke, about ten feet across, and the militiaman immediately began gasping and cursing. Cormac stepped up to the opening between boulders then and fired point-blank into the cloud with the shotgun. Almost at the same time Grenoble fired three rounds from up above—there were shouts of pain from below.

Cormac turned to fire at two men coming from his left as, holding his breath, Gary darted into the smoke, found a man crawling on the ground, oozing blood beside a fallen ax handle. Gary snatched the handle up in time to swing it at the head of another man just hunching up the path—a man whose head was obligingly thrust forward as he climbed—and felt a solid connection. The guy went down, his ax handle clattering and Gary—eyes burning from the smoke—grabbed it up and ran back to his dad. "Hold your fire, Dad!" he shouted, coughing, the smoke getting in his throat with the shout.

A hand grabbed his arm and jerked him out of the smoke cloud—his father, smiling, though his eyes were worried, as he pulled his son behind him. "Good job, son!"

"I cracked one . . ." Gary paused to cough. ". . . on the head . . . got two ax handles . . ."

He put one down and wielded the other like a bat as his lungs and eyes cleared.

"Here come two more of 'em!" Cormac hissed.

Gary found the other smoke capsule in his coat, threw it immediately—his father stepped into the opening and fired, twice. Shouts of pain—of agony, after the second round.

"You got 'em!" Gary yelled, sickened and thrilled at once. Then he heard a scuffling behind him, turned to see Harold clawing at a big, bald man with a swastika tattooed into the side of his head; Harold was clinging to the man, biting at his nose, growling in his throat like a wild animal. The man was hammering the ax handle across Harold's back. Gary turned to his dad, seeing him turned away to fire again and again across the top of a boulder at oncoming men . . .

Gary had to deal with this himself. He hefted the ax handle—his mouth dry, his senses sickeningly sharp, his stomach clutching up—and ran at the big man, who was now standing over Harold, crushing his neck with his boot. Swastika-head looked up in time to see Gary swinging the ax handle but not in time to block it. Gary swung it with all his strength right into the swastika, as if it were a bull's-eye, and felt a crunching impact. Swastika-head staggered back but didn't go down, though blood gushed from the wound. He roared like a wounded bear and raised his ax handle—Gary doubted he could block it, the guy looked too strong—

Then the ax handle exploded with a shotgun blast. Cormac had shot it away, having to fire high to make sure he didn't hit his son. The big militia thug blinked at the stub in his hand—giving Gary the chance to run forward and smash him across the top of the head, hard. This time he went down. He glanced at Harold—and looked quickly away. His neck was broken. At least he went down fighting.

Gary turned to his dad, feeling a strange jubilation—strange considering how close death was—which became a gush of warm feeling when he saw his dad nodding at him, saying, "Good job, son. Way to stay on top of it. Come on . . ."

Gary ran to Cormac's side and was immediately forced to throw his ax handle at a man who was coming at his dad from behind. He turned to grab the other one he'd picked up, while Cormac fired his last round at an-

BATMAN: DEAD WHITE 269

other thug, then turned the shotgun around and began to use it as a club . . .

But there were too many of them, coming from all sides. Gary knew they'd quickly be overwhelmed. Grenoble had run down to stand with them—but he was out of bullets.

The militia thugs moved in, grinning . . .

And a black thunderbolt fell from the sky.

Cape streaming, Batman leapt from the top of a nearby boulder, his boots connecting with two of the racist thugs, hitting each in the top of the head, knocking them flat as he used the impact like a springboard to leap up, flip in the air, coming down again between two others, his knee connecting with a chin, his elbow with the bridge of a man's nose, while shuriken spun from his fingers. He grabbed flying ax handles midair the moment he let go of the shuriken, and he flung them as additional missiles so they struck two more men down, even as—now on solid ground—he spun on his heels to slam two more with his right boot and right fist . . . ducking down and taking another charging man on his shoulders, picking the man up in his arms—

Cormac and Gary stared at that, openmouthed. Picking him up like he was a kid—

And throwing him at five other men, down the hill. All of them going down.

And the others, seeing bleeding bodies, men with guns at the top of the hill—not knowing as Cormac did they were out of ammunition—and seeing the Batman going through men like a scythe through weeds—turned and ran, in a panic, the other way.

Gary cheered, jumping up and down, his hand clasping his father's arm. Beth ran up to him, looking both hopeful and scared. "Gary!"

"*¡Cobardes!*" Esperanza boomed. "Cowards, running like rabbits! Go back! Go back and kill them! You outnumber them, you fools!"

Batman stepped over fallen, groaning men, stopping now and then to affix disposable handcuffs to their wrists, returning to Cormac at the foot of the palisade.

Gary turned to look at Harold. "I was too slow . . . I couldn't save him . . ." He felt tears welling. Darker emotions flooded him on the heels of his exhilaration—regret, despondence, hope, sorrow, fear, renewed anger. But he felt better when his father put his hands on his shoulders and said, "You did way more than almost anyone would do—you did great, son. Whatever happens—I'm proud as Hell of you."

Son and father looked at each other . . . and the barrier almost fell. But there was one thing more. Cormac could see it. Something his son wanted to tell him.

Batman was staring up at a notch in the cliff behind them. "Look—you see that notch? Beyond it . . ."

"What is it?" Grenoble asked, leaning wearily against a rock.

"The shape of it . . . a landmark I picked out earlier . . ." He looked toward the big group of men reassembling at the bottom of the hill. "There's too many of them. They'll work themselves up to charging again . . ."

"Dad—look!" Gary said. He ran over to the body of the man he'd struck down, by Harold, and grabbed a big pistol from the back of the man's belt.

"Disobeyed orders—brought along a pistol!" Grenoble said, taking it. "Good job, kid—this'll slow them down . . ."

"Use it judiciously," Batman said. He regretted not finding a way to stop the killing that had already happened. But that's the way things had been working out . . . Death followed him like the streaming of his cape . . .

"I thought they'd nailed you with those remote-firing machine guns," Grenoble said, looking Batman over.

"Took me some time—and I had to get this loose afterward." He took his grappler from his belt, telescoped it out, and made an adjustment. "I'm going to have to leave you for a while. You'll have to hold them off . . . Just on the other side of that cliff . . . there's a hillside . . . I have to get there . . ."

"Wait!" Cormac said. But Batman had already slipped away between the boulders.

"He's gone!" Beth said, coming to stand close beside Gary. "Just . . . gone! I never thought he'd . . . just abandon us!"

"We'll have to do the best we can without him," Cormac muttered. "Because here they come again . . ."

16

"*Up the hill! Kill them now! They have no more ammunition! There are many of you!*" boomed Esperanza's voice, behind Batman. He was climbing the rocks under the notch he'd seen in the cliff. An ordinary man probably wouldn't have gotten this far up—the handholds were shallow and hard to see. But Batman was nothing if not a climber.

He got forty feet up—the notch was a good distance more, the very end of the range of his grappler. The rock angled outward, over him, at this point. Impossible to continue. He didn't have the proper climbing tools with him. But there was one way, if he was fast and precise enough.

He let go of his hold—and threw himself outward from the cliff.

As he went, going backward, unable to see what was below him, he fired the grappler at the notch. It sang up, peaked, fell—and caught. He held on tight, still pitching backward, plummeting—triggering the grappler. He almost lost his grip on it, with the weight of his body jerking downward and the grappler pulling upward, feeling like his finger bones were about to pop from their sockets. But gritting his teeth against the pain, he kept his hold, and his descent stopped. He was swung first against the cliff—catching himself against it with his boots—then pulled upward by the grappler. It was pulling him slowly, however. As he realized the device was running out of power, he ruefully remembered Beth's question about the battery. "Should have stopped for a battery at Home Depot . . . ," he muttered.

"That's it, compadres! Up the hill, attack, beat them to death—but save the big black one for the noose!"

Maybe he should have stayed with them. But it would have been an exercise in futility—and he was pretty sure Cormac could handle it for a while. He had decided that Cormac Sullivan shouldn't be underestimated . . .

A gunshot echoed up the valley; another. Judging by the sound, from the same gun the boy had found. Grenoble had picked off a couple of them. With luck, that'd hold them.

Up, the cable towed him slowly up—and then stopped. It'd run out of power.

No use complaining to the manufacturer, he thought, going hand-over-hand up the cable, fast as he could. Arms aching, he got to the notch, pulled himself up, and sprinted along the top of the cliff to the hillside beyond it . . . below a spur of rock that cast a shadow over a clear-cut.

"Why are you hesitating! They have one or two bullets! You are many! Kill them!" came the shrill, amplified hectoring from the metal tower.

"Wish I could shoot that bastard out of his little Erector Set," Grenoble said. "But he's got some kind of thick plastic in front of it—looks like what they use at banks that've been robbed once too often . . ."

"No way he's going to put himself up there without that stuff being bulletproof," Cormac agreed. He shielded his eyes against the sun breaking through the clouds, gazed over the top of a low boulder below the palisade. A group of the men were sprinting—zigzagging to make poor targets—toward the open gate.

"They've got guns out there!" Grenoble said.

Cormac nodded. "That's what I think, too. They're going to get their weapons and to Hell with Esperanza . . ."

"It'll take them some time," Gary observed.

"Those others are starting up here again," Cormac said, pointing.

About sixty men had fanned out around the front and sides of the hill; the back was too sheer to climb—or to escape from without breaking your legs.

"That's it, my compadres!"

Grenoble prepared to fire his weapon . . . just seven rounds left . . . setting himself to aim across the top of a boulder, angling the muzzle to point down the hill. He cocked the big .357 . . .

"Hold on, Bill," Cormac said.

Cormac took a deep breath and shouted at the men coming, at the top of his lungs. "You men had better think before you go any further with this! Federal agents are on their way here! You saw the Batman taking your people out! He's alerted the FBI and the ATF!"

The militiamen did seem to falter at that, looking at one another.

"Where is your leader?" Cormac demanded. "Where

is he? Why isn't he here leading you? He's split on you, that's why! He's left you to face the feds!"

"Do not listen to the mud-blood child of Cain!" Esperanza's voice echoed. *"Beat them to death with joy! Each blow injures the Antichrist!"*

"Sounds like he believes that crap!" Gary said.

"He does—that's why he's still hanging around here," Cormac said.

"Two kinds of people believe that stuff," Grenoble said. "People stupid enough, and people crazy enough. He's crazy enough."

Cormac cupped his mouth with his hands and shouted again, his voice becoming hoarse: "Some of you are going to die before you take us out! Those of you who don't die are going to be prosecuted! I ask you again, where's your man White Eyes?"

"White Eyes is in the compound seeing to the great project!" Esperanza bellowed. *"Up the hill or I will report you all to him as cowards!"*

Still they milled uncertainly—till six men emerged from the gate in the wall, sunlight flashing off the auto-shotguns and machine guns in their hands. One of them opened fire immediately, spraying the hilltop.

"Get down!" Cormac shouted, pulling Gary and Beth under cover. Bullets skittered over the tops of the rocks, thunked into the palisade.

Grenoble cursed silently to himself as bullets whined close overhead. Then, loud enough to be heard over the racket, he said, "You know, I'm too damn old for this."

"Yeah, me, too," Cormac shouted back. "But then— I was never the right age for this!"

Grenoble grinned. "Okay, my brother-man—I'm the government representative here and I'm taking charge.

Get those kids up behind the wall! I'll come when I'm ready!"

Cormac nodded and signaled to Gary and Beth, cowering a few yards away. There was just enough cover to get them there, behind the palisade, all three of them almost crawling—and then he turned to look through a hole cut in the wall, saw that Grenoble had stayed below, was firing back at the onrushing gunmen. Trying to draw fire away from the teenagers, Cormac supposed. The guy had guts.

Return fire from the militia made Grenoble duck back down. A withering hail of bullets chipped away the top of the boulders, richocheted between them, chewed at the wood of the palisade.

The Brethren cheered—they began to move up the hillside . . .

Beth began to sob. Gary took her hand in his free hand—his other held an ax handle. Cormac felt even prouder of the boy then. He was taking time out to comfort someone in need—but still ready to fight. The boy had become a man.

Bullets hailed again into the palisade, in such numbers that sections of wall crumpled apart, falling beside them. They could hear men shouting as they came up to kill them. They heard boot steps.

Was Grenoble still alive?

They heard his answering gunfire then. He was hanging in. But Cormac knew that the little cover Grenoble had wouldn't last long. The centrifugal weapons and the auto-shotguns would saturate his position. He'd be dead in under a minute.

How do I end my life—and my son's life? Cormac

wondered. *Ask the boy to charge them with me? At least we'll go down fighting, side by side.*

"Gary . . . listen . . . ," he began.

Then a shadow fell over them; a rumble sounded from overhead.

He glanced up and saw a flying vehicle, about the size of a fighter jet but shaped like a triangle, flat, black. Alien spacecraft came to mind. Then he saw the jet engines, tilted downward—mobile engines, like in a Harrier Jump Jet. And he made out the subtle scalloping of the rear fins . . .

"It's Batman!" he shouted.

The Batplane was angling down toward the men on the hill, about sixty feet up, its down-angled jet engines aimed at the Brethren like flamethrowers from the sky— but still high enough that they felt only the fringes of that heat.

The militia thugs fired at the Batplane—and the bullets bounced harmlessly off its armor.

It lowered threateningly again—like a man holding a big clothes iron in his hand, about to slam it down on a cluster of cockroaches.

The Brethren got the message—as one, they turned and ran.

"*No, no, turn back, cowards!*" Esperanza howled. "*And what then if it burns a few of you, the others can still kill them!*"

Batman banked the plane over, the jets tilting up more horizontally—and flew it suddenly right at the metal tower, only angling away at the last second, so that his starboard wing slashed at the underpinnings of the structure. The tower fell, crashing down with Esperanza in it.

They heard him shouting incoherently in Spanish as he fell—then his voice cut off in midsyllable. Cormac suspected he was still alive, though. He'd be protected by the plastic shielding around his platform.

Batman continued over the wall, chivying the militiamen back toward the compound, literally herding them there. Gary and Beth started down the hill, joining Grenoble. Cormac, feeling dizzy, lurched after them.

Grenoble led the others down the hill, toward the open gate. Gary and Beth started trotting when they got to the floor of the valley, Cormac and Grenoble having to hurry to keep up, following in the tracks of the retreating men. Though none of them spoke of it, they were all afraid that mines would somehow be triggered; afraid the metal gate would close. But they passed through it without incident.

They were just outside the gate when they saw the National Guard choppers arriving, three of them, roaring over the top of the bluff . . .

"Is that really the . . . the cops?" Beth asked.

"The ATF—looks like they've got the National Guard helping out," Grenoble said. He was swaying. Feverish. But he wouldn't let Cormac support him.

"A few minutes sooner and Harold would be alive," Gary said. The dull letdown after a peak of excitement was showing in his face.

Almost like crashing from drugs, Cormac thought. *I'm going to have to keep a close eye on him for a long time.*

Grenoble stalked over to the fallen observation tower, where he found Esperanza crawling from the wreckage. He grabbed the Argentine by the collar, dragged him to his feet, decided he was more or less intact, and frog-walked him back to the others.

"All of you—" Esperanza began, eyes wild, breathing hard, spitting blood through broken teeth. "You shall—you shall all—"

He didn't get the rest out before Grenoble back-handed him, knocking him on his ass. "Shut up or I'll kill you with my bare hands."

Esperanza fell silent. Grenoble used Esperanza's belt as improvised cuffs, binding his hands behind him, and they marched him toward the compound.

Batman was hovering his plane over the bluff above the compound, watching as the gunships closed in on the men clustered inside the fences, hemming them in from the air. One group of Brethren fired a centrifugal gun at a chopper—within seconds the fire was returned with an air-to-surface missile.

A smoking crater remained where five men had stood before.

Even the centrifugal guns were no match for choppers with missiles. The remaining Brethren threw down their weapons and surrendered.

"You in the unmarked jet!" came a voice on the radio. "Land immediately, or we'll open fire!"

Batman was pretty sure he could outrun their missiles, probably survive a direct hit, with his jet's armor. But he needed to get into the compound. He had to know for sure . . .

"I'm bringing it down, just outside that broken gate," he said, into the radio.

He had no wish to tangle with "the authorities"—but he needed to look around in the Lodge, try to find White

Eyes, or get a clue as to where he'd gone. And with any luck—Gordon would be there to run interference for him.

"Gordon, you have no authority here!" said the ATF regional administrator, hooking a thumb at Batman. "This man is my prisoner!" Rance Gilman was a red-faced man with thick white hair, styled like a televangelist, yellow-tinted aviator sunglasses, and a beige Brooks Brothers suit, matching overcoat; he toyed with an enormous gold ring on his pinkie as he went on, with the air of a Supreme Court judge laying down the law. "You are not only out of your jurisdiction, Gordon, you are out of your home state."

"Batman is wanted for questioning in Gotham City," Gordon said evenly. "I wish to take him back to Gotham . . . for questioning." He turned to Batman. "Do you surrender to me?"

"Yes," said Batman, without hesitation. "I surrender to you, Gordon."

"It doesn't work that way. You've got to put in the paperwork and ask for him to be transferred to your custody. Meanwhile that mask comes off, the cuffs go on, and he goes to jail!"

Batman found another smoke capsule on his utility belt. He would have to throw it and run, knocking a couple of cops over as he went. He was only twenty steps from the Batplane. He hated to do it this way—and someone could get shot in the cross fire. Come to think of it, *he* could get shot in the cross fire. And there were other people around to complicate things—National Guardsmen with M-16s stood sentry over dozens of militia, wrists cuffed behind them, sitting in the mud, miserably waiting for the prisoner-transport buses. There were three helicopter pilots standing by their choppers just outside the compound; there were eight state police troopers standing by their cars, watching in awestruck perplexity. There was a group of ATF agents.

"I say the Batman is under federal arrest, and I'm the top of the food chain here, boys," Gilman said. "I've got questions about how he knew about all this—and how long he knew it. And what else he might be keeping from us. Then there's that plane—that thing's illegal. I'm going to order him cuffed—right now—"

"You arrest that man, and I'll howl to the press for the next ten years," said Agent Grenoble, getting out of a National Guard armored vehicle, a bandage over his gouged eye socket.

Gilman turned a scowl toward Grenoble. "You should be in a hospital, not shouting threats at administrators, Grenoble. Get to an ambulance—there's one waiting outside the gate—and leave this to us. In view of your injuries I'll overlook the threat, this once."

"You can take *overlook the threat* and shove it up your ass!" Grenoble shouted. "That man saved our lives! More than once! That man is the one who got us here!"

"It's true," Cormac said, getting out of the vehicle behind him. "Without him I'd be dead in the bottom of a mine shaft—which is something else you've got to look at. It's full of bodies."

"Who the hell are you?" Gilman demanded.

"He works with me," Gordon interceded. "He won two commendations in the Gotham PD."

"Another guy with no authority and no sense of turf," Gilman snorted.

"Let's talk about authority," said another man, just getting out of a black Humvee, the door emblazoned with DEPARTMENT OF HOMELAND SECURITY.

The newcomer was a stocky man with a round head, a seamed face, a trench coat, a bow tie over a white shirt, a comb-over going astray in the damp wind. "Wickerson," Gilman said. "You guys all of a sudden getting on the ball?"

"Some of us always were," Wickerson said, not appearing to take offense. He gestured toward Batman. "Justice Department, FBI, Department of Homeland Security have an interest in this man . . . whoever the hell he is." He looked past Batman at his plane. "Where the bejeezus did you get *that* thing? Is that a Harrier?"

"Close," Batman said. "I had it built."

"Built by whom? With money from where?"

Batman shook his head.

"So that's the way it is, is it?" Wickerson said, automatically trying to smooth his comb-over back down.

"That's the way it is," Batman said. He was glancing around the compound, wondering if White Eyes could be here still—hiding in some bunker maybe, like Hitler in Berlin. White Eyes' terrorist plans were too disrupted to carry out. But suppose, instead, he'd gotten out of the area? Suppose he went on the offensive, on his own? The hot-impact missiles could be catastrophic—even one of them.

Wickerson nodded and turned to Gilman. "The perimeter secured here?"

Gilman stared at him, probably working out the chain of command in his head. At last he sighed and said, "Yeah, yeah, it's secured. We got some men pulling in the injured ones, ID'ing the dead, up at that little playground of theirs. We got Professor Esperanza, been looking for him for two years . . ."

"You got him thanks to Batman," Cormac pointed out. Beth and Gary started to get out of the vehicle, but he waved them back in.

"Aaron Bunch got away?" Wickerson went on.

Gilman scratched his chin, unwilling to admit he didn't know who that was. "Um . . . Bunch?"

"That's the tentative ID we have for the man called White Eyes. Son of an international lawyer, Hiram Bunch, used to work for Pinochet—and for . . ." His voice trailed off.

He almost let go of something classified, Batman figured.

"Oh, yeah, Bunch. If Bunch is here," Gilman said, "we haven't found him yet."

"First order of business is to tie down the loose cannons," Gilman said. "This . . ." He nodded at Batman. "This refugee from Mardi Gras, here . . . I want custody of him."

"I heard," Wickerson said. "I'm inclined to let Gordon take custody of him for now. We have . . . we want a discussion with him later—we can have that in Gotham City. But Gordon's got to be responsible for getting him to that discussion."

He looked at Gordon. Gordon looked at Batman. Batman nodded.

"He's in my custody," Gordon said. "I'll get him there."

"We'll let it stand there for now," Wickerson said. "There are bigger fish to fry. We've got to find these hot-impact weapons Gordon warned us about."

"That could be a munitions bunker," Batman said,

pointing at the hump of concrete rising between two Quonset huts.

"You aren't going to let this guy actually call the shots?" Gilman said, in a tone of outrage.

"He's right, we should check it out," Gordon said.

"And *you*—"

"Come on, whoever's coming," Wickerson said, starting toward the bunker.

"Waitaminnut here," Gordon said, stepping over to one of the prisoners—a skinny, pale, weak-chinned skinhead with a ring of interlaced iron crosses and Christian crosses tattooed like a tonsure around his head—grabbing him by the collar, and dragging him to his feet. "That bunker wired to blow up on us?"

"Like I'm gonna tell you, you Jew bastard—"

"You don't have to. You're going in first and then we'll see what happens."

The man swallowed. Then he said, "There's a laser MachineHead set up—you don't shut it off, you break the beam, boom."

"You know where to shut it off?"

"Yeah."

"Then come on. You're going in first so you'd better get this right . . . You show us exactly how to shut it off or you get the scalp blown right off that little bald pinhead of yours, you got me?"

Ten minutes later Gordon, Wickerson, Batman, Cormac, Gilman, and the skinhead—his arms still cuffed behind him—were inspecting the interior of the bunker. It went down two levels; the top one contained racks of the auto-shotguns and centrifugal weapons. The lower section contained only a table of chemicals, mostly dried, in boxes, and, on a metal shelf affixed to the wall, a row of MAN-PADS shells.

"That them?" Wickerson asked.

Batman stared at the shells, counting them twice. "That's nineteen of them."

"There was more," said the weak-chinned skinhead, glancing at the stairs. "I get some consideration for helping you . . . you guys out, right?"

"We'll tell the judge," Wickerson said. "How many more?"

"He made twenty-one—I mean, twenty-one finished. Esperanza fired one off this morning right here in the compound to test it. Far as I know that leaves twenty."

"And one's missing," Batman said. "And so is White Eyes." He looked at the skinhead. "Isn't he."

The man nodded. "Left with Del, down the main access. Least forty minutes before you got here. Something else—them shells aren't the same as the one he used in the test. They got Ebola in them."

Wickerson's mouth dropped open. "You sure?"

"Open secret around here, dude. So you think I can get minimum security?"

"Look here," Gordon said, pulling a tarp off a table at the other end of the room. On the table was a scale model of a nuclear power plant.

"That baby's up by New York City," Wickerson said, almost whispering, licking his lips. "Oh, my Lord."

"We can ring it in with men—we can put them on alert in two minutes," Gilman said. "He hasn't got time to get there yet . . . Those MAN-PADS don't have all that much range. We can keep him out . . ."

"If that's where he went," Batman said.

"You can see right there what his target is," Gilman

pointed out irritably. "We'll ring it with men. And choppers."

"What about here, there's a hill—if he were on this hill," Wickerson said, pointing at the model.

The others crowded around to see. "We'll secure that first thing," Gilman said.

Batman was moving toward the stairs. He was very, very good at moving silently, inconspicuously.

He was out of the bunker in moments, crossing the grounds to his plane, walking in big strides but not too fast. The National Guardsmen frowned at him; the cops looked over. They'd seen him interacting freely with the big shots—they weren't sure they were supposed to detain him. But how could a guy dressed like him be legit?

As he went, Batman brooded about White Eyes. It just wasn't over as long as that tan-challenged thug was running loose. Suppose White Eyes wasn't going to the power plant? Batman knew how hard it would be to get the federal government to change its focus. He might be off on a wild-goose chase, anyway, trying to find White Eyes himself. But he also knew that White Eyes would be aware, at this point, that the feds would find his model of the nuclear power plant . . .

Back in the munitions bunker, Wilkerson was asking the skinhead, "What do you know about this power plant?"

"Nothing. I've never been down to this room—only upstairs. They were real closemouthed about it. I—hey, where's the cape guy? He's gone."

Gordon had known full well that Batman was slipping out. He tried to turn their attention back to the model. "What if White Eyes fires from the air?"

"We'll secure the airspace!" Gilman said, looking around the room. "Goddammit, where's he gone? Gordon—you're supposed to have him under arrest!"

Jim Gordon glanced at the door. In a disinterested monotone, he said, "Oh, damn. The Batman's escaped." His voice became barely audible. "Someone stop him." He shrugged, hearing the Batplane take off overhead. "Oh, well—too late."

17

Batman hunkered down by Del's body, beside the discarded camouflage netting at the little airstrip. "You're right, Alfred. It's an airstrip, and there's a body here."

"*I'm gratified to know my satellite surveillance skills are improving, sir,*" said Alfred, a voice in Batman's headset. "*I think we may . . . possibly . . . was . . .*"

"Alfred, repeat that, you're breaking up."

"*I said, sir, just after the cloud cover parted we did get a small plane leaving from that position. But it flew under clouds, again, and apparently too low for radar. We haven't been able to hack into all the radar stations in the area, however.*"

"What kind of plane?"

"*A Piper Cub, sir. The number five-three-three was visible on the fuselage.*"

"Piper Cub seems right. What heading?"

"*I'm transmitting the precise heading to the Batplane, sir. Roughly—the direction of the New York area.*"

Maybe he was going for the power plant, then. But there were other targets within range of a Piper Cub.

"Tell the authorities about the body here, and the . . . hold on."

"The what, sir?"

"I've found something else. A spotty trail of fuel. This man's shotgun was fired—I suspect he damaged the plane's fuel tank. Just how much did it leak, I wonder . . . Alfred, the feds have New York covered . . . I just remembered reading something—there's another target. If I'm right—that's where he's going." Batman shook his head dubiously. "I just hope I can make up the time we've lost."

Cormac waved to Grenoble, who lifted a hand from the gurney in the back of the ambulance. His face and upper body were heavily bandaged. There was no replacing that eye. But as Grenoble had observed, he'd "ended up a Hell of a lot better off than my partner."

Cormac saw that the ambulance medic was keeping close watch over Grenoble. He closed the door and turned to Beth and Gary just as it started to rain again.

They'd been through a great deal together. None of them so much as remarked on the rain, though it was a heavy downpour.

They walked together across the sodden compound, past the sullen, squatting prisoners, the National Guardsmen, grumbling about the rain, toward the black sedan waiting outside the gate.

"Do I have to get in that car with those cops?" Beth asked suddenly.

Cormac looked at her. "There a warrant on you?"

"No sir, there isn't."

"Then don't worry about it. I'll get you where you want to go."

She didn't say anything. Gary said it for her. "She

doesn't have anyplace to go. I mean—she *really* doesn't have anyplace to go."

Cormac looked at her. She reached out and tentatively took Gary's hand. "I was hoping . . . to stay with Gary. I mean . . . near Gary. My only friends are . . . one killed herself and the other's in juvie. I got an auntie somewhere . . . maybe she'd take me . . ."

Gary looked at her, looked at her hand in his, walked along a little farther. He swallowed hard. He drew her hand to him and put his other hand over it, too. "I want you to . . . to stay with me. If my dad says it's okay. But . . ."

She looked at him. "What?"

"You were sort of hinting . . . I mean, I'm not . . ."

"*What?*"

"I could use a best friend, that's all."

"A . . . okay. I know I'm kind of . . . white-trash-y or something."

"No, no, see . . ." He stopped—and so did the rain, almost. It eased to a drizzle. He glanced nervously around. The three of them were about thirty paces from the sedan. No one was standing near them. "I feel like . . . Dad . . . I want to tell you . . . I'm sorry I ran off. It was stupid. I was just mad. And . . . sort of embarrassed about where you found me."

Cormac nodded. "That's okay. I'm just glad we got through all this. You made me feel like . . . you really handled yourself well. I was thinking maybe you could . . . come into the family business with me. When you're ready."

"What? Be a bounty hunter?"

"I was thinking of starting my own security company.

Skip tracing, private cops, detection, the whole shebang.
If I can raise the money."

Beth listened to them, wiping wet hair from her face,
looking vaguely depressed, as if in her mind she'd already
left them both, and gone off again somewhere alone.

"Wow." Gary's smile flickered tentatively. "Yeah.
That'd be . . . yeah! I mean—I'd try it." Then the smile
fell away—just as if a bright, fluttering bird had dropped
from view. "But Dad. I'm not . . . I mean, I'm not what
you . . ."

"Oh!" Beth burst out, suddenly more cheerful. "I get
it now! Why didn't you say so!"

Cormac looked back and forth between them, baffled.
"What? Somebody tell me for Chrissakes!"

Gary shook his head and started to turn away. But
Beth took the initiative. "Mr. Sullivan—Gary's gay!"

Gary looked at her—opened his mouth to deny it.
Then closed it again. He shrugged and looked toward
his dad's stunned face, then turned away, hunching
toward the sedan.

"Gary—wait!" Cormac called out commandingly.
Gary stopped. But he didn't turn back. Cormac went to
him. "Gary—is that true? That's what you've been . . .
starting to tell me . . . all this time?"

Gary chewed his lower lip. Then he nodded.

"Are you *sure*? Like it's been there all your life?"

Gary closed his eyes and grimaced—but he nodded
again.

Cormac laughed. "Was that *all*? Jesus, boy, I don't
care! Some people like Italian food, some people like
Greek—who the Hell cares?"

Gary looked at him with tears in his eyes. "Really?"

"But—why didn't you tell me, boy?"

"Because—you're so macho and tough and . . . I don't know, I thought you'd think it was all . . ."

"Gary—you remember Murch Murcheson, was in the special forces with me? Worked with me on some of the tougher skip traces?"

"Yeah—that big guy with the scars, came to the barbecues a couple of times?"

"Yeah. Good buddy of mine. Gary, Murch is as gay as they come."

"Wha-a-at? That guy? But he's so—"

"He's tough as nails. Lots of gay guys are. And I wouldn't have cared if you were tough or not, boy. You're my son. Long as you stay off drugs, use condoms, and learn a trade, any honest trade—I'm happy! You're my son and . . . I love you." Hard to get that *I love you* stuff out, though it was true. Cormac was male after all. "That's all. That's just . . . all there is to it."

Gary wiped his eyes and said, "What about Beth? Can we keep her?"

"What, like she's a pet?"

"Like she's a sister, Dad."

Cormac pretended to look at Beth skeptically. "Yeah? You vouch for her? She'd make a good sister for you?"

"Hell yeah!"

"*Hell yeah,* what a tender endorsement. Beth—Gary vouches for you—you can stay with us, as long as you want. But you've got to follow my rules. Both of you."

Gary nodded gravely at his father. A wordless nod, a look in Gary's eyes—but Cormac knew it meant Gary was committed to a new way of life. They had almost died, fighting side by side, and somehow that had destroyed the barriers between them. Now they both understood what really mattered.

And Beth, swallowing hard, said, "I'd like to try it, Mr. Sullivan."

"Call me Cormac." He smiled and put his arms around both teens. "Come on, let's get dry and get something to eat."

Sleet fell over the small airstrip, glossed the half a dozen small craft parked there, and slashed from the wipers of the dark green SUV driving up to White Eyes' Piper Cub. The Explorer pulled up and Jenson and Hasecolna got out. Jenson was a barrel-chested Swede in a Windbreaker, his hood up, and Hasecolna was a stocky Serbian with heavy eyebrows, in watch cap and overcoat. Another vehicle was coming up the access road, a blue minivan. It picked up a man getting out of a small plane.

"Who is that?" Hasecolna asked, glaring at the minivan.

"I don't know," White Eyes said. "Not one of ours. You have to come in that vehicle?"

"Why not?" Jenson asked.

"I told you on the radio it was an emergency—protocol in an emergency is to change vehicles as they may have our standard rides watched. No time to get another . . ."

Jenson was looking at the Piper Cub. "Shotgun? You're leaking here . . ."

"Why do you think I stopped here, idiot? This airstrip hadn't been here, I'd have had to land on the freeway. We might just make it, though, driving down there. But not in that vehicle. They're looking for us . . ."

He was staring speculatively at the blue minivan as it drove near and stopped. A man opened the passenger-side window. A black man, about thirty, with short hair, glasses. With him was a white woman, a blonde, hair tied back, a round face. There was a boy in the back-seat.

A mud-blood, White Eyes thought, sizing up the kid. *Half-breed. Disgusting. But maybe this will work out, after all.*

"This is a private airstrip," the black man said. "Only people who work for Baltimore Computer can use it."

"You just fly in, did you?" White Eyes asked. "And your wife came to pick you up. Handy for all of us."

"George," the woman said, appraising the three men at the Piper Cub, leaning over to her husband. "Let's just go. Quick."

The man looked at them—then nodded. She started to put the minivan in reverse. White Eyes nodded to Jenson, who stepped up to the open van window and put a big pistol through it. Pressed the .45 to the man's temple.

"Now you turn the car off, lady, or he dies. You get in back. We take this vehicle. You are going to ride with us."

"They'll make splendid hostages," White Eyes said. "Get the goods from the plane."

Batman had pulled the Batplane up in midair, was hovering, in vertical-takeoff-and-landing mode, about two hundred feet over the edge of the commons fronting the US Capitol. But bringing the Batplane into Washington, D.C., airspace had been tricky—he'd had to elude D.C. police choppers twice. He could see a small formation of planes approaching on the radar. Fast. He touched his headset TRANSMIT button.

"Alfred—did you get Gordon on the line?"

"Yes sir—just a few moments ago. I believe he is now engaged in alerting the authorities."

"The problem is the authorities are after me now—

I'm in an unknown plane near the Capitol—I've got four interceptors on the way here—I'm getting warnings—but that looks like White Eyes getting out of a van . . . a small blue van . . ."

"A van, sir?"

"He made it to the outskirts of town and ran out of fuel, must've got one of his local scumbags to pick him up—any word on security alert for the Capitol?" All this time Batman was moving into position, angling to get between White Eyes and the Capitol.

"Not so far, sir. Is Congress in session?"

"Not exactly. I remembered reading about a ceremony on the second floor, in the rotunda—half the Senate and the most powerful congressmen from the House—and the president. And the vice president. A statue unveiling. We've got to get the word out, get them out of there. Otherwise . . ."

"Captain Gordon is trying to get the federal authorities to listen, sir—but . . ."

That was White Eyes down there all right—there were police cars racing toward the racists, and two of them were firing toward the police with centrifugal rifles as their leader picked up the MAN-PADS launcher. He was within range to hit the Capitol rotunda. If White Eyes hadn't been delayed by that leak in his fuel tank, it'd all be over by now . . .

I might still be too late. The hot-impact weapon would penetrate the rotunda and explode inside with an enormous charge, spreading death. Most of the US government wiped out at once. There was security all around them—but White Eyes was outside their perimeter.

Still, Batman was landing in between White Eyes and the launcher. Jumping out of the Batplane . . .

Stopping dead, seeing the three people whom White Eyes and his men had pulled from the van. It wasn't a van belonging to his people—they'd hijacked a mini-van. There was a young boy and his parents. A black man, a white woman. White Eyes was making them kneel in front of him.

The two parents were about the same age as Bruce Wayne's had been, that night. And the boy was about the age Bruce had been.

That night outside the opera. His parents—gunned down . . .

His men pointed a gun at the couple—and White Eyes shouted at the oncoming cops and Batman. Gesturing with their guns, even if they couldn't be heard. Their meaning was clear.

"You get any closer—I'll kill them!"

The cops pulled up short. Batman could see them arguing furiously.

White Eyes was picking up the MAN-PADS.

"Sir!" Alfred said in his headset. *"They're escorting the president and the congressional leaders out—but they're still in the rotunda! It'll take time to get them clear!"*

White Eyes was aiming the launcher . . . Batman kept walking toward them. The taller of the three gunmen was cocking his gun.

"Stay back, demon, or I kill them!"

He was only about thirty feet away now . . .

But they were going to kill them . . . *right in front of the boy.*

Shadows fell over the group on the lawn across from the Capitol—federal choppers, clustered overhead, moving into position. They were going to be too late . . .

Batman had a Batarang in each hand. He poised to throw, to leap . . .

The shadow over the people on the lawn seemed to take on thickness, a new outline. It writhed into a shape. The shape of a dark figure, a cowled figure, in a loosely sewn costume . . .

Batman's first costume, unoccupied, staring eyeless at him—standing between him and White Eyes.

He stopped dead. *I've failed. Every time I see it . . . I make a mistake. I can't make a mistake here. There's no room for error in this situation. I'm going to fail— because I can't let that thing be a part of me. Because it's death, and people die around me, like my family. It'll take me over if I let it . . . I have to stay away from it . . . I can't—I can't! It's everything dark in me and it wants to own me!*

But Batman knew he had to make his move. Teia had told him what to do.

"You," he said, starting his run, muttering it just loud enough so that only he could hear—so that he could hear himself, "are subordinate to me. I command you— you don't command me. Take your place in me. *I take you into me—where you belong!*"

And Batman, moving faster than he'd ever moved in his life, flung the Batarangs and ran, sprinting and throwing at once, leaping through the image of the shadow creature who'd haunted him—leaping into it, through it, and embracing it, all at once—

Running and leaping so hard and fast he almost caught up to his own Batarangs, which hissed home, smacking into the gunman, cracking him in the head and hands so that he staggered back, his shot going wild, while Batman was launched through the air right at the muzzle of the launcher—was upon it just as White Eyes squeezed the trigger, the Dark Knight smacking down on the barrel with both fists so that it tilted sharply at the ground, firing into the soil underfoot. The missile sizzled into the earth, burning downward to explode well underground, its substance absorbed by the clay strata under the city.

Batman flipped forward, tumbling in midair, using the impact on the weapon to drive him into a flying somersault, coming down with both feet on White Eyes' face, at the same time flicking shuriken at the other two men. Both men screamed and dropped their weapons. Stirred to action at last, the police moved in—as the young couple ran, pushing their son ahead of them—and White Eyes went over on his back.

He grabbed Batman's feet and twisted, pulling him off balance, rolling to try and get the Dark Knight under him. Batman hammered White Eyes hard on the sides of his head, both fists at once, loosening his grip, rolling free.

And Batman felt good. Strangely good. Like everything was in place inside him. Somehow, confronting the shadow, seeing it for what it was—making it a part of him, subordinate to his will—had unified him. He felt on top of his game. He was in the pocket. Batman was ready to rock.

The cops were busy with the other militiamen. White Eyes was Batman's responsibility. And Big White was already up in a crouch, charging in a psychotic fury. Batman set himself—and then jumped to one side, knowing he was outfought if he took on White Eyes, one wrestler to another. Instead he struck with his bunched fingers, using a variant of the *gunn-ting*—the scissor move that Teia had showed him—on a nerve cluster in White Eyes' right arm. Batman spun around as his adversary turned toward him—but Big White looked even paler than usual: his right arm was hanging limply. Batman sidestepped White Eyes' left hook, then struck another nerve cluster under that arm . . .

And now White Eyes' left arm hung limply.

"Steroids aren't really very impressive, Bunch," Batman said, slamming White Eyes again and again: his nose, right cheek, left temple. "Bulk means so much less than skill. And you—" One last hammering roundhouse right—hard to the jaw. "Are just . . . deadweight."

And White Eyes went down . . . out cold.

Batman cuffed the unconscious man, turned and walked calmly back to the Batplane.

"Hey you!" yelled the cops behind him. "You can't just walk away from here! Get back here! You don't have the authorization to bring that plane in here! What the Hell do you think you're doing?"

Batman turned long enough to say, "In the absence of leadership—the people do what they have to."

And he vaulted onto the Batplane's wing, jumped onto the spine of the craft, dropped into the cockpit, fired up the engines, and took off.

Bruce Wayne leapt out of the limo and pushed into the Friday-evening throng on the white-zone-for-loading-and-unloading-only, apologizing for jostling a number of Pakistani people towing their luggage, just managing not to step on several children scurrying underfoot, and almost running through the glass door before it slid open for him to go inside.

The front of Terminal 3 at the Gotham City International Airport was made of concrete columns framing a big tinted-glass wall that rose ninety-five feet to the high ceiling, where pigeons had somehow gotten in to flutter around the dusty fluorescent lighting fixtures. It was a big, airy templelike space, echoing with public-address announcements and the drone of travelers. On the far side was baggage check-in, where the airlines had cleverly laid people off and substituted touch-screen computer monitors so that customers could do the work people used to be paid for, and at the end of the rows of baggage counters was another door, through which Bruce Wayne all but sprinted to reach an escalator carrying international passengers to the second-floor gates. And here he was stopped dead by a scowling middle-aged lady in a security guard uniform and a sign saying TICKETED PASSENGERS ONLY BEYOND THIS POINT. Bruce Wayne had to follow rules that Batman could ignore. Sometimes, Bruce Wayne found that frustrating—and sometimes he found it reassuring. This was one of the frustrating occasions.

"Bruce?"

He turned to see Teia staring up at him. She was wearing yellow shorts and small white tennis shoes and a simple white top, and her hair was tied back. She had a large purse, with little mirrors sewn into its bright primary colors, which she'd bought at an outdoor market in Nepal. He'd been there, a few years before, when she'd picked it out.

"I remember that purse," he said lamely.

"Do you remember my name?"

"Hello, Teia. I . . ."

"How did you know exactly when my flight was?"

"Um—I made some inquiries. I'm sorry if it's spying . . ."

"It's kind of sweet, really, your going to so much trouble. Since it's you. But here you've caught me looking shabby . . . I'm not dressed to see you."

"You always look great. No luggage?"

"I checked it, of course."

"Oh. Yes, of course. So—before your flight, could we . . . could we have a cup of tea or . . ." He took a deep breath and said it in a rush, "Do you really have to go at all?"

She smiled wistfully. "I wish you'd asked me that two days ago."

"I . . . there was something I had to do."

"Skiing?"

"No. Something I really had to do."

"Oh. I'm sorry, I didn't mean to—" Teia glanced at a clock on the wall near the escalator, and took the ticket folder out of her purse. "I've got to go, though."

"I could buy a ticket of some kind so I could come upstairs with you."

"That's tempting. And I guess that wouldn't hurt your pocketbook much. But my plane is so soon—it wouldn't be worth it. This is . . . kind of painful for me already."

She showed no pain in her expression. But he didn't doubt her. "You sure you have to go? Maybe I'll think of a way . . ."

"A way to what?"

"I can't really talk about it right now. But . . . if you'll stay awhile . . . Then, in time . . ."

"I can't, Bruce. I have accepted a volunteer position helping refugees from Tibet. They're running from the Communists—they're in a bad way. I have made an obligation."

He nodded, feeling lonely already. Wanting to take her in his arms, crush her to him. Knowing this wasn't the time. "I wish I could come. But . . . I have an obligation, too."

"I know you do. I don't know what it is, Bruce. I know it's something important, and it's something you can't tell me about. Or you think you can't. So . . . It's all right. Bruce—that thing that was bothering you. The shape you saw. Did you meet your Mountain Ghost? Did you . . . learn anything about it?"

He nodded. "I did. It was something in me I was afraid I couldn't control. And . . . maybe it did have a life of its own. It seemed a magnet for . . . other kinds of darkness."

"Passengers who notice any unusual activity or abandoned luggage are asked to report it immediately . . ."

"What did you do about it, Bruce?" she asked, studying him.

"I saw it for what it was. I took command of it—put it where it belonged. It's part of me."

She nodded. "I thought it was something like that. Bruce—I have to go."

"Will you be in touch somehow?"

Her lips compressed. Her eyes glistened, filled with unshed tears. "Somehow."

He bent and kissed her and at last the tears fell. He tasted their salt as he prolonged the kiss as long as he could. It was Teia who drew away. She touched his face, then turned away without a word and went up the escalator, never looking back.

I could go after her. I could take the next flight. I could find her. Maybe I should. Maybe I've fulfilled my obligation. Maybe . . .

Bruce had a sensation then, as if someone, some ghostly presence, were tapping him on the shoulder. He turned—no one was there, except strangers, hurrying by, toting their luggage. But he saw what he was supposed to see. He could see it through those high glass walls:

The shape of a bat, projected by a searchlight onto the gray clouds.

"You think this guy's going to show up?" Wickerson asked, shivering in the biting wind on the roof of the Gotham PD HQ, gazing out over the nighttime glimmer of Gotham City, a grounded constellation against a field of grimy black.

"Fairly sure," said Gordon. "Since he's standing right behind you."

Wickerson turned, startled to see the Batman half silhouetted against the big signal light shining the Bat-Signal against the lowering clouds.

"You gentlemen wanted to speak to me?"

"Yeah . . . why it had to be out here, I dunno . . . ," Wickerson said, reaching into the pocket of his trench coat. "We couldn't meet in a conference room somewhere?" When Batman didn't reply, Wickerson went on, "I've got an appointment here—we just need a name on the blank line there where it says NAME OF APPOINTEE."

"What kind of appointment?" Gordon asked, shielding his pipe with a hand as he lit it.

"In recognition of what he accomplished at the Capitol, Batman is being offered an appointment as a US Marshal—and we figure you can deputize him here in town, too. Make him legal from the ground up. The word will go out so he can do his job without having to run from the police while he's running after the bad guys."

"A name—on a blank line?" Batman said. He looked at the appointment papers in Wickerson's proferred hand, but didn't take them.

"Your *real* name," Wickerson insisted. "It'll be kept confidential—just like we do with CIA agents."

Batman shook his head. "Sorry."

"Look—this is a major honor."

"I know. But . . . no names."

"Look, Wickerson," Gordon said. ". . . Dammit, this wind, can't keep this pipe lit . . . Wickerson, what I want to say is—he's shown he can be effective, and trustworthy, without our knowing who he is. Let's try it that way—if we get Batman impersonators, or whatever you're worried about, we can rethink it. For now . . . let's trust him."

Wickerson looked sharply at Batman, then said, "It's not as if we don't have a clue who he is."

Batman watched him, waiting.

"He's got to be wealthy," Wickerson went on. "*Very.* Only a few men wealthy enough and resourceful enough . . . We think we have it narrowed down to a few billionaires. Someone with unusual athletic ability—or at least high-tech know—"

"Sure," Batman said. "I got bored running Microsoft."

Gordon stared. A joke? From Batman?

Wickerson winced. "No, you're not him—too spindly, too old. But I've got a list here . . ." He found another piece of paper in his pocket and passed it to Batman. "If we know anyway . . ."

"There's a lot of names here. And none of them . . ." Batman shook his head. He passed the list to Gordon.

Gordon eyed the list skeptically. "And these three on top—Steve Young, John Giuntoli, Bruce Wayne? Come on! One's a Mormon retiree, Giuntoli and Wayne are playboys who party day and night. You're barking up the wrong tree, Wickerson."

Wickerson shrugged, snatching the paper back. "Just thought I'd see if anyone blurted, *Okay, you got me.* Well . . ." He looked at the appointment, at the folded list of names, and put them both back in his coat. "I'll put my tail on the line here—I'll go to the president. He owes you, after all. We'll see. My guess is—they'll do it your way for a while."

Batman nodded—just once. Then he turned to Gordon. "What about Burkhart, and Breen?"

Gordon ground the pipe stem between his teeth. "It's frustrating. We need someone to testify against them. The Brethren we've got weren't interfacing with them. There are still some at large . . ."

"I'll look into it." Batman reached over and flicked the switch on the Bat-Signal, so it suddenly went out, and the rooftop was abruptly darker.

Wickerson and Gordon blinked, looking at the dark searchlight—and then looked back at the place Batman had been standing a moment before . . .

He was gone. They were alone on the rooftop.

"You ever get used to that?" Wickerson asked.

"Never quite do. You drink whiskey?"

"Vodka."

"I'm buying."

Already half a block away, swinging on his grapple, Batman flipped in midair to land on a cornice, the cable rewinding into his hand. He paused there, half crouched on the rim of a Gothic-style twenty-story building, poised to leap again . . .

The wind lifted his cape to billow around him, as Batman gazed out over Gotham City . . . as he listened to the sounds of sirens; the distant rattle of gunshots . . .

And then he leapt into the void.

EPILOGUE

Striding along in the narrow alley in Gotham City's Chinatown, Red Trask was feeling almost cocky. It was a cold night, but it was good and dark. He had a score lined up, he had his gun in his pocket, and there wasn't a cop in sight.

He had given Batman the slip a couple of times, and the federal dragnet for the Bavarian Brethren had overlooked him entirely. No one had seen Batman for a couple of days. White Eyes was in federal lockup, Esperanza was shipped out to Guantánamo, but Red Trask was walking along the street free as a bird, whistling to himself, as the wind skirled bits of newspaper around his head.

Didn't have to worry about the cops, either, he thought happily. He had met with Breen and Burkhart, had promised them 20 percent of everything. He'd get a stake tonight, buy the crystal, start dealing boof down on the West Side. What was 20 percent with those guys protecting him? It was worth it. The money would roll in. Life was going to be sweet.

Up ahead was the place he was looking for—one of those Chinese medicine dumps, with the weird little roots and herbs. There was a neon sign, in a Chinese ideogram, over the shop, and, on a painted sign beneath the neon, SAM GONG'S MEDICINAL HERBS.

Word from Trask's junkie pal was that Gong kept a big stash o' cash in the back of that shop. Didn't trust banks. Five grand in there. What would one scared little chink do about him and his nine-millimeter? Nothing.

The wind picked up again, stinging his nose, sending more newspaper fluttering overhead—or was that newspaper? He got a funny prickly feeling on the back of his neck, and glanced up toward the fluttering shape.

Was that a bat flying around? Here? In this alley? No. Sure looked like a bat, though.

He shuddered. Just the sight of a bat was enough to make him think of . . . *him*.

He'd pretty much convinced himself that destiny was going to keep him out of Batman's black-gloved hands. He wasn't going to let the Bat take him, no matter what. He'd die fighting, first. Because the Bat would give him to the cops and the cops would put him in State Pen. And the worst moments of Trask's life had been in State Pen. He'd thought his childhood was pretty bad. Not compared with Cellblock 11, it wasn't. Only joining the Aryans had saved his life. And nowadays they tried to break you up, put you somewhere your gang wasn't. Which meant he'd be prey for whoever was running the place.

Maybe worse were the long nights in his bunk; the long days doing nothing. Day after day, month after month, no visitors, no lawyer to speak of. Just waiting for that interminable sentence to end. And him being so restless—as restless as they made anyone, was Red

Trask. For a guy like him, needing to be on the move all the time, prison was Hell.

No, he wasn't going back to Hell. Not for Batman, not for anyone . . .

The sign in the window of Gong's said CLOSED; the door was locked. But he could see the old guy moving around in there. That door wouldn't keep him out. One good shove with his shoulder . . .

He pulled the gun, cocked it, set himself to break down the door.

"Not tonight, Red," said a demonic voice close behind him.

Oh, no. Please, God. Not him.

"You weren't enough of a priority before," said the familiar voice. "I didn't have time to hunt you down. But things are quieter now. I'm going to make you my hobby, Trask . . ."

"No!" Trask shouted. He spun, firing the niner. But the only thing he hit was the window of an empty shop across the narrow street. Batman was nowhere to be seen.

"Where are you, dammit! Where are you?"

"Here, Trask . . ."

And the bat he'd seen earlier fluttered down into view again. He fired convulsively at it, again and again. It flew up into the shadows.

"You see, Red?" came the voice—as if from the air itself. "I'm going to be watching you, day or night, from now on . . . unless you want to cooperate with me. Just a little time in prison, Trask; you'll do the time and start fresh . . ."

"No no no no!" Trask shrieked and scurried down

the alley, firing his gun at every dark corner till the hammer was clicking on an empty chamber.

There—the Bat's shadow, falling over him from above. It was him!

Trask fumbled in his pocket for his extra clip, tried to get it into the gun as he ran, dropped it, had to scramble on his hands and knees to find it, babbling, "No no no no I won't go!"

"We can put you in that bank, Trask," came the voice from the shadows overhead. "We have a supply of fresh punks in custody who'll testify against you. You want it to be a short stretch, Trask, you'd better be willing to talk . . . I've been watching you. I saw you with Easy Molly last night on Simpson Street. And I saw you talking to Breen and Burkhart in Cohn's Deli, this afternoon. Making a deal with them. You can give them to me, Trask . . ."

"No!"

"That gun is a parole violation, Trask. We'll protect you from Burkhart and Breen—but you've got to give them to us . . ."

"No no no no no!"

Trask ran blindly to the cross street and out into traffic. Cabs honked, a truck nearly ran him down, but he made it across the street and into another labyrinth of alleys, heart hammering in his chest. He turned right, turned left, thinking, *I'm losing the Bat again, I'm doing it, I'm getting away! I'll never let him put me in jail, never, never go back to that Hell . . . I'd rather die, I'd rather . . .*

Trask came to a dead end. He was in a blind alley.

He stopped, panting, and turned . . .

To see the Bat hunched on the railing of a fire escape,

one story above him, his cape drooping down, his spiky cowl almost lost in the shadows. His eyes gleaming down at Trask . . . full of dark promise.

"Trask . . . ," came that demonic whisper. "Red Trask. I'll never let you alone. Never. I'll always be there, Trask. Unless you testify against them . . . give them to me—and I'll give you your life back."

Trask dropped the gun, sobbing. "No . . . It's Hell in there . . . I won't let you take me there . . ."

"The DA will take your testimony into account . . . You'll get through it . . ."

"No . . ."

"Oh, yes, Trask. You testify—or you're mine."

Trask swallowed, hard, looking at the dirty asphalt at his feet. He nodded. "Yes. Yes sir."

Then he went to his knees, putting his hands behind him, wrists together.

And waited for the Bat to take him to Hell.